# MAGIC OF SURGERY

GURMIT DADIALA

Copyright © 2022 by Gurmit Dadiala

All rights reserved.

This book or any portion thereof may not be reproduced or used in any manner whatsoever without the express written permission of the respective writer of the respective story except for the use of brief quotations in a book review.

The writer of the respective work holds sole responsibility for the originality of the stories and The Write Order is not responsible in any way whatsoever.

Printed in India

ISBN: 978-93-95563-73-4

First Printing, 2022

The Write Order

Koramangala, Bangalore

Karnataka-560029

THE WRITE ORDER PUBLICATIONS.

www.thewriteorder.com

*Dedicated to the Rural Surgeons*

# Table of Contents

| | |
|---|---|
| PREFACE | i |
| ACKNOWLEDGEMENTS | iii |
| TESTIMONIALS | v |
| DISCLAIMER | ix |
| PART ONE | 1 |
| JOURNEY TILL NOW | 3 |
| THE PRINCIPIUM | 7 |
| SYMPHYSIOTOMY | 9 |
| POPULARIS | 11 |
| SOME GOOD NEWS | 15 |
| D.O.T– A SURGEON'S NIGHTMARE | 21 |
| J. S. DIGPAL | 23 |
| MECKEL'S DIVERTICULUM AND AMENTIA | 29 |
| MAGANBHAI SARANG | 33 |
| URETERIC STONE | 35 |
| CUPID STRIKES | 37 |
| TRIP TO BOMBAY | 39 |
| BACK TO WORK | 49 |
| TURNING POINT | 53 |
| HERNIOPLASTY | 57 |

| | |
|---|---|
| THE YEAR OF 1984 | 61 |
| HIS LITTLE PATIENTS | 75 |
| CHANGING TIMES | 83 |
| THE SLOG OVERS | 91 |
| LAST FEW DAYS IN JIVIBEN SHAH MEMORIAL HOSPITAL | 97 |
| CORPORATE HOSPITAL CULTURE | 101 |
| HEARTBREAK AGAIN | 119 |
| GUILTY OR NOT GUILTY? | 125 |
| PART TWO | 147 |
| TEACHER DE NOVO | 151 |
| EXOMPHALOS MAJOR | 163 |
| THE WORLD IS YELLOW | 169 |
| GYNAE SURGERIES | 179 |
| SERPENS MORDEAT | 185 |
| INITIUM NOVUM | 193 |
| POENA SINE CULPA | 207 |
| POSITIVUM MUTATIO | 215 |
| MYSTERIUM RETEGIT | 231 |
| EPILOGUE | 241 |
| ABOUT THE AUTHOR | 243 |

# PREFACE

Despite being in the field of Surgery for almost half a century when one can generally predict the outcome of surgical treatment, I can not stop wondering, how a surgery can change the life of an ailing human being or even pull them out of the jaws of certain death.

The accumulated experiences inspired me to pen down a book narrating some of the unusual cases and my method of treating them, and also about the life of a surgeon. Here, I would like to clarify that the story, the lead and other characters, the hospitals he worked in, the incidents and the places are all fictitious. But I must confess, they are influenced by real-life characters or hearsay.

There are very few fortunate amongst us whose lives are utterly hunky dory. The reader would agree that the story of most of us mortals is like the game of snakes and ladders, irrespective of the kind of field they are in, and so is that of our hero in the story.

Moreover, very little is written about the life, emotions, public reaction, and peculiar status of a surgeon working in rural or mofussil areas of our country. The image of a specialist medical man in the mind of society is an affluent person, coming in and out of his chauffeur-driven luxury car with an aura around him that he is not easily reachable to a common man. My story breaks this mould of thinking.

I hope this will fulfil the expectation of readers.

Gurmit Dadiala

# ACKNOWLEDGEMENTS

With a profound sense of gratitude, I would like to thank many people for helping me conceive and complete this book.

My patients, who allowed me to serve them during the last 45 years, kept faith in me, even during my early years when I was a greenhorn, and gave me invaluable experience and satisfaction.

My two daughters, with whom I was sharing the text online- Shaily from Philadelphia and Architect Nishtha- who helped me with suggestions and editing during writing.

My wife Dr Archana, who not only allowed me uninterrupted privacy and gave me suggestions when asked; also her vast knowledge of literature was always handy.

My colleagues, who helped me with this task and also reminded me of cases which had slipped my memory. Dr Mukesh Ariwala, Dr Bharti and Dr Rajiv Rane, Dr Subhash Gupta, Dr (Late) Ramesh Gupta, Dr Jayesh Merchant, Dr Virendra Patidar, Dr Arvind Dashottar, and Dr Bhavik Patel are some of them.

Miss Divya Patidar, for sharing my burden of typing.

This book would have not seen the light of day without the help of my Publisher 'The Write Order Publications" and the very enthusiastic team of Mr Sumit Bansal, Ms Aishwarya Wanjari, the cover page designer Mr Sankhasubhro Nath and the team. The editorial team, Ms Chandni Venkatesh and Mr Rohan Kar.

# TESTIMONIALS

Dr Dadiala has compiled his medical wisdom in a book title 'Magic of Surgery'. The book is written as fiction and therefore, it is not only useful to a new surgeon, rather it is also informative for anyone who wishes to learn about his own body. The story is not only based on Dr Dadiala's experiences, it also contains his deep moral and ethical values and describes the standards all surgeon must strive for.

I hope Dr Dadiala's writing is widely available to enrich the lives of many potential readers. I wish him great success in his endeavour and also hope that he would bless us with many such works in future.

**Justice N.K. Gupta**

**Lokayukt State of Madhya Pradesh**

**Former Judge, M.P. High Court.**

This book is a fascinating in-depth analysis in the life of a surgeon and hence a must read for all medical graduates and especially aspiring surgeons. Dr G.S. Dadiala or GSD as he is known amongst friends is an ace surgeon and that too with a compassionate heart. In this book which is the summation of his vast surgical acumen and surgical skills, attitude towards patients and life, embracing the core values of life, is a pleasure to read. He vividly describes the hectic professional life, various interpersonal relationships, moral and ethical dilemmas and explaining the interesting approach towards surgical cases thus adding a unique dimension rarely found. A great storyteller he weaves his experience in a lucid style. We all hope we can pass something of value on to the gen next. GSD's effort is laudable in the true sense.

**Dr Rajeev Rane**

**MD, Senior Physician, and a Travelogue writer**

**San Francisco, USA**

Dr Dadiala is an avid storyteller. He has a flair of imagination and has a lucid way of expressing it. In this work of fiction, he has woven many aspects of surgical practice in 80s and 90s. By depicting life of a surgeon, saving lives with minimalistic diagnostic assistance of technology and basic infrastructure, he gives a fair idea about how doctors worked with dedication and strong moral character in their professional life. It is notable that the hero of the story has transient weak humane moments in his personal life but shows a strong moral character without any aberration in his professional life. In the flow of the story, he has also juxtaposed medical work culture and ground realities of general hospitals in tribal regions, trust hospitals in small towns and corporate hospital culture in metro cities; compelling the reader to wait for a while and introspect. To quote the author's words, "Those were the times when the clinicians had the liberty to treat their patients without supporting radiology or laboratory evidence. The concept of 'defensive medicine' didn't exist... only the benefit of ailing humanity used to be on the treating doctor's mind."

**Bharti Rane**

**Senior Gynaecologist, acclaimed Gujarati writer and Columnist**

Dear Dr Dadiala,

I am writing to congratulate you on the publication of your book 'Magic of Surgery'. The plot was riveting from the get go, and as the story unfolded, it was wonderful to explore the inner world of a small-town hospital, and learn about the variety of challenges a general surgeon faces and overcomes.
Thank you for enriching the literary world with such deep insight into a very specific topic.

Best Regards,

**Keval Prasad**

**Executive Vice President of Analytical R&D**


Dear Sir,

I just finished the book in one sitting, it's captivating and informative at the same time.

The only thing I wished was that Digpal and Kalpana reunite in the end. The whole story was amazingly narrated and I loved how catchy the beginning was! Honestly, in the initial 20 pages I found the story a bit slow, but gradually the story picked up a lot of pace. The characters were very nicely introduced. Each case was interesting. Every time Digpal was called to the casualty, I was thrilled and started wondering what he would face and how he would deal with it! Digpal's surgical quotes are really catchy and hold true even today. And the end took me by surprise. I am sure, all doctors, especially surgeons and even non-medicoes will enjoy this book.

Regards,

**Dr Rohan Ariwala, M.S. (Surgery)**

# DISCLAIMER

This is a work of fiction. Names, characters, events and incidents are the product of the author's imagination. Any resemblance to actual persons, living or dead, or actual events is purely coincidental; however, the cases and surgical procedures are actual, with names and places, changed. Opinions expressed are those of the characters and should not be confused with the authors.

# PART ONE

31st December 1998, when the world was looking forward to a new dawn, Digpal, standing outside the jail gates was wondering where to go. He had, leave aside a job, no place to call his home. He had savings which will fulfil his basic needs for four to 5 months. For the last few days, he was trying to recapitulate his last eighteen years of life as a general surgeon.

# JOURNEY TILL NOW

1981, it was almost midnight. He was sitting alone in the small office cum change room for doctors, in the operation theatre complex, in his scrub suit, cap and mask, the last one hanging in front of his neck; planning in his mind, the emergency surgery he was going to undertake. He was tense, which was a rare occurrence. The patient was in a coma from a bad head injury, male of 50 years related to some of the managing committee members and belonged to the local majority community. The crowd outside was swelling.

Tense he was, four years back, as first year resident posted in paediatric surgery. Those were the times when surgical super specialists were few and that too only in metro cities. In the state of Madhya Pradesh, the only paediatric surgery unit was in Medical College Indore, his parent institute. It was a very busy unit, with continuous inflow of patients. From gasping newborns to children up to 12 years of age, with all varieties of surgical emergencies; congenital anomalies, burns, polytrauma, intestinal obstructions, peritonitis, and septicaemia due to perforated appendix or gut perforations. The memory of burns sent a chill in his spine. He could never forget the Diwali night when he was the only resident on duty with two interns. He was running between casualty ward and operation theatre for the whole night. That was the night when Rajwada of Indore was dedicated to the people of India. His friends told him the Rajwada was beautifully decorated with lights, a sight worth witnessing. But he had no time to think of Diwali. The memory of a baby with 100% burns due to an accidental fall in boiling oil in which her mother was frying Diwali sweets and a 4 years old whose fingers and palm were blown off due to firecracker, burnt faces and cornea of eyes haunted him till today.

His thoughts came back to the night when he was summoned to attend to a child with a serious head injury. Sweety was a healthy 5 years old girl who fell from the balcony. She was drowsy without any external wound. He could feel a boggy swelling on the left temporal region of the head. Digpal requested an X-Ray of the skull. In those days ultrasonography and CT scans were mere terms read by postgraduates in books of recent advances, M.R.I. was unheard of. The wet film showed a horizontal fracture in the left temporal bone extending into the parietal bone. Meanwhile, her left pupil started dilating and she seemed to be slipping in a coma. Hutchinson's pupil was a bad sign. She was bleeding intracranially. Digpal could understand she had an extradural haematoma and if she would be operated upon in time, she could be saved. He had never opened the skull independently. He tried to contact his senior resident who was preparing for his masters and had eloped to the hostel.

He tried to contact his consultant who had gone for a family function and was not immediately available. Time was running out for Sweety. He decided to operate upon her and instructed the intern to arrange for a unit of blood and requested the anesthesia resident to stand by. He explained the need for surgery to the parents who looked like manual labourers. They were in shock and nodded their consent without understanding much of the explanation by the young surgeon.

That day he was tense, as he was unsure of his surgical skill as an inexperienced resident. He had never opened a skull independently before that. On the operation table, lay a child in a deep coma with a shaved head, her life and fate to be decided by an immature surgeon in making. Digpal, after painting and draping the head of the baby, infiltrated the field with local anaesthetic and the child didn't move a bit. But, with the knife in hand, he was a different person. He always thought he was born with a surgical knife, to cure and heal with its deft strokes and change the lives of thousands of people. With a clean swipe of hand he gave a hockey stick incision above the hairline, cutting skin, subcutaneous tissue, and fascia together. He and the intern quickly caught the fascia with Kocher's forceps and turned it backwards on the skull. He met with a haematoma there which he cleared. Shining skull bones and a wide fracture was facing him. With a small trephine, he made a hole in the thin bone, and as soon as he removed the disc of bone, a clot followed by blood gushed out of the hole. The Anaesthetist started pushing blood into her vein. He could see the  pulsating brain with intact meninges. He found the bleeding middle meningeal artery and ligated it with some difficulty. At that point, the girl moaned and moved a bit. The Anaesthetist injected sedation and asked him to close quickly. Even that early in his career, Digpal was known for his surgical speed. He quickly closed the wound with nylon far and near continuous sutures around a soft rolled glove drain. By the time the wound was dressed and drapes removed, the child was crying full throat! He for the first time witnessed the 'magic of surgery', through his own two hands. The magic he was going to perform many more times for the rest of his life.

But today, this 1981 night, looking into the type of injuries, he was not so sure that the result of the surgery was going to be so miraculous which was the cause of his concern. He had already done a tracheostomy in the casualty, as the patient had aspirated his own blood in his lungs. He did a bilateral craniotomy and found that the brain was badly contused and oedematous with the collection of blood below the membranes. He wasn't much hopeful when he shifted Dhirubhai back to the I.C.U. The only positive was that both the pupils were reacting equal on both sides.

At that time he didn't know that tonight's incident was going to change his status in that area for years to come.

# THE PRINCIPIUM

When he joined the hospital a few months back, there were very few surgical patients in the wards, as there was no full-time surgeon in the hospital. A visiting surgeon used to come twice a week and he did not perform any major surgeries. Most of the bad surgical emergencies were referred to a bigger neighbouring city. Digpal was young, enthusiastic, hungry to learn, and wanted to improve his surgical skills. He had a natural flair for surgery and had worked extra hard to learn during his residency.

He was allotted a small, semi-furnished one-bedroom apartment on the hospital campus. On the very first day, a thin diminutive, smiling man in golden frame glasses entered his OPD and extended his thin hand.

"I am Sarang, Maganbhai Sarang, laboratory technician. You must be the new full time surgeon! If you need any kind of help please let me know, after you are free I will take you around and introduce you to all the doctors of this hospital." Then added "Hope you stay here for a few months."

True to his word, he was there soon after OPD hours and took him around the hospital. It was a three storied building with wide passages and verandas.

It had four wings and a central core, like a butterfly with garden spaces incorporated between opposing wings. Sarang introduced him to Ravindran; the Physician with big eyes and very thick glasses, Trivedi; the fair and shortish delicate looking Paediatrician, Shobhanaben; the plump Gynaecologist, probably she was pregnant too adding to her round look, her Ophthalmologist husband, Mahesh Shah and the hefty Orthopaedic surgeon Dinkar Desai. That time he didn't know that Sarang was going to be his man Friday for years to come.

Returning back to his OPD room, Sarang indicated towards the nameplate and smiled. The plate read Dr J. S. DIGPAL M.S. (Surgery).

"What's there to smile?" Asked Digpal curiously.

"Sorry Sir, the nameplate was painted in a hurry, and we couldn't get a new plate." Then he noticed that something was painted in Gujarati, covered with fresh black paint, then his name was painted in White over it!

"I can't read Gujarati."

"Then it's good," laughed Sarang and bid him goodbye. It was after many days when he learnt some Gujarati that he could read the faint outline of the word, it was 'jajru', which meant 'toilet.' He had a hearty laugh with his residents and interns, "General surgeon is no better than a janitor, more than half of the time, we are cleaning people's drainage system!"

Gradually the number of patients started increasing and in turn, he started enjoying his work. He became popular for his concern for the patient, promptness in attending to emergencies, and good clinical diagnosis. He was particularly known for his invisible scars due to his choice of transverse crease incisions for appendectomies, hernia surgeries, and paediatric surgeries instead of the conventional oblique and vertical incisions. Word spread quickly in the area that the new surgeon is skilled and clever. The management too was happy with the increasing popularity of the hospital. He would normally have his meals in the hospital mess, which was essentially vegetarian. Sarang would invite him sometimes for homemade non-vegetarian delicacies. His wife Shabnam was an excellent cook.

# SYMPHYSIOTOMY

The Gynecologist used to go to her hometown on weekends. The gynae resident was a middle-aged local doctor, who was experienced and competent; however, when she felt a caesarean section was required, she summoned Digpal. It was fascinating, with a beautiful outcome, a new life. Technically, he didn't find it very difficult to perform the surgery.

One night, the gynae resident called him up to come immediately for a short-statured tribal woman with a contracted pelvis. She was in advanced, obstructed labor. He instructed her to prepare the patient for LSCS.

"I don't think that will be possible, the head of the baby is stuck in the outlet and the caput can be seen at the interosseous."

"Okay, I am coming." But he had no inkling of what to do in such a case. Fortunately, he had brought an obstetrics book from the hospital library to brush up on his knowledge of the subject. It was a very old edition of Munro Kerr's textbook of Obstetrics. He frantically searched for obstructed labor and found a small paragraph on symphysiotomy for outlet obstruction.

He went straight to the labor room and asked the nurse to bring a sterile minor surgery tray. After sterilizing with alcohol, he injected a local anaesthetic over the pubic symphysis and stabbed with a pointed number 11 blade towards the symphysis and divided it. At that time he wasn't sure what he was doing and what to expect, but to his and everybody's surprise, the baby slid out with great ease. The resident nurses and lower staff clapped and he too wanted to clap for himself! He went back to his bed pleased with himself but worried about the pelvis of the lady. He had separated the two pubic bones, she may develop an unstable pelvis. First thing in the morning, he went straight to the ortho surgeon Dinkar, narrated the whole story, and asked his opinion. Dinkar advised to just strap the pelvis and she will be alright. He strapped the pelvis of the lady with the wide elastic adhesive, with the advice of complete bed rest.

Later on, when Shobhna came back, he asked her if he had done the right procedure. "I have never done, seen or heard of anyone doing this procedure; only read about it in the history of obstetrics! It's obsolete now," she was surprised.

"But it served the purpose," he protested. 'No method is obsolete, it has its utility, at the right place and time'. He mused.

Incidentally, the edition of 'Munro Kerr's Operative Obstetrics' which he had referred to was from the early fifties!

# POPULARIS

The Hospital, popularly known as 'Jiviben', was the only big hospital situated in the small coastal town of Gujarat, about 20 kms from the Union Territory of Diu or Div. It was run by the affluent Jain community and was named after the mother of the biggest donor as Jiviben Shah Memorial Hospital. Most of the regular big donors were from Mumbai (Bombay at that time). A local body was elected every five years to run the day-to-day affairs of the hospital. Though the town was not very big, the hospital catered to many surrounding villages and smaller towns.

For Digpal, it was a dream place. The salary was reasonably good, he didn't have to cut corners for his basic requirements. There was a small, 1 bedroom apartment which was enough for him and the best part, he was getting a good amount of surgical work independently and without any interference.

As time went by, the workload increased and he was getting known amongst the local who's who. A coastal highway passed from the outskirts of Vidurpur and a number of vehicular trauma cases used to come to Jiviben. In joint efforts with Dinkar, they started treating these cases promptly and efficiently and the word spread far and wide in the drainage area of the hospital.

He was becoming popular in surrounding villages and would get invited to weddings and public functions. He would seldom attend these functions for two reasons; he didn't get any time from his work and secondly, he was not very comfortable in such gatherings.

One of his ex-patients in his late seventies, whose Nissen's fundoplication was done by him for reflux, insisted he come for his grandson's wedding. It was a Sunday and he made an exception. He called Sarang and asked him to accompany him. The two of them travelled on the rickety two-wheeler of Sarang to the nearby village located on the highway. The noisy venue was crowded with unknown faces. They waded through the crowd and found the old man sitting on a long easy chair, surrounded by relatives. They wished him *Namaste* with folded hands, but the old man gave Digpal a completely blank look! One of the relatives asked him,

"Who are you? Sorry, didn't recognize you."

"*Kaka* (uncle) invited him, he is Dr Digpal, surgeon at Jiviben." Sarang intruded.

"*Dada* (grandpa) developed Alzheimer's in the last few weeks, please have your meals." Requested the young man. Both of them went back into the crowd, and suddenly they noticed a couple and their daughter coming towards them.

"Are you Dr Digpal of Jiviben?" Asked the man.

"Yes," he answered with a smile. Sarang looked towards Digpal as if telling him, 'see, you are becoming popular'.

"You had operated upon my mother two months back." Said the middle-aged man.

"How's *Ba* (mother) now, she must be doing well?" Digpal asked.

"Oh! Don't you remember? She died the same day in the ICU after you did her surgery," replied the man, surprised. Digpal's smile vanished, "Yes, now I remember, very sorry for that." And they both excused themselves and proceeded towards a corner. "Let's leave, I am getting bored." Digpal whispered in Sarang's ear.

"What about lunch, then?" Sarang didn't want to miss the goodies and sweets displayed on the buffet counter.

"We will eat at Ballu's dhaba on the highway. You get delicious chicken preparations there."

"Will do." Answered Sarang reluctantly.

In hindsight, he remembered a 78 year old obese lady brought straight to OT as an emergency case, as it was his surgery day. It was a busy operation day with an interval appendicectomy, two Bassini's repairs for hernia, a gastrojejunostomy with vagotomy and so on. Those were the times when cimetidine or proton pump inhibitors were not available and the incidence of peptic ulcers and their complications like bleeding, pyloric stenosis, and even hourglass stomach were not uncommon and the only cure was surgery.

He had his own way of doing GJ/V. After opening the upper abdomen with a midline incision, he would pull down the stomach and feel the taut vagus nerve, hook it on a mixter's forceps and divide. His logic was that the oesophagus is a muscular structure which will stretch by pulling down, but the nerve won't, which in turn stands out clearly. After gastrojejunostomy he used to make a small hole in the high point of the fundus and pass two feeding tubes through that; one of them stays in the pyloric canal, to drain the stomach postoperatively and another passes through the anastomotic stoma into the jejunum. The second one was used for feeding. This way the patient would hardly need any intravenous fluids postoperatively and could be fed through the second tube, and the nasogastric tube was avoided by the first tube. The patient was not only more comfortable but would also save money on IV fluids.

That day, as he was about to close the abdomen of a GJ/V patient, an intern came and whispered in his ear, "There are two emergencies, I have called them in the OT." He told the assistant to close and went straight to the OT lobby to examine the cases in his scrubs only. The first one was a middle-aged female with vomiting and distention, and an erect X-Ray showed multiple air fluid levels with an empty colon. A simple straightforward case of small gut obstruction. He explained to the relatives, who agreed immediately to surgery. On exploration, it turned out to be obstruction due to an omental band, which he divided and the patient recovered uneventfully. The other case was not all that straightforward. Again a female, obese, known diabetic, and hypertensive. 78 years of age with marked tachycardia, hypotension, and distended, tender abdomen. These were the early eighties and investigative facilities were very basic in smaller places. Clinicians had to rely mostly on their clinical acumen. For surgeons the dictum was, 'when in doubt, open and see!' This was one of those cases. She could have had peritonitis, obstruction, or acute pancreatitis.

She was in bad shape and her chances of survival were bleak. Digpal explained to them the risk of surgery and prognosis and asked if he could take the chance. With some reluctance, the relatives agreed for exploratory laparotomy. Though Harish, the Anaesthetist, was not very happy with Digpal's decision as she looked toxic with marked tachycardia, leukocytosis, high blood sugar, high blood urea, and creatinine; he agreed reluctantly. On exploration, the abdominal cavity was full of hemorrhagic fluid, digested fat, and oedematous viscera. It was acute hemorrhagic pancreatitis. Harish told him to wind up quickly as the patient was sinking. He quickly washed the cavity, placed drains in both 'gutters', and closed the abdomen with a thick nylon suture and some tension sutures. Her respiration didn't resume and they shifted her to the ICU with an endotracheal tube and ambu's bag. She died after 6 hours. She was the lady, who was the mother of the family Digpal and Sarang met at the wedding function.

## SOME GOOD NEWS

Meanwhile, Dhirubhai, the head injury patient on whom he had done bilateral craniotomy, was stable though still unconscious but responding to painful stimuli. there was an occasional eye-opening as well. After more than three weeks Digpal removed his tracheostomy and was satisfied with his recovery. But the relatives were not, for two reasons: One- they thought that the recovery was very slow. Second- they were rich and renowned, getting treated in a small town general hospital by a young general surgeon was not their idea of good treatment. So, they decided to fly him to Mumbai (Bombay, those days) to be treated by a renowned Neurosurgeon. Digpal felt all his hard work going into the drain, the patient was to definitely improve over time, but the credit will be taken away from him. He refused to discharge him and told them sternly that they could go only against his advice. (Known as DAMA amongst medical circles i.e. Discharged Against Medical Advice.) The relatives complied and took the patient away, accusing him of rude behaviour. 'So much for society's gratitude towards doctors', thought Digpal.

John was an employee on whom no designation would fit. He was almost a permanent fixture in the operation theatre. He had no formal education but knew every detail of autoclaving, sterilization techniques, surgical instruments and their uses, anaesthesia equipment, and everything else pertaining to surgery. He was middle-aged, unmarried, hard-working, and an alcohol addict. He would start getting tremors in his hands when not drunk. He was respected by all and nobody ever minded his drinking habit. He would generally give his opinion about a new surgeon within a week and it was considered perfect.

Digpal used to begin his surgical operations from six in the morning, John would come at 4 AM. He would bring out sterilised drums from the autoclave machine and if nurses were a bit late, he would start arranging surgical instruments on the trollies, check oxygen and nitrous oxide cylinders, and top-up Ether and Trilene in the bottles. After a week of Digpal joining Jiviben, during surgery, John was standing on a short stool behind him and murmured, "He is doing a good job, he has good hands and mind," and the surgeon felt as if he received his postgrad once again!

Immersed in his work, Digpal had almost forgotten Dhirubhai, the head injury patient who had taken discharge against advice. After four days of him leaving for Bombay when Digpal was busy examining patients in OPD, he noticed two of Dhirubhai's relatives peeping from the door asking for permission to come in. After He signalled them to come in, one of them said politely, "We want to admit our Father again under your care." Digpal agreed reluctantly but was surprised with the change in their behaviour. They were very rude when they had taken forced discharge. The secret was revealed by one of his interns who happened to be related to them. When they had consulted the senior Neurosurgeon of Bombay Hospital, a straightforward Parsi gentleman, he didn't mince words and told them bluntly in Gujarati, "*Ahiyan shu karva laiva chho? Tamara gam na surgeone ketlu saaru treatment karelu chhe.*" (Why have you brought him here, the surgeon of your town has done such a good job) And this was a game changer! Since Dhirubhai was a big businessman, the word spread in the town about the new surgeon. Till then only poor and middle-class people used to come to him for elective surgery, now patients from the affluent class too started pouring in donations started increasing and Jiviben Hospital was considered a decent destination for getting treated. Digpal had completed his first year in the hospital. He was given a raise in salary and the management offered him the post of Medical Superintendent, which he accepted as he had learnt some working knowledge of Gujarati, though still he mixed many Hindi words in his conversation. The new responsibility made his busy life busier.

Digpal had a special liking for paediatric surgery. He loved his little patients, but he felt a bit handicapped in that field, as the hospital didn't have the kind of facilities needed for difficult neonatal surgeries. The instruments for paediatric work were non-existent, NICU was not well geared to handle post-op cases and the nurses were not adequately trained. With existing instruments he could manage surgeries like appendectomies, congenital hernia, and trauma on older children, but couldn't do many other neonatal surgeries and congenital anomalies and neonatal surgeries. Those were the times when antenatal care was not available to a large number of women resulting in too many congenital defects; even neural tube defects too were pretty common for want of folic acid. He decided to go to Bombay one of these days and hand-pick instruments himself, but something happened which postponed his visit to the metro and for good it was!

Mr. Pratap Singh Sisodia was Superintendent of Police of the district, of which Vidurpur was the taluka and it came under his jurisdiction. His image was of an efficient and strict IPS officer. His eldest daughter had cleared her MBBS from Jamnagar medical college. Her mother wanted her to stay at home during her Internship. The reputation of Jiviben Hospital had reached police headquarters as well and the parents decided to enroll their daughter, Kalpana at Jiviben for 1 year's internship; as it was easy to commute every day from home to the hospital.

The list of new interns was placed on Digpal's table for assigning them to different departments, from where they would be rotated every 2 months. On the first day, he called them to his administrative office to brief them on the working pattern, punctuality and so on. New interns were six in number and at the reporting time of 9 AM, only five were present.

"Where is the 6th one?" He asked.

"Sir, she is Kalpana Sisodia, must be on her way." Informed one of the interns.

Digpal briefed them about the rotation system and the different departments each one was posted in.

"You all have to be punctual and be in the hospital before your seniors." Digpal explained. "Don't think these are paid holidays, as it is popular belief amongst medicose."

In India, the one year internship is thought to be an easy going period when not much sincerity is expected, but Digpal thought otherwise. As he was about to tell them to disperse, a very beautiful, fair, tall girl, with big brown eyes and long black hair entered his office without asking for his permission, accompanied by a police constable, who saluted him and stood there. "Yes?" Digpal asked with a question mark on his face.

"She is Sisodia *saheb's* daughter, joining here for learning," the constable said in Gujarati.

"Are you going to work with her in the hospital?" Digpal asked sarcastically.

"No *saheb*, she will work here," stammered the constable.

"Then, what are you doing here?" Asked Digpal.

Constable saluted and hurried out. All the interns laughed mutely, except Kalpana.

"You must come on time madam," he told firmly, "this won't be tolerated, and it doesn't matter who is your Father. You are posted in gynae for two months, after that in Surgery. You may leave now."

Even during the short encounter he couldn't ignore the beauty of this intern. She was taller than average, fair, classically beautiful features, well shaped brown eyes, long black brown hair, and a well proportioned body. He shook his head trying to shake away her image and continued with his official work. However, whenever the gynae team crossed the surgical team he couldn't help giving her a flying look, not to give an impression of staring towards her, which the residents and interns did without hesitation. One of the residents whispered, "What a bod!"

"Obviously, she was the best athlete in the college," answered one of the interns, "but beware, you know, who her Father is."

But then, he hardly had any time to think and brood upon the beauty of an intern. That particular day, the Ortho surgeon was on leave, and it was his operation day. He thought he could use the opportunity to post one of his waiting thoracic cases. It was a case of a large opacity in the left side of thoracic cavity, thought to be a pleural effusion. It was referred to him by the Physician Ravindran, a very sincere and knowledgeable colleague. He would sometimes take Digpal's help for tapping difficult pleural and pericardial effusions. In this particular case too after a failed aspiration, the Physician sent the patient to Digpal, but he too found it a dry tap. After careful review of the average quality X-Ray, he noticed that unlike an effusion, it was not an opacity with uniform density, but was blotched at places. He decided to do a diagnostic thoracotomy, and discussed this with Ravindran who seconded his decision. But before he could instruct the OT staff to prepare for the surgery, a resident posted in casualty was seen hurrying towards him.

"Sir before you go to the OT, have a look at this lad in casualty; he is bad, marked tachycardia, hypotension, high fever and rigid abdomen," told the resident in one breath, "and I have already pushed 4 pints of fluids."

Digpal rushed to casualty, and yes, the boy was in septic shock. He instructed the resident to prepare him for emergency laparotomy, and take a high risk consent. He explained to the worried parents and relatives about the condition of the boy, they in turn agreed after some discussion amongst them. Then he rushed towards the OT; called up the OT nurse and told her to prepare for an emergency laparotomy and entered the doctor's office cum change room to discuss the case with Harish, the Anaesthesiologist, who always insisted on being called so, instead of an Anaesthetist. They decided to post the thoracotomy case after the laparotomy.

Digpal opened the patient with a mid-right paramedian incision, where he found the peritoneal cavity to be full of foul-smelling pus. It must be from lower GI, he thought. He had a habit of speaking continuously during surgery, "In a young man with peritonitis and foul smelling pus, think appendicular perforation first." And there it was, the appendix was gangrenous, perforated at the base, with gangrene extending into the wall of the coecum. Almost two square cm of the cecal wall was gangrenous. He did a thorough peritoneal lavage with normal saline solution; then deftly removed the appendix with the gangrenous part of the coecal wall. There was hardly any bleeding as the feeding vessels and veins had already thrombosed. "Give me a malecot's catheter no.34, sister." He told a bit loudly,

"Sir, you are not going to stitch back the coecum?"

"You know what is the peculiarity of coecum? It has the highest intraluminal pressure in the whole GI tract, forward pressure from the ileum and the ileocecal valve is a non-return valve and backward gravitational pressure from ascending colon. If you attempt to repair, the sutures are going to blow-away post-operatively and your patient will be worse than preoperative status and you will lose him." While talking he placed the flower of malecot's catheter delicately in the inflamed coecum, put a loose catgut suture on the cecal wall near the entry point of the catheter; and brought the catheter out through a stab incision in the right iliac fossa. he then placed drains on both the flanks and closed the abdomen. "The patient is already better," said Harish smilingly, "that peritoneal lavage did good to him, the BP is stable and pulse rate is coming down." He had developed a good rapport with Harish, they admired each other for their competence.

The patient was shifted to recovery and the nurse started preparing for the thoracotomy.

# D.O.T– A SURGEON'S NIGHTMARE

Farhan was barely 20, and 32 kg, an emaciated son of a tonga owner, Abdul. He had been receiving anti-tubercular treatment for the last three years and that was only worsening his condition, hence the decision to perform a diagnostic thoracotomy.

Harish was not very happy with the patient's general condition, but Digpal told him it was only a diagnostic thoracotomy and Harish agreed; he induced and intubated the patient and gave him a shot of tubocurarine as a muscle relaxant. The surgeon put a 3 inch intercostal incision, and what he saw gave him a small jolt.There was a glistening, moving, peristaltic small gut in the thoracic cavity.

"Looks like a diaphragmatic hernia. Harish, will you allow me to repair it?" Asked Digpal and the answer was just "Hmm," a reluctant 'yes' by Harish. He further extended the incision; and lo and behold, the spleen too was in the thoracic cavity. There were adhesions between the lungs and the gut.

"I will have to open abdomen too; to reduce the content in abdomen and perform a splenectomy," said Digpal.

"Patient is already sinking, his heart has stopped," Harish hissed. He injected Mephentin, with no effect; adrenaline injection, no response. Digpal put his hand in the thoracic cavity and pushed and pumped the heart between his fingers and the patient's sternum. There was some feeble activity in the heart, and then it stopped again. They kept on trying to revive the patient without any result. It was more than 3 hours that Farhan was in the OT, and the crowd started swelling outside the OT Complex. Ultimately they had to abandon any further attempt of resuscitation and Digpal quickly closed the chest.

Both the surgeon and Anaesthetist were hugely disappointed and saddened by the young death. Now the next big question was breaking the news to the relatives, and who else but the surgeon had to do that? Digpal might be an excellent surgeon, but he wasn't great at communicating with relatives; he was poor at mincing words and was too straightforward.

John advised him not to go out and face the crowd, "They can become violent," he warned. Digpal removed his operating gown and went out of the OT, called up Abdul, who knew him well, as he had ridden his tonga many times. By the surgeon's expressions, Abdul guessed the mishap.

"Sorry Abdulbhai, we have lost Farhan, we couldn't save him," informed Digpal.

The mob of about 50 people started murmuring, one of them shouted angrily, "You have killed our brother." Abdul raised his hand and spoke firmly, "It is not doctor *saheb's* fault, this is Allah's will. We have nothing against you doctor *saheb, shukriya.*"

Digpal bowed his head and went into the OT doctor's room to change, but for many days, and more during nights when he was alone, he couldn't forget the sad incident and kept on analysing what he should have or should not have done.

After that dreadful incident, life was back on track with a continuous inflow of patients. There used to be some cases, where Shobhna, the gynaecologist needed his help if there was an associated surgical problem during operations. Similarly, when he was operating on female patients and some abnormality turned up with female genital organs, he would call up Shobhna; who was invariably accompanied by Kalpana. He would give a flying glance towards her as if he had not noticed her presence; but women are good at judging these glances. She too adored his surgical skills, his confidence and his knowledge. Only after 15 days now she would be posted with him in the department of surgery; and Digpal was eagerly waiting for that.

## J. S. DIGPAL

After his occasional encounter with Kalpana, Digpal became a bit self-conscious. He would stand in front of a full-length mirror and try to analyse himself. He was an inch shorter than 6 feet, darker in complexion than an average wheatish Indian; not very muscular or macho physique; thin built, and his chest bones were slightly prominent in the middle due to childhood malnutrition. On his bare chest, a rickety rosary of calcium deficiency was visible. The only positive was his balanced facial features, a sharp nose, shallow divide of the chin, black pupils in the middle of medium size eyes, which missed nothing and a thick lock of black hair. He had a peculiar birthmark on the root of his neck on the left side and it looked as if a lady was sitting on knees and hip joints fully flexed with open hair and head thrown backwards. He preferred to stay clean shaven and his stubble grew very quickly.

Though he looked thin, he was tough, as he had grown up in an orphanage, where life was pretty structured and it was a continuous struggle to get your full quota of food and maintain your superiority among other children. It was impossible to have any food choice in the orphanage, so he was not fussy about the food he got to eat. He would make his own tea and breakfast in his apartment and take meals in the hospital mess, where students, nurses and patient's relatives took their meals. It was basic and not very tasty but it didn't matter to him.

Since it was a Christian mission orphanage, the children would get meat on Sunday for their lunch and it used to be a big day for them. The quantity used to be limited and they invariably used to have quarrels on Sundays for pieces of meat. There used to be thin, fiery curry in which you had to search for pieces but it used to be their best meal of the week. He badly missed non-vegetarian food in the mess, and in Gujarat, people felt uneasy if you ask about the availability of non-vegetarian food. Here again, Sarang came to his rescue. Though a Hindu sailor by the community, his wife Shabnam was a Muslim and cooked delicious non-vegetarian preparations and often invited Digpal for that. Sarang had started treating him like his younger brother, but being brought up in an orphanage, Digpal's understanding of affection, attachment and reciprocation of love had not developed fully. After a few months, he found a non-vegetarian joint in a Muslim area, where food was cheap and tasted good, and he didn't mind the poor hygienic conditions.

One evening, while Sarang and Digpal were chatting over a drink and it was the third peg of rum, Sarang asked about his background. He slowly opened up in front of his only friend in the town and confessed that he wrote his name in reverse and that it is- Digpal Singh Joseph.

"So you are a Christian by religion?" Asked Sarang, surprised.

"I don't know," answered Digpal.

"Then why such a surname?"

He was brought up in an orphanage, 'God's own children', run by a Christian mission near Indore. Father Samuel was the main caretaker of the mission, which had a Church, an orphanage and a school up to 12th std. Sister Maria and Sister Sofia were two nuns who helped Father Samuel. Sayed Ahmed Ali used to look after the accounts of the mission.

As per Father Samuel, he was abandoned by someone on the steps of the Church when he was a newborn; wrapped in a white cloth; there was no thread, cross or tabiz to indicate his religion. He was a full term healthy baby, the only mark on his body was that dark peculiarly shaped birthmark on his neck, like a lady's profile in a sitting position with open hair thrown backwards. "We surgeons call it a port wine stain but because of my dark

complexion it looks dark black," smiled Digpal.

Most of the orphans were either taken back by their parents, who had left them in the orphanage due to poverty, or were adopted by childless rich Indians or foreigners. Somehow he was not chosen for adoption. But unlike most children, he was bright in studies and stood on merit in the state board. Mr. Digpal Singh Chouhan was a regular donor and visitor of the orphanage, he was a local zamindar, he liked him and his name and when he was to be admitted in 1st std, when asked, he told his name is Digpal Singh. Since the name of the mission was St. Joseph Church and School, 'Joseph' was added with his name.

Father Samuel tried to convince him to get baptised in Christianity, but he was adamant and told he had no faith and belief in god and he just didn't want to embrace any religion for the sake of it.

Sayed Ahmed Ali too explained the principles of Islam, the uncomplicated one god theory and preaching of the Quran-e-Sharif. He liked the idea but refused to be labelled to any particular faith. During their secondary school tenure; he opted for Sanskrit as a third language and studied Bhagavad Gita. He was very impressed with Gita's preachings. But again he thought, he is ok with his agnostic status.

Children who completed their schooling had to leave the orphanage. As he got admission to the most reputed medical college in the state, he shifted to the medical hostel and becoming a doctor and if possible a surgeon, was his dream. Dr Banerjee, who used to visit the orphanage once a month for routine check-ups of the children rendered his services free of charge to the mission. And from his childhood, he was in awe of Dr Banerjee, idolised him and wanted to become a doctor. When sitting alone he would proudly see his long thin fingers, one of the very few positives of his physique, and imagine himself holding a surgical scalpel in them.

He was getting a merit cum poverty scholarship which was barely enough to pay for his food bill and some sundry expenses. Since he had no extra money to spend in the college canteen or hotels or movies, he avoided going out with his classmates. He couldn't make any friends but he had to continue hard work and studies to get good marks in examinations, otherwise, his scholarship would be discontinued. Purchasing expensive medical books was impossible for him; that made him sit for long hours in the college library. Sometimes an occasional donation from the zamindar would come in handy; he would generally ask about his progress and any monetary requirement. He scored well in his MBBS examination and after passing out; the stipend of internship and then of residency solved his financial vows.

After completing his master's in surgery, he frantically searched for a job, when he came across this advertisement for the vacancy of a surgeon. He didn't know where Vidurpur was situated, except that it was in Gujarat, and he had some idea about how to reach there. He caught a bus to Ahmedabad and from there he could get an old state transport bus for Vidurpur. He was quickly selected, as neither of the parties had any choice. The salary of Rs. 1200 sounded wonderful to him; he liked the hospital, the peaceful quiet town and he joined immediately.

Before he left Indore, he went to the mission to bid goodbye and seek blessings from Father Samuel, Sisters Maria and Sofia, Sayed Ahmed Ali, Dr Banerjee and Thakur Digpal Singh Chauhan.

In the end, he went to meet his professor, Dr C.P. Tripathi

touched his feet and informed him about his job. "Always remember, never think that you have become a surgeon, this degree is only a license for beginning to become a surgeon. The process of learning surgery will never stop till the last day of your professional life." Said the wise professor and he never forgot that, and when he did, he had to learn the lesson the harsh way.

# MECKEL'S DIVERTICULUM AND AMENTIA

He was in OT performing an appendectomy on a 16 year old girl. He almost always used a transverse crease incision, a bit low in females, so that it is not visible when they wear a saree or other dresses. In those pre-ultrasonography days, it was not unusual to get an occasional surprise on exploration. Encounters with ovarian torsion, tubo-ovarian inflammatory mass, ectopic pregnancies, and ileocecal tuberculosis were not too uncommon. He felt a transverse incision can be extended to perform even a major procedure if need be. His incision would rarely be more than 2 inches in young females for a routine appendectomy.

While he was exploring mesentery and ileum, for co-morbidity and Meckel's diverticulum; his thoughts went back to residency days and Ruchita Nadkarni. She was an 18 year old girl, slim with slightly prominent upper incisors and was average looking. She had acute appendicitis and he took her up for an emergency appendectomy. While exploring the ileum he found a large Meckel's diverticulum, 2 feet proximal from the ileocecal junction. He had a theoretical idea about Meckel's diverticulum but had never seen such a big one. He called a senior resident to have a look who in turn said that since the base of the diverticulum is bigger than the width of the ileum, better to do a resection and anastomosis, to remove any possible ectopic tissue. He gave his opinion and left the OT. Digpal did a resection anastomosis and appendectomy in that patient and was too happy with the opportunity he got for performing a major procedure independently, and that too during his first year of residency. Postoperatively he would take extra care of her and her parents. Since resection was done she required IV fluid for 2-3 days. After 48 hours she started having distension of the abdomen, no bowel sounds, raised pulse rate and fever. During rounds, he asked the consultant to please examine her and guide him. The senior man told him to do proper nasogastric suction and add potassium to the drip; it may just be a prolonged postoperative intestinal ileus. After another 2 days her condition started deteriorating further. He would sit near her bed whenever he got time. On rounds once again he insisted his professor examine her, which he did and told him to post her for laparotomy. Then he asked Digpal,

"Who did her surgery?"

"Sir, I did during my emergency."

"You know her anastomosis seems to have leaked and she will need blood for re-exploration, she is looking anaemic."

"Yes Sir," he answered meekly.

Ruchita's blood group turned out to be an uncommon one, AB positive, which was not available in the blood bank, but incidentally, Digpals's group was the same. He happily donated blood for her. The boss did the laparotomy through a big right paramedian incision; the anastomosis was leaking. He performed a re-do and subsequently, she recovered completely. During the postoperative period, Digpal felt so guilty that he spent more and more time with her. He felt sorry for the suffering she underwent; an additional long scar on her young abdomen. But it was not the same for Ruchita and her parents. Her parents thanked him profusely for his attention and blood donation, and Ruchita's feelings took a different turn. She started liking the young doctor. During the last dressing before discharge, when they were alone for some time, she held his hand and told "You are a very nice person doctor, can we keep on meeting even after I recover completely?" Digpal was not ready for this "Well, you can come for follow-up whenever you have any problem."

Ruchita had thought he had also started liking her but his answer disappointed her. The infatuation gradually weaned off but Digpal could never forget her leaked anastomosis.

Digpal was closing the appendectomy case which was a straightforward one. He always told his assistants, to respect the tissues, don't apply tight sutures, our job is to only approximate the cut margins; healing will be done by nature. "Tight sutures are a sign of a surgeon's insecurity, it will only make the margins ischaemic, delay the healing, increase fibrosis and subsequently it will be an ugly but weak scar."

Then there was this case of Govindbhai Bhandari, another one with a huge Meckel's diverticulum, the heaviest he ever witnessed! Bhandari, a 45 year old, male, presented with classical signs of acute small gut obstruction. Digpal opened him up through a right paramedian incision. To his surprise, the loop of ileum was disappearing in the pelvis. When he brought it out, it was twisted on itself and a 3 x 5 inches Meckel's diverticulum, filled with fluid, giving it a globular shape was the culprit. From there, the surgery was simple, he did a resection and anastomosis of the small gut and closed it.

Postoperatively, for five days Govindbhai's abdomen was silent. He added more potassium and calcium to the drip, but the gut refused to move. He suspected probably his anastomosis had leaked, but there were no signs of septicaemia. However he lost his patience on the seventh postop day, and re-explored the abdomen. To his surprise, everything looked fine. He did a small ileo-transverse shunt, to reduce distention from the small gut, and closed the abdomen, hoping for the best. Govindbhai's gut started moving after 48 hours, but Digpal kept on wondering, what was the cause of intractable paralytic ileus! Before the patient was to be discharged, past midnight something struck his thought process; he could hardly wait for dawn. In the morning, he went straight to the wards and asked Govindbhai to stand, and close his eyes. The surgeon had to catch hold of him to prevent his fall!

"That explains," he spoke aloud and instructed the nurse to send the patient's blood for a VDRL test; which subsequently turned out to be strongly positive. 'Riddle solved, it was ileus due to autonomic neuropathy of syphilitic etiology'! he inferred.

# MAGANBHAI SARANG

Sarang's full name was Maganbhai Jhinabhai Sarang, but he was known as Sarangbhai or Sarang saheb. Though he was only a laboratory technician but was very popular among people of that area. Thin, petite, ever smiling, ready to help anyone; and used to wear golden frame glasses. He was in Jiviben for the last 20 years, was only a higher secondary pass and had learnt the techniques of his job in this hospital only from his seniors and visiting pathologists. He belonged to a poor family which owned a small fishing boat and would generally sail for fishermen in the Arabian Sea. His first wife belonged to his own community. She died 16 years back due to carcinoma of the breast.

His second wife Shabnam was accompanying her Father Mahboob when the latter was admitted for prostatic surgery in hospital. She came in contact with Sarang during that period and they started liking each other. Their marriage was not a straightforward affair. Sarang refused to convert to Islam and Shabnam's Father and other relatives did not agree to this relationship. Shabnam's mother had died 10 years back during her 7th delivery. Mahboob was poor and had 6 children to look after. After much convincing from sensible people of both communities, they agreed to a court marriage and that the two of them would retain their own religion. Now they had been married for 15 years and had a 14 year old son, Sahil and were happy together.

Sarang had many acquaintances but no close friends. Since he had met Digpal he immediately liked the tall, dark young man who didn't speak much; except when he was talking about surgery; had no religious beliefs; was straight forward and lacked any tact or diplomacy. Gradually they became close friends in spite of the age difference. Sarang was very proud of their friendship, after all, Digpal was a surgeon and Sarang knew he subsequently would become the Superintendent of the hospital, which he did after one year of him joining Jiviben.

Generally, they would go out together and after a year Digpal purchased a second-hand scooter on which they would go to the nearby Union Territory of Diu, where beaches were beautiful, alcohol was available cheap and seafood was in abundance.

Shabnam too started treating Digpal as a family member, she was only a year older than him but he respected her and addressed her as Bhabhi. For the first time in life, Digpal felt he had a family.

## URETERIC STONE

Those were the times when ureteric endoscopy was not developed and was available only in metro cities and the complication rate of Dormia basket was very high. Once again it was a long tiring operation list and one obese contractor was to be operated for a long date palm seed calculus in the lowest part of Ureter, and the lower end of stone was stuck in the intramural part of the ureter. It required a lot of retraction and exposure of this awkward space of body. It was the last case of the day; Digpal removed the calculus and sutured the ureter with thin interrupted catgut sutures; placed a retroperitoneal drain and instructed the resident to place foley's self-retaining catheter in the bladder. As soon as Digpal left the OT, the resident instructed the intern to introduce the catheter and went away for lunch. And it was for the first time the intern was introducing foley's catheter on his own.

During the evening round, Digpal observed that there was a little blood stained urine in the bag and the patient was complaining of pain. He ordered the nurse to inject another shot of analgesic and added an additional pint of IV fluids.

At 8 PM when he was about to have his dinner, it was a senior staff nurse on the intercom and she sounded worried. She said the patient is passing frank blood in the catheter and is in a lot of pain. He instructed her to shift the patient to OT and called up the OT nurse to keep a trolley ready for re-exploration. He wondered if there was a major bleeder in the uretric wall which he had missed. He couldn't eat and rushed to the OT, on the way rang the bell of Harish's apartment and told him to come to OT.

He examined the obese patient on the table and noticed that the foley's catheter is longer than expected. And the patient's lower abdomen looks swollen with urine coming out of the drain.

He removed the foley's catheter and the patient passed urine with great force, spraying blood stained urine on Digpal and the nurse standing near him. Actually the intern did not introduce the catheter fully up to the urinary bladder and inflated it in the perineal urethra resulting in it's rupture and retention of urine. The surgeon had to re-introduce a fresh foley's catheter to stop the bleeding from urethra and drain the urine from bladder.

After this episode he found it difficult to believe his juniors, even for minor procedures, which didn't make him popular amongst them.

## CUPID STRIKES

Gradually Digpal was in good rapport with his colleague consultants; Mahesh and Shobhna, who had a newborn baby and Dinkar Desai, the Orthopedic surgeon. He too was a bachelor and both of them would sometimes go to Diu together. Ravindran was a typical studious physician with excellent theoretical knowledge and with his thick glasses and Harrison near his chest gave him the look of one. Trivedi the Paediatrician was married, his wife was a homemaker and a son of 2 years, they didn't mix much with others.

But, what was changing Digpal's life was the new entrant Kalpana Sisodia the intern. Now she was rotated to the surgery department and Digpal tried very hard to treat her like other interns; tried to ignore her, and even reprimand her occasionally for coming late on duty. She was generally present in OT, when he was operating and was interested in scrubbing to assist too but Digpal kept on keeping her out of the operating team for some days. One day in a female patient he suddenly looked towards her and said, "Go scrub." It was a case of a large mesenteric cyst. After exploration he gave an incision over the cyst with a tinted scalpel to delicately cut only the thin mesentery. Kalpana was awed to see the skill and accuracy of the surgeon. She had assisted some gynec operations but nothing as fine as this. He carefully separated the mesentery from the thin wall cyst putting his fingers between the two layers and a complete cyst about 10 x 10 inches filled with clear fluid came out intact, without a drop of bleeding. "A ruptured cyst is a surgeon's ruptured ego." He said smilingly while keeping the cyst carefully in a big kidney tray, which John was holding in his extended hand in anticipation. John was fond of showing the removed pathologies to the anxious relatives standing outside the OT and would receive tips from them, for his evening dose of booze. Digpal closed the mesentery with thin catgut, putting interrupted sutures.

"Why are we not using continuous sutures Sir, to give it a smoother finish?"

He was happy she asked something and he always enjoyed explaining, "We have to leave some gaps for the oozing serum from the space formed by removed cyst or it will be trapped inside and collect between the leaves of mesentery." When she was removing her gown and gloves, this ordinary looking, dark, thin surgeon started looking attractive to her.

Gradually Kalpana volunteered to assist Digpal in most of the cases, if not as first, then as a second assistant.

## TRIP TO BOMBAY

The hospital ran mainly on donations; majority of it coming from NRIs of the town but generally it was always on brink and short of money. He somehow could convince the management to purchase paediatric instruments and some upgraded gadgets for OT.

During one of his trips to Diu, he hesitantly confided in Sarang about his liking for Kalpana and Sarang jumped on the revelation. "Don't be too late in telling her, in a few months her internship will be over and she will be gone for PG and her parents will get her married," advised Sarang.

He talked of his plans of going to the metro with his juniors. After the OPD, finding him alone, Kalpana entered his office and asked hesitantly, "Sir, have you ever been to Bombay?" He moved his head in negative. "My uncle stays in Andheri and I have been to Bombay many times. Will you mind if I accompany you? I can be a good guide," she said smilingly.

What else would he have asked for? Happy inside, apparently he said, "Well, but the management has sanctioned travel expenditure for only one; that too in second class, and no taxi fare. We have to use local trains only."

"Fine with me, I will sponsor my own trip, will ask for my parent's permission and join you."

"Jump on the wagon then."

Kalpana convinced her parents to visit her uncle and he decided to catch a train to Bombay from Ahmedabad; where they reached by state transport bus. Both of them with their backpacks boarded an unreserved compartment, luckily the train was not very crowded.

It was a 9 hour journey to Bombay. They talked about surgery, different career options after MBBS, then literature, movies, and politics. And about then Prime Minister, Mrs. Indira Gandhi, whom they both adored. Then tired, Kalpana on the window seat started dozing off and kept her head on his shoulder. He sat stiff, wide awake, having a feeling, he could not understand himself. He never had been so near to a girl whom he liked; currents of excitement running through him, he sat there unmoved, fearing she may wake up and move her head away.

His thoughts and her sleep were disturbed by the cacophony of Borivali station. "Next stop will be Andheri," she informed. "You come with me and stay at my uncle's place, they have a big apartment at Lokhandwala and they won't mind." He declined her offer and told her he will stay at the YMCA hostel and the next morning they will coordinate for instrument shopping. It was around 10 PM and Digpal noticed, the city didn't look like it was going to sleep at all.

As was decided they both reached the Churchgate station at 10 AM. Even at that hour it was warm and humid; October though it was, which is considered the beginning of winters, but is hot in this part of India. The fast life, high rise buildings, local trains, crowd, were all very fascinating to Digpal. He had never been to a metro city before and Kalpana was absolutely at home.

"It's quite a city. High rises, the sea..."

"Yes," smiled Kalpana, noticing that he had never been to such a big city, "almost like New York, only the later is cleaner, less noisy, the high rise buildings are taller and subway train is less crowded."

"Oh! Have you seen New York?" He asked, a bit surprised.

"Two years back our family, my parents and younger brother; all four of us went vacationing; on east coast tour of America; we go abroad every alternative year."

Digpal could only mutter "Oh," and mused, even coming to

Bombay is a big deal for him, can't even think of an overseas trip and he didn't believe in unrealistic dreams.

They walked to Princess Street, famous for all kinds of surgical instruments, hospital equipment and medicines. They reached a big instrument shop; it was a typical Indian style shop where the long display counter was facing the road. The customer had to climb two steps to stand on a two feet wide clearance in front of the counter on which a large number of surgical instruments were lying cluttered– the forceps, hemostats, needle holders, retractors, and scissors of all sizes and shapes. The customer had to choose, haggle the price, take his goods and pay there only in cash. Digpal was excited to see the surgical instruments like a woman in front of a jewellery shop. Kalpana could read the joy on his face, his dimple becoming deeper on his dark face. Suddenly his attention was diverted towards some hot discussion between one of the owners of the shop and a person holding a small suitcase, which was partially open, and surgical instruments peeping through it. Apparently, the person with the suitcase was demanding his overdue money and the shopkeeper was trying to convince him to come on a later date for payment.

"You're all thieves and cheats, I came all the way from Jalandhar to sell you these cheap instruments and you are selling at three times the price, telling your customers, they are Bombay made." He started shouting in a heavy Punjabi accent then the shopkeeper tried to hush him, meanwhile a salesman addressed Digpal "Own hospital or government?"

"Trust hospital," replied Digpal.

"Don't worry, we will give cut on your purchase." The salesperson offered. Digpal had heard the conversation between the man with suitcase and shopkeeper and the offer for cut further repelled him.

"No, thanks, will see later." And descended back from shop

"We give highest commission in the market," shouted the salesman as Digpal almost came down the shop and told Kalpana, "let's go somewhere else, they are cheats, trying to bribe me and sell poor quality instruments."

"But they all will be like this, it's business."

"Let's go."

A middle aged man, very dark in complexion standing on the pavement, started walking alongside Digpal, "I manufacture good quality instruments, *Sar*." The man coming near him told in a heavy South Indian accent. Digpal was startled for a second, then asked,

"Where is the shop?"

"*Sar*, I am Verghese, we have a small manufacturing unit in Thane, you come with me and see for yourself."

"Don't rely on a stranger just like that," whispered Kalpana.

Digpal looked toward Verghese and then told Kalpana, "I will go with him."

"I too will accompany you, Thane is another end of Bombay," she replied.

"I will pay for the taxi up to VT, from there we will catch a local for Thane." Verghese offered.

All 3 of them went to Victoria Terminus by cab. It's a grand building, 'so beautiful', thought Digpal. They reached Thane in less than an hour by local train.

Verghese's manufacturing unit was a small one, about 8 people working for him, some, on machines and two of them giving finishing touches by hand with fine instruments, sand paper and iron files. The quality was really excellent; Verghese would personally go to all machine men, give them instructions and check all finished products.

Then the trio sat in his small office and Digpal gave him his list of instruments, mainly paediatric, baby mosquito forceps, adson forceps, cat's paw, baby allis, three inch and four inch needle holders, hook retractors, right and left raspatory for cleft palate, paediatric urethral dilators, baby sigmoidoscope and so on. "We get very good filter coffee here, you try it," offered Verghese.

"I love South Indian filter coffee." Both Kalpana and Digpal said in unison.

The coffee came in stainless steel glasses and a bowl, typical of the south and it was nice, strong and refreshing. Then they started discussing the prices, "Ours is a charitable hospital, runs on donations, we are generally short of funds, even our salaries are also very modest. You will have to give us a discount," requested Digpal. As he told 'we', Verghese asked curiously "Madam is your..." and left the sentence halfway. "Oh, sorry I didn't introduce Dr Kalpana Sisodia, she is my colleague."

"I am his junior, learning from him." Kalpana intervened.

"Regarding pricing, *Sar*, we directly selling from factory, so no expense of showrooms and salesmen, property very costly in Bombay, we sell on small margin and no cuts to purchase officer, that's why we don't deal with government hospitals. But you are different, everybody saying, give bill for more money and give us the margins. I like you *Sar*."

Kalpana could feel Digpal's passion for work and few needs. What must be his family background, she wondered. They finalised the deal, placed the order after Verghese completed the formalities.

From Thane they caught a local train to reach VT station again. It was almost 4 PM and they both were hungry. Digpal, though not easily tired, was a bit hassled by the crowd, the noise and the pollution. They entered a small Udupi restaurant near station.

"Will it be ok with you Kaplana?" He quizzed her.

"I am hungry and these small restaurants of Bombay serve fresh and delicious food."

It was a crowded place with narrow benches and tables and was not meant for leisurely meals. Service was fast, people were in a hurry and so were they. After the meal, they had a good cup of South Indian coffee again and took a cab for Marine lines, to meet one of the renowned surgeons of Bombay Hospital, Dr R.K. Jhavar; who turned out to be an easy mannered amicable person, in his early 60s.

When Digpal was leaving Indore, his professor had told him to meet Dr Jhavar for guidance. When the latter came to know that he was Dr Tripathi's favourite student, he was keen to help him by all means. He gave Digpal many practical tips about Hepato-Biliary Pancreatic surgeries, and ano-rectal surgeries and so on. Digpal was a keen listener and tried to absorb as much as possible while Kalpana was all eyes for Digpal. In the end, Digpal asked, "Sir, one of the most intriguing problems is recurrent hernia. Whatever the technique I use, some patients come back with recurrence. What to do about it?"

"Right time to ask this question young man. Even the best of surgeons face this problem of recurrent hernia. Last week only I had been to the US for a conference and a surgeon there presented a paper on reinforcement of the posterior wall of inguinal canal by a synthetic mesh and the best part of it is that unlike Bassini's it's a tensionless reinforcement. Later I contacted that surgeon and he told me that he had been using a mesh called Marlex's mesh with excellent results."

Digpal came almost to the edge of the chair to catch every word, "And if you are so keen to try, I have a spare unsterilised piece of mesh for you to try. You can cut it, autoclave it, and use it. But I am not sure how successful it will be in Indian conditions, I too have yet to try."

"Sir, I will be too happy to try and share the experience with you," he almost jumped at the idea. Dr Jhavar gave him a 12 x 12 inch Marlex mesh, while holding the pack from the senior teacher, he didn't know he was going to change the face of hernia surgery, in that part of the country for which he will not get any credit from the surgical fraternity.

It was already dark and the local trains towards the suburbs were choc-o-block. Whatever little money he had, he kept it in his trouser pocket in a wallet and some small bills in the top pocket. Their return ticket was in a suitcase in the YMCA hostel room. They had to let go three trains before boarding the fourth one, Kalpana was better than him in the art of boarding the trains. He had never seen such a density of homo sapiens.

"Come on, let's go up to *Mama's* (maternal uncle) home. You can have a cup of coffee and go back, the local train towards south Bombay will be empty at this hour, you will enjoy the ride." She offered, which he agreed hesitantly. He didn't want to part with her; but he was not comfortable meeting people socially, that too of a higher economic status. As if reading his mind she added, "*Mama Mami* are out for a movie and won't return before 10." Digpal was relieved and happy.

They hired a rickshaw for Lokhandwala complex, on reaching the high rise building complex; while getting down, he read the fare on the meter and put his hand in his pocket and his fingers touched his thigh, his pocket was neatly cut by a blade and his wallet was missing. Kalpana didn't notice the change in expressions of Digpal and murmured peeping into her purse "I have the change," and paid the driver.

His excitement of sitting in proximity of the beautiful girl in an auto rickshaw, accidently touching her body on bumps and sharp curves of the road and anticipation of getting some time with her in the empty apartment, was watered down by loss of wallet.

It was a 10th floor penthouse with luxurious interiors. She told him to relax and went to the washroom "Do you want to freshen up?" Asked Kalpana

"I am ok," he said and sat on the soft sofa. The tapestry was pure white and he was afraid it may be spoiled by him sitting on it.

She came back with 2 glasses of water, her face was glowing after the day long Bombay pollution was washed away. He couldn't move his eyes away from her face and figure and he felt he was no match for her. He thought he was dark and thin, with no family, caste or religion. He must stop seeing unrealistic dreams. He shook his head and her feminine fragrance woke him out of his thoughts, she was sitting near him on the sofa and asked softly, "Why are you shaking your head? You are much more handsome than your looks, in spite of your meager salary, you are honest, upright, an extraordinary surgeon and above all, a very fine human being." Digpal smiled, getting back some of his confidence and stretched his arms on the back of the sofa on the side where Kalpana was sitting.

Suddenly they fell silent, his hand wrapped around her shoulder, her hand was on his other hand, and by some unknown force, their torsos came near each other, and their lips locked with each other. He felt, he was floating in the air. This was something he had never felt before. Kalpana too, was probably in the same condition. Digpal was the first to recover. With a jerk, he took his head away, and told himself, 'what are you doing, you fool, you don't deserve her'. She held his hand tight, and asked in a husky voice, "What happened? I know you like me, I had read that in your eyes, the very first day." With other hand, she kept caressing his birthmark, on the root of his neck, which looked like the silhouette of a lady sitting on knees, with head thrown back.

"Is it a tattoo?"

"No, it's a birthmark."

"Let's go inside." She said, as if intoxicated. He too was excited, and the proximity of the lovely lady was driving him crazy, but he answered in a cold voice, "We are ok here."

"Then, why did you bother to come to uncle's house?" She reacted, a bit angrily.

"Kalpana, you are beautiful, intelligent, from a reputed family and will be a consultant in a few years, and yes, I love you. But I think we should give more time to understand each other. I don't want you to make hasty decisions."

She rushed to the kitchen, to conceal her tears. Started preparing coffee, and thought, in a way, he is right; I know, he is a good, honest and upright human and a fine Surgeon too, but is this enough? I have no idea about his family background, caste, and religion.

When she came back to the sitting room, she was almost normal, except with slightly congested eyes, wearing a formal smile. He was not that good at shaming and small talk; was sitting on the edge of the sofa, with a somber face. They took their cup of coffee in silence. He wasn't great at small talks, she broke the silence.

"In the morning you board the train from the centre, it stops at Borivali. I will join you there," he just nodded his head. He finished his coffee and got up.

"It's getting late, I must be leaving now."

Coming out of the building, he had almost forgotten that he had lost his wallet and he had a small amount in his upper pocket; as only the thoughts of Kalpana were occupying his mind. On the main road when an auto rickshaw screeched near him and asked "*Kidhar ko saheb?* (where to Sir?)" He answered in negative and decided to walk back to his YMCA hostel. It was a good 20 kms walk but his life till now had made him tough.

This reminded him of an incident from his childhood. Sometimes the orphanage officials would take them to nearby cities, generally to Indore. Apparently it was to take the orphans for an outing in the city; but during these trips they were given a band to play, a receipt book of the orphanage and the children had to beg for donations from the public. Some would pay a small amount, others would sympathise with the children, saying, 'tch poor orphans', but many of them insulted them and told them to stay away from them. During one such trip, when they were passing from the road in front of the imposing seven storied building of Maharaja Yashwantrao hospital, he left his group, entered the hospital compound, and stood mesmerized in front of the hospital building. Medical students, doctors in their white coats, nurses and other staff, patients and relatives, were moving from and to the building. He was only 11 years old at that time, but imagined himself to be a doctor someday and get trained in this gorgeous hospital. Nobody in the group noticed that he was missing and they left for the orphanage, which was 25 kms from there, by a bus. When Digpal came out of his day dreaming, he noticed that he was alone. That day too, he was alone and hungry and had to walk back to the orphanage, a distance of 25 kms.

On this day too, he kept walking on the S.V. road parallel to the railway track towards South, until he could see the familiar Bombay Central area. His thin long legs brought him back to the hostel in almost 3 hours. He was tired and hungry, the mess had already closed. He gulped down half a bottle of water and tried to sleep.

Next day, all throughout the return journey, they didn't talk much except for the Bombay crowd, local trains and hot and humid weather of the maximum city. Big consolation was, proximity to each other and an occasional touch when the train moved laterally.

# BACK TO WORK

On the way back from Ahmedabad to Vidurpur on bus, Kalpana got down at the district headquarters. A police constable was already waiting to escort her to her home. Digpal was not that fortunate, he got down at the small bus stand of his adopted town with his backsack, tired and hungry. As he hit the only main road of the town, a scooter stopped near him. The omnipresent Sarang was there with his little rattling scooter which looked like a Mercedes at that time. "Hop on Sir, I was expecting you to be here," and Sarang's non-stop chatter was music to his ears. He updated him on hospital news and how badly he was missed during those 2 days in the hospital. But all Digpal wanted just now was something to eat and then doze off in his familiar bed for a long deep sleep.

As soon as they entered the campus gate of the hospital, John, who always wore white instead of dusky green of other ward boys, came running towards them, "Sir, before you go home, have a look at an emergency case. It's a stab injury and he is bad."

He never doubted John's observation, he left the bag at reception and rushed to casualty. A young man in his twenties lay on stretcher, perspiring, anxious, and though the casualty resident had started a ringer lactate drip, his pulse was thready and fast and pallor in conjunctiva. There were two penetrating stab wounds on abdomen, not more than 2 inches in width with minimal bleeding from the wounds.

"Push him more fluid, send blood for CBC and blood grouping and cross matching and prepare the patient for surgery, he will need at least 2 units of blood," instructed Digpal.

"Already sent blood for cross matching, Sir." Resident replied

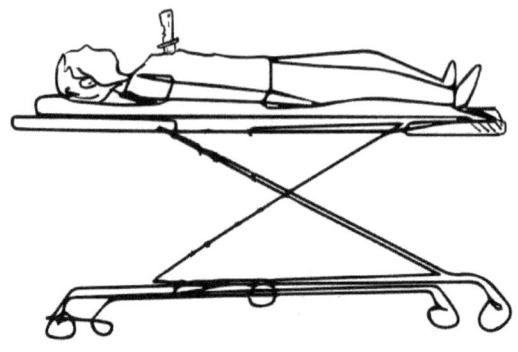

"I will be back in half an hour, shift the patient to OT."

He rushed to his apartment, washed-up, had a quick cup of tea with powdered milk, as he had no refrigerator to keep fresh milk and rushed back to OT. Harish was already there and was preparing his anaesthesia drugs sodium pentothal, pethidine, atropine, succinylcholine, to intubate the patient and then checking ether and trilene in the bottles.

By the time Digpal scrubbed, Harish had already intubated the patient. There was no time to waste. Digpal, post painting and draping with a clean swipe on the midline, opened skin and linea-alba and reached peritoneum which looked dark– a sign of intraperitoneal hemorrhage. He carefully opened the peritoneum between two hemostats with an oblique knife blade no.15. He had seen during his residency, his colleagues sometimes nicking the gut in a hurry to open the peritoneum. He sucked out blood with a perforated sump suction and told the assistant to strongly retract the abdominal wall towards the left upper quadrant. He could see some cuts in small intestine but that can wait, he thought. There was a large clot in the left hypochondrium, as he removed it, blood started spurting from the hilum of the spleen. The stab had severed the splenic vessels right at the entry of splenic hilum. He quickly pinched the splenic vessel between left thumb and finger and with the right hand he went around the convex surface of the spleen to blindly break free the organ by breaking the ligaments and delivered it to the wound. After making sure he is not pinching the pancreatic tail with the splenic pedicle, he applied double clamps on the proximal part of the pedicle, severed the remaining vessels and delivered the injured spleen out. Harish smiled, "The blood pressure is coming up, it's 100/60. You know from incision to spleen removal, you took 9 minutes. We can party this evening."

Harish was always looking for the opportunity to have a few drinks with him and Digpal too used to join them gleefully.

"I am still not done, greedy fellow. A lot is to be done yet." Shot back Digpal.

He carefully explored the whole abdomen, there were 16 perforations in the small intestine with a cut in mesentery. Fortunately, mesenteric vessels were spared. He repaired all the intestinal cuts with connel's and lambard sutures, using 00 atraumatic catgut. Then washed the abdomen with isotonic saline and closed linea-alba with interrupted sutures. He always insisted that while closing, a correct amount of tension on tissues is very important. When it comes to strength, interrupted sutures were more reliable then continuous, irrespective of the material used. Distance of entry of suture must be 1 cm from the edge and distance between 2 sutures should not be more than 1.5 cm. Tight sutures could be counter-productive.

The Patient recovered uneventfully. He had to go to the court, two years after this surgery as an expert witness. After his deposition the judge asked curiously, "Off the record doctor, was this patient as bad as Amitabh Bachhan?" That was the time when the famous actor was in the ICU in critical condition and was the center of concern for the whole country.

"Sir," replied the surgeon, "this patient's injuries were many times more serious than the superstar's, the latter probably had only two perforations in the small gut and my patient had sixteen cuts, plus injury to the spleen!"

"Then how come your patient recovered uneventfully?"

"Many medical reasons; age of patient, associated diseases, early decision of surgery, no VIP syndrome. In short because he was a poor person, operated by an unknown surgeon."

# TURNING POINT

"This is my last week in this hospital. My internship will be over here and then I will be completing it in another three months in rural posting," one afternoon when he was sitting in his administrative office alone, signing some papers, Kalpana barged in and told him so quickly in one breath, as if afraid, that she may not be able to complete her sentence without interruption. Before Digpal could respond she shot again, "I want to meet you alone; is it OK if I come to your home tomorrow during lunch break?"

He didn't know what to say, but she was out of his office without listening to his response. He kept on wondering, what is the future of their relationship? Some thoughts again and again started hitting his thinking process. She was beautiful, intelligent, and belonged to a well-known family. He was no match for her. He should stop this right here and now. But she was irresistible, she was his dream girl. He is not going to love anyone so passionately again, if she won't be in his life. He vaguely understood the Indian psyche, traditions and systems. The idea of religion and caste was so deep rooted in the Indian mind, that leave aside matrimonial relationships, even on meeting a stranger the biggest curiosity is his/her caste. ' We have pre-formed ideas about language groups and caste', he thought. "There are upper upper caste and upper and lower cast, then lower caste and upper lower, and lower lower caste; its mind boggling." Even education has not changed these biases and prejudices. Once the bride/bridegroom is of the same caste then comes the family background and history of the family. If the mother's cousin sister, 30 years back, married out of caste, the niece may be disqualified for a good bridegroom. Strangely, amassing fortune by bribes and unfair means is considered a positive point and Digpal didn't score well on that point either.

He could guess why Kalpana wants to come to his apartment; to ask for his firm commitment before leaving the hospital, and weighing vis-à-vis his status with her, he outright disqualifies for their relationship, he thought. And even if they get married there will be incidents of embarrassment for both of them throughout their life. He will clearly refuse and end this forever.

And she came earlier than expected during the lunch break. He had just come out of the bathroom wearing only a vest and a towel wrapped around his thin waist and was heading towards the bedroom to change. He felt two arms wrapping around his chest and the feminine softness on his back before he could react. She pushed him on the bed and jumped on him, giggling all the time. "Shocked? Aren't you?"

"Hey what are you doing?" He asked in a choking voice.

"You should keep the main door bolted from inside, but now it is," she said laughingly

"There is nothing worth taking away from my home." He smiled back.

The proximity of his dream girl made him dizzy but then the reality of the vast gap between his and her status brought him back to senses. Gently but firmly he held her by her arms and lifted her up from him, took her out of his bedroom and closed the door from inside. She shouted from outside, "You cheat, how can you throw me out of the room?" And kept thumping the door. "Relax, you go sit in the drawing room, I am coming in five minutes," he shouted back.

After a while they were sitting in the drawing room, Digpal had prepared omelet, bread and tea for both of them and she started gorging on that. "I am very hungry, aren't you?"

"What do you know about me?" He asked suddenly on a serious note.

"All I know is, I love you, and that is enough for me to be with you for the rest of my life," she added, "and your name Digpal

Singh indicates you belong to our community, so my parents too won't have any objection."

"Kalpana, my full name is Digpal Singh Joseph, I write my name in reverse order." Kalpana's smile vanished, keeping her cup back on table, surprise in her voice, she asked, "Are you a Christian? You never told me."

"I don't know my religion or caste. I was brought up in an orphanage. I was left on the steps of an orphanage as a newborn, nobody has any idea about my parents." Digpal was relieved after telling the truth about himself but Kalpana was silent. For some time; none of the two spoke a word. Then Kalpana got up and left quickly; stood near the threshold, turned and said, "I don't think I have the courage to ask my parents, they will never agree."

He stood in the door seeing her leaving his house and probably from his life forever. He felt some part of his body and soul was leaving him and deep in his thoughts he left his residence for his evening OPD. He had the feeling that it would be difficult for him to come out of this trauma; but the pain and suffering of patients made him forget his own.

# HERNIOPLASTY

Hernia surgery is one of the commonest elective surgeries done in all hospitals. That evening too he had some patients of inguinal hernia. As the backlog was gradually increasing, he had to give them appointments for another month, sometimes for after 5 to 6 weeks. Almost nearing the end of the day a thin oldish looking man, about 60 years old, entered his OPD. His expiration was longer than inspiration, with a wheeze, and he had a hand on his groin. He looked very uncomfortable. While the resident was writing history, he told him to strip off. He was asthmatic with a tense swelling on right groin and two supra inguinal scars traversing over the swelling. There was no abdominal distention, swelling too was not very tense. There was a history of hernia surgery done twice at different places. The patient was cursing in a broken speech, typical of asthmatics; that all his savings are spent in surgery; that he is a poor retired primary school teacher and both his sons are fed up with his ailments. Carbon dioxide in his blood was making him even more irritable. Digpal noticed that his hernia side testicle was missing. Probably during the second surgery the surgeon removed the testes to prevent recurrence, but the adamant hernia recurred all the same.

Digpal instructed the residents to admit the patient, send a call to Ravindran for his medical problems and if declared fit, prepare for surgery in an emergency. At 10 PM at night, the resident informed him that the hernia had reduced and emergency surgery was not required. Digpal posted the patient in the next day's operative list, but he couldn't sleep. A conventional Bassini's repair is not going to solve this patient's problem and then he remembered the synthetic mesh, so kindly given to him by the senior surgeon of Bombay. He got up from the bed and went straight to OT, the nurse was surprised to see him at that time. With a straight scissors he cut the piece of mesh about 5x8 cm and gave it to the nurse and told, "In the morning give this to John, tell him to double autoclave this with the hernia set and don't open the drum till I come in the OT."

"What are you going to do with this?"

He smiled naughtily, "I will put it inside the patient's scrotum to make him more masculine! Need this for the hubby?" The young nurse blushed and he left the OT.

He could hardly sleep in the night, opening patient up, layer by layer, dissecting, placing the mesh in, suturing in his imagination. It was his usual habit; he would always run a movie of the surgery he was going to do in his mind and when in doubt, refer to his operative surgery book. But unfortunately for a mesh hernioplasty no guidance of any kind was available at that time. The biggest advantage of this was, it kept the thoughts of Kalpana away from him; albeit only temporarily.

Next morning the first two cases were paediatric, and the third one to be operated on was the recurrent hernia. Before surgery he went to see the patient, found out his name was Narendrabhai Desai and tried to explain to him, "Narendra *kaka*, since you are getting this hernia time and again, I want to try a new operation, I will put a synthetic..."

"Doctor, I don't want to know anything," Narendrabhai interrupted him, "all I want is I must be cured of this damn thing; do whatever you want to or I have no will left to live anymore."

He patted the shoulder of the patient and left for OT.

After finishing the paediatric cases, the hernia patient Mr. Narendrabhai was anaesthetised by Harish with intrathecal spinal injection. The resident catheterised him, which was a routine in all past middle aged patients to be operated under spinal anaesthesia; and he thought it is better to catheterise under full aseptic precautions in OT rather than in bed, if the patient develops retentions. He thoroughly scrubbed the patient and again scrubbed himself. He was always very fussy about the no touch technique of wearing gloves and painting the operative site centripetally.

"Small precautions give big dividends," was his dictum.

He did not excise the old supra inguinal scars. He despised the conventional oblique incision which he considered ugly and gave a 'ridge effect', as all the layers are cut and sutured back in the same direction. He preferred a bit of high transverse crease incision in the skin, subcutaneous tissue and fascia; then retract downwards to expose external oblique aponeurosis. Opened the aponeurosis in the direction of fibers, to reach the inguinal canal. In this particular case, since an orchiectomy had been done on the last occasion, the canal was almost obliterated. He could see some nylon sutures which had cut through and a gap had formed and the hernial sac could be seen coming through it. He removed all nylon sutures, opened the sac, checked its inside and transfixed it at its neck and amputated the redundant sac. With his finger he gently made space between the conjugant tendon and the peritoneum and inserted the edge of the mesh in that space, then below the pubic tubercle medially and entered in the internal ring laterally. Then sutured the mesh all around with conjoint tendon, periosteum of pubic tubercle and inguinal ligament with interrupted 00 polypropylene sutures; all the time taking care of urinary bladder, femoral vessels and inferior epigastric vessels. Once the mesh was securely fixed on the defect, he sutured back all the layers over it. The surgery was totally bloodless, he took care to stop all bleeding points, which he would normally ignore. After meticulously closing the skin and dressing the patient himself, he addressed the patient, "Narendrabhai you are going to be fine this time." The patient was groggy with sedation but still smiled and thanked him.

"You seem to have made history, Digpal," Harish said.

"We all did," replied the surgeon.

He kept the patient in hospital until his sutures were removed and the wound healed. Narendrabhai didn't mind staying in the hospital for a full 8 days.

After this first mesh hernioplasty he kept on doing this, in all recurrent hernias, almost one per week. But, as was to happen, the sheet of mesh got used up. Fortunately, he could find an importer in Bombay, who provided him with more mesh on a regular basis. He kept on widening his indications of doing mesh plasty. He would do it in all direct inguinal hernia, in all middle aged and older patients. Then he started doing mesh plasty in ventral hernia as well. As time went by he did different experimentations with mesh, but that was much later. Subsequently in a state conference, he demonstrated, live, a mesh hernioplasty which created a lot of interest in surgeons of the state and many started doing it too. Later on, this repair, a tension free repair of hernia with a mesh was known as Lichtenstein mesh repair of hernia and became a gold standard of hernia repair. Digpal remained an obscure, unknown hernia surgeon for the larger world; only well known in the small western corner of his country, and he didn't mind it.

But in spite of all this and continuous flow of emergencies too, he could not take away the memory and pangs of pain of Kalpana's lost love from his mind. His nights kept on becoming more and more sleepless.

# THE YEAR OF 1984

1984 was a fateful year for Digpal. That was the year when he lost his best friend and guide. That was the year when he live demonstrated hernioplasty in a state conference, and had a small piece of recognition. That was the year when the country lost her bold and strong leader, the Prime Minister Mrs. Indira Gandhi, murdered by her own body guards, the backlash by people of a particular political party and genocide of thousands of Sikhs, and a year when finally the curtains were down on his love story.

First things first, the unfortunate Sunday when he was invited by a Dr Kanani for a wet party. He had helped Kanani, who was a medical officer in a Primary Health Center, 15 kms from Vidurpur. Kanani used to do tubal ligations, a national family planning program in his PHC under local anesthesia. During one tubal ligation, he inadvertently injured the small intestine and then the loop of intestine sank inside the abdominal cavity and he couldn't find it. Then in a hurry to close the abdomen, his needle broke and the broken piece was lost in the rectus muscle fibers. He loaded the patient in an ambulance and brought her to Jeeviben hospital. That was the first time Kanani met Digpal. The former was very worried and tense; Digpal assured him that his patient will be okay and he will not let the incident leak out to the authorities and relatives. Under spinal anesthesia, Digpal reopened the incision, found and removed the broken needle from the rectus muscle, fished out the injured intestine, repaired it, gave peritoneal wash and completed the tubal ligation. The patient recovered uneventfully. In that reference it was a thanksgiving party to the young surgeon. Kanani had arranged for delicious chicken preparations and Scotch whisky, which was not easy to arrange in the dry state of Gujarat. They sat there chit chatting for a few hours and he reached Vidurpur late in the afternoon.

On the road in front of the hospital, there was a small crowd, a few vehicles and a fire brigade vehicle and an ambulance. As soon as he reached there some people came running towards him, "Come quick doctor." The crowd made way for him and what he saw was a shocking sight. Three bodies lay supine, motionless on the ground, near an open sewer hole. Two unknown persons, who looked like labourers soiled in the mud and the third a diminutive thin fair man, without his golden frame glasses, the man who meant so much to him, so talkative, silenced forever. So many people animatedly spoke together about what happened and that said a lot about the type of character Sarang was. The 2 labourers went down the sewer opening to clean the drainage line and could be seen falling unconscious from above. Sarang at that time was passing from there. The ever curious and helpful person that he was, he volunteered to bring them up. He went down holding the rope, and instructed people who were outside to pull on his instruction. But as soon as he climbed down, he too lost his senses from the poisonous gasses, lost his grip from the rope and fell in the sewer. By the time the fire brigade team arrived and brought all three out, they were already dead. Digpal was numbed with shock. He got all three loaded in the ambulance to take them to the government hospital for mandatory postmortem and followed them on his scooter. After Postmortem, Sarang's body was brought back to his home. Shabnam was sitting at the door with a few ladies of the hospital staff, and his teenage son Sahil stood outside looking lost.

Digpal was not great with social skills. He couldn't think coherently, what to do and what to say on such occasions. He would always look toward Sarang for advice on such issues. Sitting outside Sarang's house, the memories of the diminutive man kept rolling in his memory like a movie. He used to have all news and gossip handy with him, some very difficult emergency cases had been saved due to timely advice and information by him.

He remembered an unusual case he had operated a few months ago. Around 7 PM, post OPD, a group of doctors were sitting and chatting in a space arranged with cement benches in quadrilateral manner and Sarang suddenly rushed towards them, shouting, "Sir, come quickly to casualty with Harish Sir." The urgency in his voice was alarming enough not to ask further questions.

Newly joined pathologist Gopal Sanghvi too got up, "I too will come, the patient may need transfusion." Gopal was a handsome, fresh pathologist from Rajasthan, enthusiastic and hardworking. The surgery resident, too, accompanied them as they reached casualty. There were no patients, nurses there were dressing a teenage boy with minor injuries. "Why this fake call Sarang?" Inquired an irritated Digpal.

"There was a scuffle near the train station and a gunda stabbed a young man. He must be coming," and before he could complete his sentence, there were noises outside and a small group of people and a ward boy rushed in a hefty man about 26 years on a gurney. At the thoracic inlet, at the root of the neck a knife handle could be seen projecting. Apparently the whole knife blade was in the chest up to the hilt! His breathing was labored and he was drenched in perspiration. Strangely, very little blood was oozing at the point of entry of the knife. His pulse was thin and he looked pale. Digpal did a quick venesection from which Gopal collected blood for routine test and group cross matching.

"Let's take him to OT, I will intubate him," suggested Harish. Everybody quickly agreed and the patient was shifted to OT. Many years later Digpal mused, their speed and efficiency in that era could dwarf the most modern, well oiled machinery of future corporate hospitals. They didn't know the name, address, financial status and details of the patient and he was already lying on the operative table!

Harish intubated the patient and Digpal did a quick intercostal thoracotomy. There was no time to go through the rib bed, the usual approach. The knife blade could be seen in the thoracic inlet, cutting through the upper lobe of the lung and as he retracted the lung, he could see it brushing the major vessels coming out of the heart and the tip of the knife disappearing in the spine. Once confirmed that only small vessels and the lung was injured, they tried to remove the knife. A new young surgeon Suresh Kumar had recently joined the hospital as junior Surgeon, and he was assisting Digpal in that particular case. They tried to remove the knife, but it didn't budge. The surgeons wanted to remove it straight out, any kind of lateral movement could injure major vessels. Suresh Kumar had done a stint in orthopedic surgery during his residency. He suggested, "Let's apply the femur nail extractor to remove its blade."

"That's an excellent idea," agreed the senior surgeon. They hooked the shoulders of the knife handle in the extracter, and with repeated outward hammering, the knife came out. There were some spurts after the knife came out. Surprisingly, the tip of the knife was bent at an angle. Such was the force of the assault that the tip had entered the spine and had gotten impacted there. Digpal kept the drainage tube, connected it to an underwater seal and closed the chest. Blood came rushing out and then gradually reduced. "Can he bleed again and will we have to open him again if there is fresh bleeding?" Asked Suresh Kumar.

"There is an interesting story in this connection. A nurse, Sister Sheiga notices that when the drainage tube is warm to feel, that patient collapses quickly and must be opened to stop the bleeding and this is called Sister Sheiga sign." Digpal chuckled.

The patient recovered smoothly, his vitals were normal within a few hours and there was only a slight pinkish hue in the drainage. The whole team of doctors was in a celebratory mood. Digpal ordered some 'faffadas and jalebis' from a nearby shanty. But did their celebratory mood last long?

The stab injury patient improved steadily. Next evening's round brought a shocking revelation. When Digpal asked, "How are you doing Babulal?"

"I can't feel a thing below my belly button; can't move a muscle below that level, and get any sense of pee!" To their disappointment, they discovered he had developed complete paraplegia. His spinal cord was fully transacted due to the stab injury at the thoracic level.

After complete recovery from the injury he was shifted to the paraplegia rehabilitation centre in Ahmedabad. The magic of surgery doesn't always work or works only partially, at times.

Nights were always bad for Digpal. Since Suresh Kumar, his younger colleague, had joined the hospital, his emergency work had become lighter. But that made things worse for him. The memories of Kalpana and their last afternoon meeting would pass through his mind repeatedly and made him more and more emotionally and physically deprived. He longed for a female by his side. He would get up groggy in the morning, but his strong will power always controlled his urge to find refuge in alcohol or tranquillizers.

He sometimes would visit Maganbhai's house, to see if Shabnum or her teenage son needed any help. On her request, he got her a seat in the Nursing training school run by the Hospital and was allowed to retain her quarters in the hospital campus. During one casual visit, when her son had gone out playing, she asked him to stay for a cup of tea, and he didn't mind. For the first time he noticed, that even in her thirties, she had a toned body, a full figure, and a shining, healthy dark complexion. No wonder Sarang fell for her! Women have a sharp sense of reading men's eyes and intentions. She could read Digpal's probing eyes and covered her bosom with 'dupatta', consciously. When she was serving tea to him on the low table, his eyes were again stuck on her cleavage. He caught her wrist and their eyes met. She didn't resist or pull away her hand, only said in a low voice, "This is 'gunah' doctor, you were always Magan's younger brother for me, and still are." Digpal loosened his grip, he felt so ashamed of himself that he left the tea untouched and rushed out of her home in a hurry.

He was so embarrassed that he couldn't go to her quarters for quite some time, but kept a vigil on Sahil's progress and her nursing training. Whenever he went to the market, he would purchase extra vegetables and fruits, and send them to Sarang's house.

He mustered the courage to go to Sarang's house after a month. Sahil, with a cricket bat in hand, threw a 'namaste uncle' towards him, and ran outside, shouting, "Have a 20-20 match today, will be back after 3 hours."

"Will make a cup of tea and some snacks for you, you have come after a long time," she said with a smile, closing the door, "a lot of flies outside, have to keep the door closed."

She went inside the kitchen and he took a detailed visual round of the room. A small two seat sofa with two plastic chairs at right angles to it, a plastic central table in the middle and a settee in front of the sofa, covered by a thin cotton mattress, was laid in the small sitting room cum dining room. On the wall, above the settee, was hanging a colour picture of a smiling Maganbhai, his bright eyes shining behind glasses in a golden frame, a sandalwood garland hanging over it. He stood in front of the picture, willing it to talk to him.

Engrossed in his thoughts, he couldn't hear the sound of footsteps, he felt something soft pressing on his back, and two arms around his waist. He felt her warm breath near his neck. "He is no more Digpal, but we are still alive," Shabnum whispered. For some moments, he felt intoxicated and dizzy, then regaining his senses, he slowly turned around, facing her, and removed her arms from his waist. Shabnum was a tall healthy lady, her medium sized eyes looked red and round cheeks flushed. She was wearing a pink kurti (top) on a magenta petticoat and no chunni. For a while Digpal seemed to lose control of himself, then spoke in a stammering voice, "You were right that day, Maganbhai was like an elder brother to me."

"You like me, don't you? I am only a year older than you, we have a life left to live."

Digpal thought for a while, "You are right, and I am not

answerable to anybody, except my own conscience. But I am not very sure. You too give it a long thought."

"Okay, but I don't have a lot of time to waste, I am finding it difficult to bring up Sahil single handed."

He let go of her arms, "Seems, will have to go back hungry today too."

And they both laughed, she headed towards the kitchen and came back with some dhokla and tea, looking towards him lovingly, gorging on the food.

Back in his apartment, he tried to read a book unsuccessfully, turned on the radio, closed his eyes and dozed off.

It was past midnight when he was woken up by the harsh ring of the intercom. Kumar was on the line, "There is an old man in uraemic coma, seems to be obstructive uropathy."

"You can deal with it Suresh," he replied in a sleepy voice.

"They are insisting you come. They have shifted him from a private surgeon's hospital. Eminent people of Vidurpur, big builders, the whole clan is here."

"These VIPs are a pain in the wrong place, am coming," he muttered, washed his face and was out in two minutes, without closing his apartment door.

Kumar was right, the whole lot was there. Sons, daughters, daughters-in-law and some grandchildren; some of them yawning. 'It seems they are thinking, this is the old man's last day'. He wondered.

He despised too many attendants with a patient. 'I will examine and refer him to a bigger centre for further treatment, they have money aplenty', he thought.

When he entered the casualty, he could smell the uraemic odor. The old man was lying still with fever and tachycardia. A feeding tube was jutting out of his nostril, and a number 14 foley's catheter connected to a urine bag had drained a small amount of purulent urine. Per rectum examination revealed a large soft to firm prostate.

"We must do a suprapubic cystostomy now. I will talk to the relatives."

"His blood urea is 200, do you think he has any chance?" Kumar had doubts.

"It is only obstructive uropathy, inadequately drained. He will recover."

The relatives proved to be exceptionally well behaved and courteous, they readily agreed to whatever he deemed correct.

He did a suprapubic cystostomy, placed a wide bore Malecot's catheter in the bladder and removed the urethral cath. Before placing the catheter, he thoroughly explored the urinary bladder from inside, he had a large prostate jutting in the bladder with trabeculations of the bladder wall-a sign of long standing obstruction to outflow. There was no calculus or diverticulum, nor any sign of malignancy.

He went for rounds after 24 hours. The two sons were standing outside near the door of the patient's room, with wide welcoming grins. "You did a miracle doctor, we had heard a lot about you, we are very impressed by your skill," said the elder one. "Let me check him." Digpal said and entered the room. Ramjibhai Prajapaty, the man brought unconscious, had opened his eyes and was speaking in slurred speech and went back in stupor. In another week, Ramjibhai was fully conscious, eating a full diet and was forming copious amounts of urine! Ramjibhai and his sons and relatives thanked him profusely. Digpal just smiled and answered, "I did nothing great, it's just... magic of surgery."

"We will remove his Prostate after a fortnight, meanwhile if you want to take him home, you can."

"We will keep him here, till he is completely cured and will pay the hospital bill, whatever it is," said the elder son, who was an architect in a nearby big city.

'Surgery is a funny thing, you get heaps of praise and credit for a very simple job, or none for a very complicated surgery'! mused Digpal.

After three weeks, once Ramjibhai was declared fit for surgery, he was taken for Freyer's prostatectomy, the most commonly performed method during those days. Patient is operated in supine position, unlike TURP. Harish injected a spinal anesthesia. Digpal preferred standing on the left side for pelvic surgeries, with Kumar in front of him, as assistant and audience for his running commentary.

"I am removing the Malecot, extending the incision transversely. Now let's explore bladder with finger, will give a circular incision on bladder mucosa over the prostate, you can use cautery as well, now will put my index in internal meatus and break the anterior commissure, you put your finger in and get the feel." He removed his finger and offered Suresh to put his finger in the meatus. "Now with a circular sweep, I am separating the adenoma from false capsule, and lo, the villain is out," he placed the large gland in a kidney tray offered by John, who in turn slipped out to exhibit it in front of anxious relatives, and receive his tip for the evening booze. The team inside packed the fossa with roller gauze and waited for a few minutes, then introduced a number 18 Foley's in the bladder with a balloon in the empty fossa. He applied a gentle traction to the cath and fixed it near the iliac crest and flank with a broad adhesive.

"I am seeing this for the first time. In our institute, a string used to be tied to the cath, and a small weight tied to it, hanging from rail of the bed." Suresh commented.

"And restrict the patient's movements?" Quipped the senior man, "Since this part is not very mobile and even if patient is ambulatory, the balloon is not disturbed."

Ramjibhai recovered completely in another ten days, and

went home happily. As for Digpal, he had added another good family to his tally of friends.

Amongst their routine elective surgeries, they had an obese middle aged lady with a large incisional hernia through a previous hysterectomy. Suresh insisted on assisting in that case and learning the technique in detail.

Harish injected a long acting spinal anaesthetic. They were face to face with a large abdomen, looking larger due to a big hernia, only partially reduced by the relaxation of spinal injection. "This signifies two facts, one the hernia is not fully reducible, second, be prepared for extensive intestinal adhesions and a prolonged surgery."

While incising, he continued, "You must make an elliptical incision, and try to avoid the thinned out part of skin over the hernia, the gut may be adherent to the under surface and you may land inside the luman. Once the field is soiled, it is not fit for mesh repair." Then he carefully dissected away the skin ellipse and opened the peritoneum from the part, where it looked free of adhesions.

"Don't be too enthusiastic in lysing all the adhesions, new ones will form, and they may cause obstruction. Use all the patience you have, don't try to show off your speed."

In little over two hours, they could clear the hernia ring, and reduce the contents in the abdomen, close the peritoneum and start clearing a space between peritoneum and ring.

"This reminds me of Ballu, I mean Balbir singh, 110 kg, with a large post appendectomy hernia."

"You mean the Sardarji, who owns the Shere Punjab hotel? Food there is really delicious and affordable." Kumar chuckled.

"Yes it is, and he is a jolly good man. He didn't have many adhesions, I had placed a 12 x 12 inches mesh in him."

While dissecting a space below the ring, Kumar asked

curiously, "Can't we put a mesh over the sheath? It will be simpler."

"I won't unless there is some overwhelming reason. It must always be an inlay graft, which gives a huge mechanical advantage. Think!"

He inserted the margins of mesh well below the ring, passed one suture in all four sides, away from the edge of the ring through the mesh and then sutured the margins of the ring, with 0 number polypropylene in continuous fashion. Placed one suction drain on each side, and when satisfied, asked Kumar to close her, "See still a lot of abdominal wall left to approximate."

As he was relaxing in the doctor's room in OT, an excited intern rushed in,

"Sir, Prime minister Indira Gandhi has been murdered!"

He changed and came out, everybody looked disturbed, the whole country seemed to be in shock from losing their strong and beloved leader, on that fateful day of 31st October, 1984.

As he was crossing through the campus towards his apartment, he saw a small procession coming out of Sarang's house. It was led by a short thin middle aged man, wearing a gaudy *sherwani*, a net skull cap, sporting a short beard coloured orange-red by henna and teeth stained by tobacco chewing; followed by Shabnum in a glittering *salwar kameez* and *chunni* over her head, wearing silver and some gold ornaments. Behind them were two teenage boys and a girl in early 20s grinning and chatting. Lagging behind was Sahil, with his head hanging on his chest. Digpal stopped him and asked, "What's this?"

"*Ammi* got married to Shabbirbhai, a rich poultry owner. The two boys and the lady are children from his first wife. Uncle I don't like this but what can I do?"

'What a day'! thought Digpal, 'don't know what more is in store'.

When he reached his apartment, he found a folded piece of paper tucked in the door handle. He settled on the sofa and opened the paper. It read-

'Dear Digpal, I know this will be an unpleasant surprise for you, but I had to think about my life and the future of my child. You will understand that you don't imagine the rest of your life with me, and you will soon forget me, but you will always remain in my thoughts and *dua* (prayers)'.

The letter was not signed and it was not required. How very right she was, he couldn't imagine his life with anyone except Kalpana, but that was not to be!

He kept a cushion on one end of the sofa, and lay down with shoes on, closed his eyes and soon dozed off.

He was rudely woken up by the shrill sound of the intercom. He could hear a panicky resident on the line, "A tractor trolley has toppled and more then two dozen labourers are injured." Without saying anything, he immediately got up, splashed water on his face and hurried towards the casualty.

Before he entered the casualty, he had to wade through a small crowd composed of relatives, friends, other labourers, and onlookers. Inside the 30 x 30 feet, four bed casualty, the injured, the doctors, nursing staff and ward boys, seemed to have occupied every inch of the space. On the beds were badly injured, moaning patients, on the two gurney's were 2 dirt covered men, unconscious and already intubated and connected to ambu's bags. Harish was checking the connections of the apparatus. Orthopaedic resident was applying temporary splints on fractured limbs. When Digpal looked towards him, he said, "I have informed Dinkar Sir, must be on his way." 'Not everybody sleeps with shoes on'. Digpal mused. The 3 nurses were managing intravenous fluids and injecting drugs as per instructions. Rest of the less serious ones were sitting on the floor with gauze pads pressed on their wounds, their repairs could wait. At that moment Kumar too entered the casualty, throwing a 'sorry' towards Digpal, and they both started assessing the injured.

They did three laparotomies, a splenectomy, repaired a lacerated liver and two intestinal and mesenteric tears, left a renal injury untouched, then repaired all the bad wounds till wee hours. During the whole night, Kalpana or any of the happenings of the previous day did not cross his mind. How the pain of others wounds can make you forget yours!

After finishing off the surgeries, they went to ICU to review head injury patients. One of them, the driver of the tractor, had expired. The other two were doing well, and were fighting their ET tubes. Digpal told the resident to remove their tubes and give oxygen through a mask.

When he came outside, most of the accompanying people were tired of crying and were drinking their morning tea in small cups. On the stairs, a middle aged man and a young lady were sobbing continuously. The watchman informed, they were the deceased driver's Father and wife respectively. Digpal went near them wanting to console, but couldn't find words. He just rested his hand on the old man's shoulder, then left silently for his residence.

He reached his apartment, drained physically and emotionally. All he wanted was to have a good cup of tea and put his legs up, but that was not to be.

In a hurry to leave, he had not bolted the door and forgotten the pot of milk on the kitchen platform, and the cat cleaned it off gleefully. When something like this happened, he had the habit of smiling to himself, rather sarcastically. He sat with a black cup of tea, and switched on the radio. Black and white TVs had arrived in India by that time, but were a luxury, and obviously our chief surgeon couldn't afford it. The news on radio kept on repeating every detail of the Prime Minister's death, and how the whole country was mourning the demise of their beloved leader. The PM was assassinated by her own bodyguards, who belonged to the Sikh community. Anticipating something bad, he sprang up from his sofa, picked up his scooter and headed towards Balbir Singh's dhaba. It was already 10 in the morning and the whole town was closed like a snail shell. Roads were deserted, and shutters of Ballu's dhaba were down, probably for the first time since its inception.

He went towards the backside of the building, where only a small wooden door was half ajar. Ballu, his wife Paramjeet and 5 year old son were sitting in front of the small B&W television, in which there were more grains and stripes than a clear picture. The generally cheerful and jolly Ballu was in a sad mood. "Is everything okay?" Digpal quizzed.

"All well in Gujarat, except, I received some threatening calls and insulting communal remarks. But bad news from Delhi, U.P., Bihar and M.P. Killings, arsenal and looting has begun, and the police are not doing anything to prevent it. I am told that it is being instigated by some leaders of the ruling party. Now the hooligans will get an open play field to loot the generally prosperous community." Ballu was sad and angry, at the same time.

"This is deplorable, come on, let's go to the Gurudwara." Digpal held Ballu's fat arm.

Though Digpal was not religiously inclined, he liked the cleanliness, the serene atmosphere and peace of Gurudwara. He loved the '*kadha prasad*' and *langar* (community meal); and volunteered many times to clean utensils and organise the shoes of the devotees. What impressed him most was, nobody bothered about his caste or religion, the most embarrassing questions.

They sat in front of the holy book for some time, and sat for *langar* on the floor with others. The food was simple but delicious, he was hungry and devoured it like a starved man. That probably was the only bright spot of the day!

He stayed with Balbir and family until afternoon, came back to his home and slipped into deep sleep.

## HIS LITTLE PATIENTS

It was Monday and Digpal was getting ready for morning OPD, when the doorbell rang. Before he could open the door, Harish rushed in, pushing the door, "Did you have tea? I need a cup."

"Yup, I did. If you want, go help yourself. Gimme half a cup too."

They both sat with their cups and some Monaco biscuits, which Harish hunted from the kitchen cupboard. Harish broke the silence.

"Before you see my resignation on your office table, I thought I should break the news to you first hand. I am leaving the job."

"Didn't you have anything better to say first thing in the morning?" Digpal was surprised and disappointed at the same time. Both of them didn't speak for a while. After a pause Digpal asked, "What do you plan to do now?"

"I am shifting to Bhuj, and will start private practice there. It's a good city, and hardly any competition in Anesthesia. Moreover I am so good at my work, you know." Harish let out a small laugh but Digpal didn't even smile. He had become so used to Harish's presence in OT, and they had become good friends too.

Both were quiet for a while, than Digpal spoke finally-

"Okay then, if you have already decided, what can I say? But before you go, we must go to Diu to celebrate your exodus. This weekend should be fine, I will talk to Dinkar as well." In response Harish smiled ear to ear.

During Harish's resignation period only, another Anaesthetist, Ronak Jain joined the Hospital. He was trained in

Bombay and was very competent, specially for neonates and smaller children, he had a deft and delicate approach.

Life seemed to be coming back on track. A good number of paediatric cases started pouring in. Congenital anomalies like cleft of lip and palate, neural tube defects- meningoceles of different sizes, shapes and location, from frontal region to lumbosacral part, hypospadias and an occasional epispadias, undescended testes, and so on. There used to be some very challenging cases like tracheo esophageal fistula. He operated on a few, but stopped doing so once he realised that results are almost always going to be dismal for want of proper neonatal care. Vidurpur was too small a place to get that kind of care.

Good antenatal care and Folic acid were not available to most of the pregnant women, which was responsible for neural tube defects. He vividly remembered a case of a newborn baby girl, with meningoencephalocele, bigger than the baby's size! The parents brought her with little hope of getting her cured. They were so scared of the rupture of the huge cyst that they couldn't handle her properly. Digpal confessed he had never seen something of that scale, leave aside operating on it. He explained to the parents that the baby may die on the table during surgery. The parents were not ready to go back home, and were ready for any eventuality.

Ronak too was reluctant, but then took up the challenge. He intubated her smoothly, and put the baby in an exaggerated head up position, to minimize CSF loss. Digpal slowly and carefully dissected away skin from the thin sac, and all of a sudden, the thinned out meninges gave way, CSF started gushing out, and the baby's heart stopped. Ronak swiftly started cardiac massage, holding her delicate chest, between his thumb and fingers.There was a combined sigh of relief when the little heart started beating again. The rest was uneventful, repair was leakproof, the wound healed completely in a week's time and the smiling parents took the playful baby home on the tenth day. By that time the baby had not been named, as they were not sure of her survival.

When she was brought for follow-up after a fortnight, the resident sitting opposite Digpal asked if now she had a name? The mother said, "Yes, she is Digansha. We have named her after doctor *saheb*."

'It's a huge return for getting this unique experience.' Digpal thought.

He would get very disturbed and angry with parents who neglected congenital anomalies for many years. Specially painless anomalies hidden under the pants, like hypospadias, undescended testes, ectopic anal openings and other minor anomalies. When advised, they would say the child is too small for surgery, and the child will be harmed. The hapless minor has to suffer due to the ignorant guardians and many a times, misadvising semi-educated practitioners.

Parents would bring their grown-up children with underdeveloped undescended testis, non functioning and with risk of teratogenicity. Most of the corrective procedures were done in stages and tested the patience of the child, parents and the surgeon.

But all said and done, he loved his little patients and developed an affectionate connection with them.

In the ensuing years till 1989, many things changed. Most of his consultant colleagues left the hospital to settle in private practice at different places as per their choice. Managing committees kept on changing every couple of years and he couldn't develop much camaraderie with the new generation doctors. But his work kept on increasing and his name and fame crossed district borders. For elective surgery there was an average waiting period of 2 to 3 months. Suresh Kumar had left and was replaced by a very enthusiastic young surgeon from Vadodara, Mukesh Khatri, later on he came to know that Mukesh belonged to Surat and Wanted to settle down there subsequently. They developed an immediate liking for each other, Mukesh longed to learn and Digpal wanted a sincere and reliable junior.

What did not change was the memory of Kalpana, which kept on keeping him awake during nights for hours. Her beautiful face, her sweet voice, her big eyes, the look she gave him, her intelligence and understanding. Only thing he didn't like was the lack of courage to face her parents and the society, about their relationship. She even did not want him to ever come to her home to ask for her hand. His attraction for Shabnam was only physical and he soon forgot her.

It was usual for a small group of doctors to stand in front of the clearance near the main gate of the hospital and chit chat about the day's happenings after the evening OPD. On one such evening when Mukesh and Digpal were discussing a choledocoduodenostomy done in the morning; they saw a young couple running towards the entrance with a child in the Father's lap of around 1 to 2 years, panic written on their faces. Mukesh stopped them and asked, "What happened?"

"The baby has swallowed something and now he is not breathing," replied the Father, almost crying. Both the doctors quickly examined the child while he was still in his Father's arms. The baby was blue, listless, no respiration and the heartbeat was very feeble and irregular. "There is no ENT surgeon in the hospital," muttered Mukesh. Grabbing the child from the Fathers arms, Digpal ran towards the operation theatre which was on the ground floor only; this small procession followed him. On the way, Mukesh asked the mother, "Was he playing with something before this happened?"

"Yes, he was playing with chess pieces," replied the mother. Digpal put the listless baby on the operation table, introduced the laryngoscope blade in the oral cavity. Mukesh, with a chest piece of stethoscope, whispered, "His heart has stopped!"

"Keep pumping the chest," shouted Digpal.

He could see a circular foreign body in the laryngeal inlet, covering the opening and both the vocal cords. He caught the foreign body with Megle's forceps, the tip slipped, he tried again but the foreign body was impacted so firmly, it did not budge.

"Give me a Kocher's forceps, quick." He shouted. The OT nurse handed him a Kocher's forceps, a sturdy instrument with lock and teeth at the tip. He firmly held the foreign body with the toothed tip of Kocher's and steadily pulled it out, and a pawn of chess came out with a swish! He put in an airway and started giving positive pressure oxygen intermittently. Mukesh stopped the cardiac massage and smiled, "It's beating on its own!" Gradually the baby's colour started changing and then suddenly the baby gave out a loud cry, pushed Digpal's hand away from his face and gagged on the air way, which Digpal removed in a semicircular movement. "Oh boy!" Digpal took a deep breath and noticed he himself was not breathing for quite some time. 'What a way to end the day', thought Mukesh, or this is what he thought.

As they were passing through the corridor of casualty, they noticed a small crowd of young boys, all teenagers in whites, one of them holding a cricket bat with one of the leg pads still on. A boy was lying on the table looking pale, perspiring and in agony, but was not moving or tossing.

"He was hit by a cricket ball on the side of abdomen, and has severe pain and cannot stand up." Told a very tense looking boy holding a bat in his hand. The resident there already had a drip of lactated ringer's solution ready. Mukesh and Digpal did a quick examination. The boy was in shock with a thready pulse and very low blood pressure.

"Get his blood work-up and grouping cross matching done immediately and inform OT for laparotomy," instructed Digpal "and call his parents." Facing the boys he said, "Any of you above 18 should be ready to donate blood for him, his spleen seems to have ruptured and he has lost a lot of blood."

"We are not finished with the day as yet," murmured Mukesh. The boy was lean and thin. In two knife strokes, Digpal reached the peritoneum through a left paramedian incision. It was looking dark, an indication of hemoperitoneum or blood in the abdominal cavity. He quickly opened all the layers, ignoring small bleeders in the abdominal wall. The abdominal cavity was filled with blood. Without bothering to suck out blood and clots, he pinched the splenic pedicle between his left thumb and fingers. "Now suck out the blood," he asked Mukesh, who deftly put a perforated suction cannula in the abdominal cavity and retracted the muscle towards the left of the patient and they could see the shattered spleen. Digpal double ligated the pedicle and removed the spleen. Some very small fragments remained in the peritoneal cavity,

"They will embed in the peritoneum and grow into tiny spleens; useful." A resident rushed in and informed the Anaesthetist, "We have only one blood for him, his blood group is AB positive."

"We will need at least one more, if not two." The Anaesthetist replied. "Mukesh, please close the abdomen and keep a drain in the left paracolic gutter, I am going to the blood bank, my group is AB positive." Digpal hurriedly removed gloves and gown and headed to the lab in his scrubs, got his blood cross matched and donated a bottle of blood for him.

The next day's list was a typical general surgery list– One sub-total thyroidectomy, a congenital hernia, two mesh hernioplasty, one elective appendix, two hydroceles and a fissure in ano. Raunak Mehta was an efficient and competent Anaesthetist and ran two operation theatres simultaneously.

Mukesh was interested in scrubbing with him in the cases of thyroidectomy and congenital hernia of a child, and he wanted his senior to explain every step of the surgery. As was the norm, the first case was the child with Hernia.

Digpal began with the incision, "Children are not small adults. Unlike adults, the incision should be a small transverse incision just above the pubic tubercle, instead of supra inguinal. In infants and younger children, the two inguinal rings are almost superimposed, the inguinal canal is not developed. After subcutaneous tissue, you straight away encounter the spermatic cord; don't handle it, just lift it on a haemostat, and slowly dissect with two plain forceps, and see, the glistening white sac is right there. Dissect it till its neck, transfix and cut. So simple, no need to do anything else just close."

'He makes things look so simple', thought Mukesh.

Next day was a grand round day, when they didn't post any elective surgeries. In front of the two bed sharing room, named a semispecial in that Hospital, there seemed to be some hot discussion going on. Heated words were being exchanged between two small groups, one headed by a muscular man and another by a middle aged bearded man. The hospital admin was trying to pacify both the parties, with little success. As they found out, the bearded man was Father of Abid, the injured teenager, and the other fellow was Father of Sanjay singh the fast bowler whose ball had hit Abid.

Seeing the surgical team, they fell silent and made way for them to enter the room. Abid was doing very well. Satisfied, they came out and faced the small group.

"Abid is recovering well, and will be sent home in a couple of days" Digpal explained, "He is a strong boy and will be able to play again after about six weeks. By the way, have you heard the name of Nari Contractor?"

"Yes Sir, the great Indian opening batsman," some of the boys spoke in unison. Digpal continued, "He was hit on the head with a bouncer by West Indian fast bowler Griffith. Due to the serious injury, Nari's international cricket career was finished, but still, he held no grudge against Griffith! Why? Because Nari was a true sportsman, and he knew it's all part of the game. Abid's shot could have injured Sanjay or any other player."

The surgical team proceeded to complete the round. Digpal hoped the two warring parties would see reason and stop accusing each other, otherwise, it didn't take much for religious hatred turning into riots. It always surprised him how people thought in terms of religion, caste, language groups. He couldn't understand because he belonged to none. But at that time, he had more important tasks at hand than being philosophical.

The next patient was in a deluxe (luxury) room. A 75 years old male, whose Freyer's prostatectomy was done a month ago by Digpal, and was discharged on the seventh postoperative day. "I admitted him again last evening. His suprapubic leak refuses to stop, I have introduced Foley's again." Mukesh briefed quickly, before entering the room. The patient's son who sounded like an NRI was in a foul mood, probably because he had to extend his stay in India.

"Why is my Father's wound not healing? Was the operation done properly? I had told my Father to go to Bombay for surgery, but he had so much faith in you." He spoke in an irritated tone. Digpal tried to console him, "We will solve the problem, don't worry." But he had no clue about the solution. He was sure there was no forgotten foreign body in the depths of the wound. During the rounds, Digpal suddenly said, "Let's start anti-tubercular treatment in that case."

"Without any evidence?" Mukesh asked.

"Yes, without any evidence."

By the end of the following week, the fistula healed completely.

Digpal explained to his team, "Tuberculosis is so common in our country, that we can commence AKT empirically if we are convinced, it is sometimes difficult to prove by investigations."

Those were the times when the clinician had the liberty to treat their patients without supporting radiology or laboratory evidence. The concept of 'defensive medicine' didn't exist and the state had not slapped the consumer protection act yet in the medical field. Only the benefit of ailing humanity used to be on the treating doctor's mind.

# CHANGING TIMES

As the time went by, the management personnel of the hospital trust kept on changing, as they were elected bodies, and the new management did not go along well with the ways of Digpal. All other doctors were young and the managing committee members could behave high handedly with them, but not with Digpal. Some of the donors had big egos and they treated doctors as ordinary employees. Moreover, some members felt that they were paying a very high salary to Digpal; a new surgeon would cost much less.

It was the early nineties, things were changing in the surgical field as well. A new breed of surgeons, called super specialists were coming up, Neurosurgeons, Onco surgeons, Paediatric surgeons and so on; Neuro and Cardio thoracic surgery branches were already developed. A new variety of surgeons were rising on the horizon, called Laparoscopic surgeons, which would make open surgery and surgeons outdated, but that was much later. Rich patients started preferring these super-specialists over their tried and tested General surgeon.

Newer diagnostic gadgets were making their entry, first at bigger centres and then in mid sized cities and towns. The most remarkable was ultrasonography, which was going to change the way surgeons would reach diagnosis and decide the line of treatment, especially in abdominal problems. Computer Assisted Tomography was used mainly in bigger cities for intracranial pathologies and had greatly aided in treatment and prediction of outcome of head injuries.

The surgical list too was changing its character. The number of exploratory laparotomies was reducing due to USG diagnosis. Good antenatal care was reducing the number of congenital anomalies, and major anomalies could be diagnosed in early pregnancy, which in turn could be terminated in such cases. This proved to be a curse as well to the society. Antenatal sex determination became rampant in certain communities, and their love for male offsprings resulted in the killing of daughters in wombs. This ugly practice was going to change the lopsided sex ratio, leading to numerous social and legal problems in the future.

There wasn't much change in the working pattern of the surgical department at Jiviben hospital, but the undercurrents were flowing against Digpal. Management didn't have to wait very long to take action against Digpal.

On one of the weekend evenings, a drunk relative of a managing committee member came to the casualty with minor head injury. The casualty medical officer informed Mukesh, who in turn examined him and found that he had only a concussion and a small wound on his forehead. The young man was accompanied by his friends, most of them drunk. They insisted that since the patient is a VIP, he must be examined by a senior surgeon. Mukesh called up Digpal, "Is he bad?"

"Not at all, I am admitting him for observation."

"I don't think I need to come." Digpal hung up the phone.

The next day was a long operation list, as usual. The President of the managing committee sent a man in OT to summon Digpal, as soon as possible. "I can come only after completing all the operations." He told the messenger and sent him back.

The operation list was complete by afternoon, Digpal was tired and hungry, and he forgot about the president's message.

The following morning when he reached his office, an envelope was waiting on his table. The letter in it read-

'Dear Dr Digpal,

You are instructed to attend an emergency meeting of the managing committee at 5 PM sharp today in the president's office, without fail'.

It was signed by the president.

In the evening, Digpal wore his best dress, a blue necktie and a doctor's white coat. The governing council members, fifteen of them, were sitting in a semicircle, many of them thirsty for his blood. A chair in the centre was placed facing them all. The president was a kind old man, who liked Digpal. "Please have a seat doctor," he instructed.

The secretary cleared his throat and began, "Dr Digpal, lately there had been complaints of your rude behaviour and avoiding to attend VIP patients, you don't take regular rounds of deluxe rooms as well."

"And you are not attending patients at the proper time." Jumped in a semi bald, pot bellied short man. Digpal recalled doing his fistulectomy, after which he had expected the surgeon to examine his wound, early in morning, after he had his bath. But Digpal never obliged, there were more important things to do in OT at that time.

"You didn't examine my nephew, who came in with a serious head injury on Saturday night, and you let your assistant treat him." Fumed another middle aged member, who had earned a fortune in illegal sand mining.

"Doctor, please explain and apologize for your behaviour," the President urged him in a mild tone.

"We gave him this job and allowed him to work freely in this hospital, even though he is an outsider." Shot a sixty-plus old man with a nodding head. His wife's radical mastectomy was done by Digpal for stage III carcinoma of breast seven years back, and she was still disease-free.

The secretary intruded again, "You have worked very hard to bring this hospital to great heights, if you apologize, everything will be forgotten." He didn't want to lose a good surgeon for baseless complaints.

Digpal answered slowly and firmly, choosing every word carefully, "I am thankful for the opportunity given to me for serving the ailing humanity of this region. As per my appointment preconditions, I herewith tender my resignation and my notice period of three months begins from today." He pulled out a paper from his coat pocket, and placed it on the table, turned and left the room before anybody could react.

It was evening, he was feeling light headed and free. He drove to Ballu's dhaba, where Ballu, without speaking a word, took him straight to the first floor room. Ballu closed the door, pulled the curtains, arranged two glasses, lemonade, peanuts and a bottle of vodka on the table. None of the two spoke a word. Ballu poured the drink, and both started sipping in silence. When Ballu poured a second drink, he spoke in his usual jovial style. "Now tell, what's the matter?" Digpal was surprised at his insight, observation and understanding.

"I have resigned from Jiviben." His voice was low.

"What? Are you crazy?" Then regaining back his usual mood, he slapped Digpal's thigh, "*Koi gall nahi* (doesn't matter). There are no dearth of opportunities for a surgeon like you, you have earned a good name here, and can start practice as well."

"No Ballu, I don't have the aptitude and mindset of a private practitioner. Can't become a businessman."

"Not all private practitioners are businessmen, anyway if you are not comfortable, forget it."

They kept on drinking and talking till midnight, and after four pegs, he forgot about the resignation and began talking about Kalpana and how much he missed her.

Next day in OPD he informed his junior colleague Mukesh, his residents and interns that this was his last month in this hospital and he wanted that all the patients waiting for elective surgeries be operated before he is relieved of the job. He requested Mukesh to give further appointments only to those patients whom he himself was confident to operate upon.

"Means I should refuse paediatric cases, major malignancy surgeries, hiatus hernia and many more?" Mukesh asked.

"Your free will dear."

For our man, work was the best ointment for all wounds. He immersed himself in Surgeries, rounds, dressings, OPD and brainstorming with his team like nothing had changed. Only when he would come back to his modest apartment, which he had started liking and was home to him for the last 13 years, the uncertain future would start haunting him.

One evening, a couple of days after the resignation, he noticed a well dressed young man in a blue blazer and a matching tie, waiting in front of his apartment. The stranger smiled and offered his hand, "I am Vineet... Vineet Kapadia, can we talk for a while?"

"I am Digpal, yes sure, please come in." He responded and guided him toward the single sofa and two-plastic chair drawing room. Without discussing the purpose of the visit, he placed two glasses of water on the table, sat on a chair and glanced toward Vineet with a question in his eyes.

"Well, I am H.R. manager of Golden group of Hospitals. The head office and main Hospital is in Rajkot. We came to know that you have resigned from Jiviben hospital." 'News spreads fast in a small town', thought Digpal. "Yes, that's true, and I am on a three month notice period."

"The owner of Golden Hospital will be pleased to have you in their hospital. The pay package will be many times more than what you are getting here, plus 50% of operation charges of all the patients, irrespective of the category and 10% of the investigations advised by you."

There was silence for a few minutes, "I need some time to think."

"Take your time, I am leaving my card here, you can contact me when you make up your mind." Vineet got up, shook hands with Digpal, and while leaving stopped at the threshold, turned and smiled, "You can negotiate your salary at the time of meeting the chairman." He left and Digpal sank in the sofa, repeating the Clever man's words in his mind and how he was baiting him, stressing so much on the money part.

For the next few days, he kept mulling over the prospect of joining the Golden Group of Hospital. Every day he would call a friend to seek their advice. He badly missed Sarang at this time, he would have rightly advised him. He called up Harish, he responded after giving a thought, "Go for it dear, it's a lucrative offer and you will come out of that small well of Vidurpur, you will shine in a bigger field. See, how happy I am in Bhuj!" Almost every friend and well wisher expressed similar thoughts.

One evening, he suddenly remembered Ankita, his batchmate. She was his first crush; he liked her for her qualities but the relationship could never go beyond exchange of notes from classrooms, discussing some books or general talk. Ankita Sinha was a reasonably good looking girl, though not beautiful in the popular sense. She wore thick glasses through which her beautiful big eyes seemed to be reading you Inside out. She was a voracious reader of a wide variety of literature. He always felt a bit small in front of her, probably that was the folly of his own personality. She was reserved by nature, had few friends and those too only girls. He was the only exception. They kept on meeting occasionally from first MBBS, till they cleared the graduation. She never showed any liking for him or was good at hiding it!

He could never muster enough courage to express his feelings. She was from a well educated, cultured family of Delhi and her Father was a government officer. The disparity of status, his orphanage background and inferiority complex, came in the way of taking their relationship to the next level, but, he confessed to himself, he was never as crazy for her, as he was for Kalpana.

He adored the Intelligence and analytical mind of Ankita and thought she could advise him without bias. He had lost contact with her after MBBS, as she went to Delhi for an internship. He searched her number from the batch directory, hesitated for a while, kept the index finger in the dial for a minute then started dialling. After a few rings, he heard a girl child's sweet voice, "Hello, I am Dolly, I will call Mommy." And he could hear small running steps. After a while he heard the familiar voice, "Hello! Whom do you want to talk to?" He was a bit nervous and was about to stammer talking to her, then collected himself and introduced himself, and asked about her. She informed him that she did her MD in Pathology from Lady Hardinge medical college, Delhi, and married a cardiologist. They have two daughters, she is very happy and her husband's name is DP Mathur.

"Ah! the famous cardiologist doctor DP Mathur?"

"Yes, Digant is my husband."

"He must be keeping very busy, are you happy?"

"Digant is a very caring and understanding husband and loving Father." Digpal felt a twinge of jealousy.

"You didn't call me to ask about me?" 'She is too clever', he thought and told her everything about his job, his single status, his failed love affair, resignation from the job and the offer in detail.

"You can join there, no harm but as far as I know you, you won't survive in the job for more than two years. There is one way-ask them to remove the offer of 10% from the investigation charges. Your moral won't let you take the kick backs. Maybe then you can work there with more peace of mind."

"Thanks a lot Ankita for the valuable advice."

"My pleasure," and without giving him a further chance to continue the conversation she hung the receiver. 'I don't matter for her any more, or never mattered', he thought.

# THE SLOG OVERS

The load of elective surgeries had increased tremendously, as he wanted to finish off all waiting cases. One of the operative days during a Nissen's fundoplication, he found the spleen was adherent to the fundus of the stomach.

"What will we do now?" Asked Mukesh

"Let's knockout the spleen, otherwise we won't be able to wrap the stomach around the lower end of the esophagus, to form an ink pot, to prevent regurgitation."

They had already introduced an autoclaved flatus tube in the esophagus through the mouth, with the help of the Anaesthetist, so that the plication did not become too tight. Then they removed the spleen and wrapped the upper part of the fundus, to suture it on the right side of the esophagus, with thick silk sutures. Satisfied, he told Mukesh to close the abdomen.

Then there was a second stage hypospadias. He sat down and slowly made a tube from penile skin with a 6-0 chromic catgut. It needed patience and accuracy. Mukesh and Kumar before him never bothered to learn that. He felt there is too much headache and little returns monetarily, also the high fistula rate is an embarrassment to the surgeon. Mukesh subsequently wanted to start private practice in Surat, where he belonged, and had a perfect aptitude. Most of the congenital anomalies were common in low economics status population, that's why it didn't interest most practitioners; but Digpal enjoyed them, not knowing at that time that this attitude will be a bone of contention in his future.

Rest of the cases that day were hernioplasty for ventral hernia, a lumbar sympathectomy, a renal pelvic stag horn stone, and an elective appendectomy plus a few minor surgeries. In the OPD, every now and then, his patients and their relatives would urge him not to leave Vidurpur or even if he wanted to leave Jiviben, start private practice in the same town. Some of them even came with the offer of renting out their newly constructed commercial buildings to start practice and not to worry about the rent.

Then there was this patient, a young female around 30 years, all skin and bones, who came with her husband. He had seen him in the market, running a small makeshift shop of roasted peanuts and chickpeas. He could gather from his accent that he was from Uttar Pradesh. He was almost crying, "My wife has been losing weight since last 1 year, runs a fever every evening," but he was a poor man and could not afford expensive treatment.

"I had examined her last evening, got her routine work up, X-ray of chest and abdomen done." Informed Mukesh. "She has tuberculosis written all over her," whispered Digpal. They went through the investigations. She was anemic with very high ESR, RBCs in urine, normal X-ray chest, but most interesting was X-ray of abdomen which showed a white opacity on the left side of spine, exactly the shape and size of a kidney but higher up then its normal position.

"We must operate before you leave, it's a calcified tuberculous kidney for sure." Mukesh was excited. "Before surgery we must have an intravenous Urogram, to know the status of the other kidney, " commented Digpal. "Get it done today only, if we can arrange blood it can be posted in tomorrow's list." The IV urogram surprised both the surgeons, she had both Kidneys intact and functioning! The calcified kidney like shadow was lying a bit above and medial to the functioning left kidney.

Next day the lady was taken for surgery and on retroperitoneal dissection, a hard calcified kidney with atrophic ureter, with blood supply from small size vessels coming from the left renal artery could be seen. The calcified organ was removed uneventfully. Later on, it was reported to be a calcified tuberculous kidney by the pathologist. With anti tubercular and supportive treatment, she started recovering quickly and gained weight. This was the only person with a third kidney in his career, which ensured free supply of roasted peanuts for the whole department until he lived in Vidurpur.

That evening he searched for the visiting card of Vineet Kapadia, the HR man of Golden Hospital, called him up and expressed interest in joining their hospital, "Only thing I want is, the offer of 10% cut from investigation removed from the conditions."

"That you can discuss with the chairman during the interview." replied the HR manager. After half an hour his phone rang, "I am Vineet again doctor, can you come to our hospital at 11 AM on Sunday to meet our Chairman? Please be on time, the chairman is very particular about timings."

"I am never late," was the curt reply. Digpal reached Rajkot at 10:30, it was a good 3 hours drive from Vidurpur in his second hand Maruti van. The full name of the Hospital, 'Golden group of hospitals and Research Centre' was inscribed in Golden letters prominently on the second floor elevation. It was a world apart from Jiviben Hospital! As he stood in front of the huge glass door of Golden Hospital, the sliding door parted in the centre and opened automatically. He entered the reception area where he was caressed by the cold Breeze of central air conditioning. Noticing him enter, a smart young lady in a knee length, tight blue skirt and beige top left the reception counter short and wished him 'good morning'.

"I am doctor Digpal..." and before he could complete his sentence, she interrupted with a smile, "the chairman's office is on 5th floor, he will see you at 11 AM sharp. The lift cluster is straight ahead exactly in the middle of passage, on both the sides."

As he was crossing the Reception area, he noticed a big board on the right wall with a long list of specialists and super specialists, their timings and days of availability. Next to it at eye level was the signage for reaching different departments. Then there was a large waiting area for OPD patients and relatives, furnished with airport-like chairs. On one side four wheelchairs and four gurneys were parked. He noticed they were hydraulic gurneys with side rails, fitted with oxygen cylinders and Masks.

He crossed the waiting area and reached the elevator cluster, took a lift marked 'for doctors', to 5th floor. There, he was received by another young lady in the same uniform, she guided him to a closed lounge by the side of an office with a golden plate, marked 'CHAIRMAN' on it. The lounge was furnished with comfortable sofas, draped with leather upholstery. A glass of water and a big cup of coffee with sugar cubes in a separate dish were kept on the central table.

The girl said, "It's 15 minutes to 11, doctor, make yourself comfortable." He was a bit hungry from the drive. He downed the glass of water in one go and sipped away the cup of coffee. Exactly at 11, the same girl entered and announced, "The chairman is waiting for you."

He had anticipated a gray haired middle-aged or past middle-aged gentleman in a three piece designer suit with a cigar in his mouth, but he turned out to be a young, trim, very fair complexioned man in his thirties donning a T-shirt and jeans. As Digpal entered, he got up and extended his hand, "I am Pramod Soni; welcome doctor Digpal."

"Thanks Sir." Was the short reply of the surgeon, who was not as relaxed as the other man.

"I guess you accepted our offer. I will be very happy to have a surgeon like you in our hospital." Then they talked about the salary and removing the condition of the 10% payback on investigations. "That is to encourage our consultants to advise necessary investigations for the benefit of patients. Anyway, if you don't want that we can waive that off." Said Pramod smilingly. 'He is a liar and businessman to the core' he thought. "I would prefer that 10% be passed on to the patient and be deducted from their charges."

The chairman did not like the idea, but he didn't want to let go of this man. He will bring clients from Vidurpur and surrounding villages. He said politely, "Fine with us doctor. You will be provided residence in residents quarters till you get your own decent house. Welcome to the Golden family. "Thanks Sir, it will take me 15 days to wind up from there and join after that." Digpal told.

So, he was in for a new chapter of his life.

# LAST FEW DAYS IN JIVIBEN SHAH MEMORIAL HOSPITAL

There was another one more week to go by in Jiviben and Digpal's operative lists were full with appointments for elective surgeries. Apart from this, there were cases which were not actually urgent but required early surgery.

Jethabhai was one such case. He was diabetic with a pus discharging sinus lateral to left pubic tubercle. The sinus was repeatedly curated, dressed regularly, antibiotics were given cyclically, as per culture and sensitivity tests; even anti tubercular treatment was prescribed, without any result. He had been moving from pillar to post for a year. What was omitted was a small piece of history, that his right sided mesh hernioplasty was done by a practitioner in a neighbouring city, two months before development of sinus.

The surgical team decided to do a sonogram to assess the extent of sinus. When radio opaque dye was injected in the sinus, it clearly demarcated the mesh on the right inguinal region. Jethabhai was convinced for surgical removal of the mesh, which was the nidus of infection. His diabetes was controlled by Insulin, mesh removed and with proper dressings, his sinus and wound healed completely.

Then, there were sporadic cases of elephantiasis of lower limb coming in due to filarial infestation. Patients would come in where they could hardly lift the affected limb because of the excessive weight. Most of the existing methods were disappointing and made the limb uglier. During his residency, he had assisted a case where one of his teachers ligated the femoral artery, resulting in remarkable decrease in size and weight of limb, though his professor was not sure of long term results. In some of the patients he tried the ligation, and the results were encouraging. He had heard it being referred to as Dixit's ligation. Since he was afraid of possible gangrene, he would ligate femoral, below profunda femoris artery, to ensure collateral blood supply to the limb. On one occasion, he had the opportunity to talk to Dr Dixit, Professor at Surat medical college, himself. When he talked of his fear, he patted his back and said, "Tie it above the profunda, young man, the results will be better and no harm will be done."

These were encouraging words, and he followed the old professor's advice. During his last week at Jiviben, he called all the waiting elephantiasis patients for surgery. At that time he did not know that he would not operate a single such case for another six to seven year, because the rich and affording seldom suffer from such problems.

The last week in Jiviben was studded with farewell parties and emotional speeches for him. Surprisingly, even the managing committee threw a farewell dinner party for the surgeon. Nurses union, interns and residents, and consultants arranged his farewell. During these farewells, such good words were spoken for his qualities, which he too was otherwise unaware of. These are the ways of this world, he wondered; when someone leaves a place or the world, even the qualities he or she never possessed are spoken of, in flowery language. The lies and falsehood that exist in society were so very apparent.

During this period, he could not repair all his post hypospadias repair fistulae, and so promised to do so in Golden hospital, free of charge.

On the penultimate day, when he stepped into his administrative office, the secretary and president of the trust were waiting for him. After the initial exchange of formalities, the secretary quickly came to the point, "Doctor, you have worked hard to bring this hospital to this level, we don't want you to leave. You reconsider your decision, I will convince the committee to increase your salary as well."

Digpal was surprised by this change of heart.

"Thanks a lot *kaka* (Gujarati for uncle), but I am sorry, I have made up my mind to leave. Moreover I have committed to another hospital management, to join there."

The duo wished him good luck and left. Only time will tell, whether his decision to join Golden hospital was correct, or a blunder!

The last two days were packed with activity. He had to pack his meager belongings and complete his commitments of elective surgeries. On the penultimate day, he was to remove a staghorn calculus of one Prakash More, a hefty central reserve police jawan from Maharashtra. The calculus was occupying the whole drainage system, the calyces and the pelvis of the kidney. After exposing and freeing the kidney, he turned the organ interiorly. While incising the pelvis of kidney, he could feel the gritty stone with his scalpel. He gently tried to dislocate the calculus, which refused to move. He had to cut it in the middle with a bone cutter. The upper half was delivered without much hassle, but the lower half didn't come out, as the rounded tips of stone were bigger than the necks of calices. He lost patience and gave a slight tug to the calculus, and it came out, but the kidney started bleeding profusely. He kept the kidney compressed for some time, when released, it started bleeding again. He considered pinching the renal artery, but was afraid it may damage the kidney. Should he go ahead with nephrectomy, to save the young man's life, he wondered.

"We must take consent of his wife before considering removal of kidney." Mukesh commented. Digpal kept quiet, then holding the kidney in a wet mop, instructed the resident to arrange for a unit of blood and take a written consent for nephrectomy from next of kin. Meanwhile he asked the circulating nurse to give him a pair of sterile gloves filled with ice.While waiting for the blood and consent, he placed the ice filled gloves around the kidney.

"Blood will be ready in twenty minutes; his wife is crying since I mentioned kidney removal." Resident informed.

Both the surgeons stood still for more then ten minutes; and when they removed the ice packs and wet mop, the bleeding completely stopped!

"Does he have hypotension?" Digpal asked anxiously.

"He is stable." The Anaesthetist grinned.

He closed the pelvis and the wound around a drain. Prakash More went home and recovered after a week, but that was after Digpal had already left the hospital. Fortunately, he could leave Vidurpur without the weight of complication on his conscience.

Leaving Jiviben was an emotional event. With the help of John, some nurses and wardboys, he loaded his meager belongings on a small three-wheel loading truck and fragile belongings in his Maruti van. With a heavy heart and moist eyes, a small crowd of doctors, nurses, other staff, some relatives of patients and stray dogs of the campus bid him goodbye.

Ballu insisted on accompanying him and loaded his rolly polly body in the van. Initially, he was to stay in one of the resident's quarters, until he found some decent accommodation in the city.

# CORPORATE HOSPITAL CULTURE

Digpal's consulting room in Golden Hospital was in stark contrast to the 10 x 15 feet OPD of Jiviben hospital. The latter had an one old ceiling fan, one big laminated table, revolving chair for the surgeon, a stool for patients and on the two sides, residents and the junior surgeon accommodated themselves. There were two examination tables, on which the residents and junior surgeon would write history and examine the patients. If needed, they would summon Digpal to have a look. History taking and examination was done quickly, investigations advised, appointment for elective surgery was given. Patients requiring admission were advised accordingly. Everything was swift and in the crowded OPD, there was order in chaos. Very few patients or the relatives would counter the doctors or object to the dates of appointments given.

The consulting room at Golden Hospital was air conditioned, rather the whole Hospital building was centrally air conditioned. There were comfortable waiting chairs with newspapers and magazines on the side tables. There was a secretary, common for three Consultants, the surgeon, the physician and the ENT surgeon. She would enter the data of the patients in the software and was responsible for giving appointments for further consultations and surgery. There was a nurse with each consultant to help them during examination of the patients.

Digpal was impressed with the setup and his imported revolving chair gave him the feeling of being a big consultant! For the initial few days, there were very few patients; most of them were old operated cases in the same hospital with scar pain and other minor complaints. He observed that the pain threshold was far lower than the patients reporting at Jiviben hospital. On the second day, there was a call on the intercom that there was a case of acute abdominal pain. The patient was shifted on a gurney to his consulting room for immediate attention. The young man was in agony, rolling and tossing, with his right palm on right iliac fossa of abdomen and the thumb on the flank. He was accompanied by his wife, who anxiously asked,

"Doctor, can a person have two appendixes? His was removed only two months back."

"Relax and let me examine first." The surgeon replied.

The history was very clear; he had severe and sudden pain in right lower abdomen, had vomiting, and the pain was radiating to his right testicle too. He was operated by an eminent visiting surgeon. two months back. The young man informed, "I had exactly similar pain two months back and an emergency appendectomy was done. I was okay for two months but the pain has returned. Digpal instructed the nurse to shift him to the treatment room, inject an analgesic and antispasmodic then shift the patient for investigations. The previous record showed slightly raised blood count, an ambiguous urine report and ultrasonography showing Appendix with presence of probe tenderness. The histopath read sub acute appendicitis.

This was a straightforward case of right sided ureteric stone, at lower 1/3rd of ureter. The diagnosis was later confirmed by investigations. This seemed to be intentional mis-diagnosis at the previous instance. This was his initial lesson to understand the commercial aspect of surgery. The urinary colic case settled by conservative management and the patient was discharged on the third day.

Then there was this executive from a multinational company who had a minor head injury and a one centimetre lacerated wound, on the Frontal region, which was repaired in casualty. Digpal examined him and admitted him for overnight observation. Next morning, found him absolutely normal and instructed the resident to discharge him. "Sir, won't you refer him to a neurosurgeon? It's a routine here that all head injury patients are to be referred to neuro." Asked the resident, who was there for quite some time.

"I don't think it's required." Quipped the surgeon.

As soon as he went back to his office, the intercom rang, "Dr Digpal your head injury patient was seen by the neurosurgeon and advised a brain scan. Please refer the patients to relevant specialties for better service to the society." It was the hospital admin on the line. Digpal uttered a short, "Okay."

He was gradually learning the ways of corporate medicine. There was a full time resident surgeon who had finished his Masters only a year ago, Jainil Patel, young, enthusiastic and hard working. Digpal was second on call for emergencies. Jainil would attend to all surgical emergencies and would inform him on phone if his opinion is required. He rarely had to go to the hospital at odd hours.

Compared to Jiviben, life was quieter, professionally. Most of the patients would come for consultation with prior appointments; most of the surgeries he was doing were planned surgeries. He would get enough time for talking to the patient, and do a thorough clinical examination; investigative facilities in the hospital were good and he was getting a good pay packet. Within a few months he sold his old Maruti van and purchased a Honda car. He started looking for a good apartment, he calculated that he can afford EMI for that. Still he was lonely. He had developed some new acquaintances but couldn't feel close to anyone.

Digpal had entered his forties with no close local friends and no love life. Junior nurses used to rotate in different departments in the hospital. A new nurse was posted in his consulting room. Charming, always smiling, with a spring in her gait. Darker in complexion than an average Indian, her face was childish with a small upturned nose. She seemed to be from the southern part of India, her lapel plate read Joseline Breganza. When introduced for the first time, she said charmingly, "Call me Jose, Dr Joseph."

Hardly anyone ever addressed him as 'doctor Joseph', wondered Digpal. Jose addresses him this way, thinking he is a Christian.

"Call me Digpal, Jose." Replied the surgeon.

That day onwards, they got along well. Whenever OPD was lean, they would talk on different topics, but rarely about their personal lives. Strangely, he did not deny that he is not Christian! She was quite talkative, and within a few days revealed that she had been married for four years and her husband was in the Middle East, working as a cab driver. She was from Goa and lived with her mother in the nurses quarters. Her husband never came back from the Middle East after their wedding, called her occasionally and promised every time that he would come during X-mas and take her along with him. By now she had stopped believing him. Priti Nanavati was a full time gynaecologist, fair, petite and full of energy. She was fresh from Medical School and was hungry to learn.

Another difference from Jiviben was, whenever during a laparotomy a gynec pathology was encountered, it was mandatory to call the Gynecologist. In Jiviben. He could operate any gynae case he wished to, or if the Gynecologist was not available. In Golden hospital, during a laparotomy if any abnormality was encountered in the female reproductive system, or an incidental tubectomy had to be done, he would just inform Priti, write her name on paper, and operate. She never objected.
Digpal and Jainil planned to operate upon a middle aged lady with a big incisional hernia and left sided hydronephrosis, due to obstruction at lower end of ureter. She was operated on two years back for a large uterine fibroid, and her hysterectomy was done at that time. The USG report showed a cyst in the pelvis.

"Sir, it seems we will have to request the senior Gynecologist to assist us in this case, she is in gynec OT right now, why don't you go and meet her personally?" The younger men suggested and Digpal agreed.

"By the way, what is her name?"

"She is Mrs K.S. Rathore, wife of an IPS officer." Informed Jainil.

When he entered the operation theatre, the gynec team was closing the abdomen. The Gynecologist's back was towards him, her rich lock of hair neatly tied in a bun, covered with a surgical cap. The middle string of the gown was tied at the level of her thin waist, making her figure more pronounced. He missed a beat, even though her back was towards her, and she had donned surgical gear, he recognised her unmistakably!

He muttered a husky "Excuse me," and walked to the head end of the table where the lady Anaesthetist was chatting with the all-female operative team. On listening to his voice, her hands with needle holder and thumb forceps stopped for a moment, which nobody else noticed, except him.

"I am Digpal, the senior surgeon here. I want to discuss a case with you, will wait for you in the doctor's room." She just nodded and he left for the adjoining doctor's room. His heart was beating very quickly, even a major surgery never made him so nervous. He stood up as she entered, she had removed her mask, cap and gown and was looking beautiful as ever even in her Scrub suit. She had lost a kilo or two, wondered Digpal.

"Sorry for keeping you waiting, doctor." Was the impersonal remark. There was no 'Sir' or Digpal in that. She sometimes used to address him as 'Pal' when they used to be alone. But something was amiss on the beautiful face. The omnipresent smile was missing, the bubbly chirpy girl with wide curious eyes was missing. His surgically trained eyes didn't miss a faint Blue discoloration near the left zygomatic area, in spite of makeup to conceal that. For a few minutes, only two of them were in the room.

"How are you Kalpana?" He asked. At the same time, Priti entered the room with other residents, and she promptly asked, "You had come to discuss some case?" Digpal, in brief, described the history and probable diagnosis and they agreed to post the case after three days in surgical OT.

"I can manage on my own, but I want your presence in OT for some time, for statutory reasons," he smiled.

"I know you easily can," for the first time she sounded familiar, "but I would like to scrub."

"My pleasure." Digpal stood up to leave.

"Can we have a cup of coffee together after surgery?"

"Depends," she replied with uncertainty.

The next 3 days were difficult for him. He found out that after completing her internship she did her PG in Obstetrics and Gynecology from BJ medical college in Ahmedabad. She was considered a very bright student and skilled surgeon as a resident. Soon after her PG, she was married to a very handsome IPS officer, Surendra Singh Rathore from a distinguished family of Jamnagar. She worked for two years in the Civil Hospital of Jamnagar, and the last three years she had been attached to Golden group of hospitals, as Mr Rathore was posted in Rajkot. They had no kids as yet. During those three days, he felt like a teenager before his first date!

Finally, on the day of surgery he asked Jainil to finish off with minor cases in another OT. He reached the change room half an hour before scheduled time, changed into his scrubs and kept on turning the pages of patients' records without reading them. Kalpana came in time, they briefly discussed incision and steps of surgery. They decided to open through a Pfannenstiel incision, excising the old scar inside an ellipse. There was no muscle between skin and peritoneum. There were extensive intestinal adhesions, which Digpal patiently divided with sharp and blunt dissection. Kalpana preferred to assist like Jiviben Hospital days. Their excitement of meeting after such a long interval had vanished and they were working on the case, like true professionals. It took them a long time to clear the abdomen and pelvis of adhesions. There was a three inch by three inch ovarian cyst lying on the ureter.

"Would you like to remove this?" Digpal asked.

"No you do it, I will assist only Sir." While saying that she smiled behind the Mask, he guessed.

"I don't think this is the cause of hydronephrosis," he commented. She remained silent. After removing the cyst, he gave a linear incision parallel to the ureter in the peritoneum.

"That is a lot of periureteric fibrosis and the ureter is kinked." He murmured, and slowly dissected free the thin walled tube from surrounding Fibrosis.

"This should relieve the obstruction." They repaired the hernia defect with a big mesh, fixing it as an inlay graft, then they closed the wound around two section drains. "Now we deserve a large cup of tea." He offered peeling off his gloves.

"Sure." Her sentences were becoming few and shorter, he noticed.

In the OT sideroom she asked about the Jiviben hospital. He informed her about Sarang's death and Shabnam's remarriage. She was sad for a while.

"Did you get married?" She asked suddenly.

"I wanted to, but the girl I loved rejected me. I am losing hope now." He spoke in jest. "Moreover, I have started liking my own cooking." Both of them laughed and they started chatting like old days. He said something and she lifted her hand to give a high five, laughingly. Her hand stopped midair and her laughter stopped abruptly. He followed her eyes and noticed someone standing at the door. A handsome, fair, nearly 6 feet tall heavy shouldered police officer, cap in hand, was looking towards them with cold gray eyes and a smile on his lips. Kalpana got up from her chair, as if she was scared of this man.

"You are quite late today, so while returning from the Police

Headquarter, I thought I'd pick you up." The officer addressed Kalpana with a smile which did not reach his small gray eyes.

"The surgery turned out to be more complicated and longer than anticipated, we just finished." Kalpana explained, as if she was clarifying her guilty position. "He is doctor Digpal Singh, senior surgeon here."

"I am Rathore, Surendra Singh Rathore IPS and her lucky husband." He said and extended his hand towards digpal.

"Pleasure meeting you, Sir." Digpal extended his thin long hand. While shaking hands, he felt if the officer squeezed his thin hand any further, He will be out of work for a month! Fortunately, he didn't.

"You seem to know each other already," quizzed Rathore.

'He must be a good police officer'. Digpal thought.

"Yes, I was an intern under him in Vidurpur." Kalpana responded quickly. Digpal had a gut feeling that Mr Rathore didn't like him much, and Kalpana too looked tense in his presence. They bid goodbye to each other and left to join their own chores.

After a week, once again they crossed in the hospital corridor with their respective assistants and exchanged smiles, but even in a quick glance he noticed another faint blue discoloration on her face. 'Does she have some hemorrhagic disorder or...' he didn't want to think about anything else. After a few days, he got another chance to meet her in the hospital canteen. She was sitting alone, waiting for her coffee. He pulled a chair in front of her and asked,

"May I?"

"Sure you may," she invited him smilingly, "you will have tea I think."

"You still remember?" She didn't answer, looked distraught and absent minded.

"Is everything alright? How is Mr.Rathore?" He quizzed.

"Hmm, okay." He felt she didn't want to reply.

They talked about patients and workings of this Hospital.

Suddenly he asked, "Are you happy in your marriage?" She had not expected this question.

"Well… it's ok." She wanted to avoid replying.

"You can tell me, Kalpana." And placed his hand on her hand reassuringly.

She pulled her hand away and answered firmly, "Don't try to see cracks, you have no chance." But somehow conviction was missing in her voice.

"You are not planning kids for the time being, I suppose," he poked further. This time she did not retort and kept quiet for a while. He noticed her eyes were slightly moist. She spoke slowly, "My in-laws are blaming me for not having children. I got myself investigated, everything is normal. He doesn't want to get himself checked.If I insist, he becomes very angry. Frankly, I am scared of him."

'Now I understand the blue black marks on her face', thought Digpal. "But if you want I should not suffer anymore, stop interfering in my life and unless really required for professional reasons, don't try to meet me. He found out from his sources about our relationship from Vidarpur; such things don't remain a secret. I have finished my coffee, goodbye for now." He just sat there motionless, sad, angry, disappointed all at the same time.

It was Saturday and he had no work after lunch in the hospital. He used to take his lunch in the hospital mess and then leave for the small apartment in the hospital campus. That day he skipped lunch and left for Vidurpur, by evening he was at Ballu's Shere Punjab Dhaba where the round figure of Ballu was seen on the counter table as a permanent fixture. As soon as he noticed Digpal from a distance, he began shouting, "*Oye yaraa* c'mon. Seen after a long time." Then observing him closely, added, "Why such a long face?"

"Will tell you everything when we sit together, can you come to Diu for dinner?"

"Fine with me, will tell my son to sit at the counter; anything for you dear."

After an hour they left for Diu. During the hour long drive Digpal was silent, only Ballu kept on chattering, that he has no faith in any other doctor in Vidurpur, after he has left half of Jiviben Hospital is empty, and so on.

In Diu, after they downed two large pegs, Ballu said, "*Ab bol*, (tell me now) and Digpal slowly described his meeting with Kalpana, about her marital life, husband and that he was very concerned about Kalpana. Ballu let him speak, and didn't give any opinion. They kept drinking till midnight; in the end Ballu said, "Kalpana is not in your life now, let her suffer her own fate and you better move on."

"I know, but I can't see her suffer, I love her so much." Digpal's speech was slurred. They both were drunk, but Ballu, being a seasoned one, was able to hold himself. Digpal didn't seem to be in control of himself. Ballu drove till Vidurpur, then asked, "Should I drop you to Rajkot?"

"I will have a strong black coffee, I'm okay, don't worry I will reach home alive." By the time he reached the hospital campus, it was past midnight. Somehow he parked the car and came out staggering. He felt he was losing balance and was about to fall when two arms encircled his lower chest and prevented his fall. He heard a female voice assuring him, "it's okay, it's okay. I won't let you fall, doctor. I will take you to your room," and shouted, "Mom you go sleep, and don't lock the door from inside."

In the room Jose put him on the bed, removed his shoes, trousers and shirt and covered him with a sheet. She was about to leave, when she heard him moaning, "Don't leave me." And then blabbered some incoherent sentences, turned and slept. Jose thought for a while, then removed her own dress, found an old shirt of Digpal, wore that and slept in the same bed by the side of Digpal, who feeling her presence, turned and put his arm on her. She kissed him on the cheek, and caressed his back. She wanted to make love to him; she was married, alone and her husband didn't seem to be coming back. She lovingly looked towards his face and saw a hundred dreams in those few minutes. But he was deep asleep unaware of her presence and emotions.

He woke up groggy with a throbbing headache and was shocked to see Jose sleeping in his bed, in his shirt, with nothing below that. He himself too, was in his vest and undies. He quickly got up, drank a glass of water and went to the bathroom to freshen up, where he noticed marks of lipstick on his cheeks. She was still asleep, her baby-like face, slightly dark in complexion, and the red lipstick still on her lips, was looking beautiful and inviting. 'Did anything happen in the night between us?' He wondered.

He didn't remember anything beyond the parking of his car on the hospital campus. "Hey Jose! what are you doing in my bed?" He asked in a low voice, patting her arm. She half opened her eyes, held his arm and pulled him in the bed. Before he could speak anything, she put her lips on his and covered both of them with a sheet.

For the next few days, they both pretended as if nothing ever happened between them, but Jose kept on planning that if Winston, her husband, did not turn up this X-mas too, she would propose to Dr Joseph and divorce her husband.

Next evening when he was about to prepare his dinner, his phone rang, "Sir come quickly, there is a baby and she is bad." He rushed to casualty. Anxious parents were standing outside the casualty. Junior surgeon Jainil and a surgical resident and nurse were trying to find a vein to start an IV line. The baby was around 7 to 8 months, chubby and severely dehydrated, her breathing was fast and she was lying listless. The mother informed, 'Rumi was okay, and suddenly since last 2 days she had been crying and vomiting and now passing a small amount of red coloured stools, today she is running a fever as well.'

He placed his fingers on her pulse, it was fast, thready and irregular. He could feel a vague mass on the right side of abdomen. He introduced his finger for per rectal examination, the finger stall was soiled with a mix of blood and mucus, like a red jelly. Meanwhile, they started a paediatric solution drip and a shot of antibiotics.

"She has intussusception, but it seems it's too late to save her." Digpal murmured, "Will talk to her parents." He informed them that she was seriously ill and they will have to operate on her, but chances of her survival were bleak. The baby's Father was a young man with a small beard, looking completely lost. All he could say was, "Do whatever you can, rest depends on Allah." And lifted both his hands towards the sky.

He called the senior Anaesthetist for the child's surgery, she was experienced and competent. He opened the abdomen with a mid right paramedian incision- the peritoneum was filled with darkish hemorrhagic fluid. The terminal ileum was disappearing in the ascending colon and the whole mass had turned black.

"Irreversible gangrene has already set in, and will have to resect the gangrenous intestine and ascending colon." He told Jainil who was assisting him. Resection and anastomosis was done and peritoneum was given a good wash with ringer lactate solution. With good intensive care, blood transfusion and higher antibiotics, she was on oral fluids on day 4 and was sitting playfully in the mother's lap on the 5th day. He and his whole unit were delighted by the success of surgery, and the day Rumi was discharged, his unit had a small celebration in the hospital canteen. 'Would she have survived in Jiviben?' He wondered. Such tertiary care hospitals are a blessing for gravely ill patients, provided they can afford them. But was it a blessing for him too? He was monetarily better off, he could easily pay the EMIi for his new car and was looking for a decent apartment in a plush area on Kalawad road. He could afford good food and clothes, a fortnightly trip to Diu and good quality liquor. Was he happy ? No. There were dark areas in his psyche. There were unanswered questions about himself. Who was he, who left him on the church steps and why? To which religion, caste, language group or family he belonged? Then there was the permanent pain of losing his love, to a senseless system of caste and family's social standing.

Professionally too, many a times he felt frustrated and limited, due to changing ethics, one upmanship, dishonest practices, too much reliance on super specialists, leg pulling by co professionals and so on. Patient transaction also was different then what he was getting at Vidurpur, where generally they were poor or middle class, loyal and faithful, in contrast to upper middle class and rich patients of Golden hospital. Most of them had no faith in any doctor, and were fussy and demanding. The hospital had a few general ward beds to maintain its "service to society" image. He wasn't very comfortable in this kind of set-up, and the management could smell it.

The following week was uneventful, both on surgical and personal front, except that he had zeroed down on a two bedroom apartment, applied for a loan from the bank, which was easily approved; afterall he was senior surgeon of a reputed hospital.

Rumi was brought for follow-up in his consulting. She had recovered completely and was alert and playful in her mother's lap. Parents looked very satisfied with the treatment. The Father Rafiq and mother Zarin thanked him repeatedly. Zarin hesitantly placed a well wrapped packet on his table.

"What is this?" The surgeon asked.

"*Doctor saab*, I'm a prawn merchant from Veraval. These are export quality prawns. I came to know you are non-vegetarian, so..." He spoke in a low voice, as even a mention of non-vegetarian food was a taboo in that part of the country, and more so in that hospital, whose owners were strictly vegetarian. Digpal looked towards Jose, who immediately understood what he wanted. She took away the packet quietly.

In the evening, Jose came near him and whispered, "I will cook your dinner, and bring it to your place at 9 PM, and will stay overnight, okay?"

"No, it's not okay." She thought he was joking.

That evening he took a lengthy shower, applied his best deo, changed bed sheets, placed a pack of condoms below the pillow, cleaned the dining table and switched on his music player. Still there was another hour to go, and time seemed to tick away very slowly.

He thought he had time to set the table before she came, and as he headed towards the crockery cupboard, the shrill ring of the phone stopped him there.

"Injury on neck, bleeding profusely." There was urgency in the casualty doctor's voice. He rushed to casualty, leaving everything status quo.

Jainil was standing by the side of the table, compressing the neck wound with a large pad. There was a pool of blood below the table. The nurse had already started an IV line.

"Vitals?"

"80/60, 110/minute, SPO2 98%."

"Pupils?"

"Equal and reacting, glass injury, hit by broken bottle in a street brawl."

"Carotids seem to have escaped."

Digpal moved the pad and blood started gushing out from the upper end, he swiftly pressed it again.

"It's Jugular, give me a hemostat, quick." He kept the upper end of the wound pressed and swiftly clamped the lower end, which was not bleeding!

"He could have sucked in air from the lower end, and air embolism would kill him quickly." Then he clamped the bleeding upper end. "Jainil, please tie both the ends, minor bleeders and repair the wound."

When he walked back to his apartment, taking long strides, the main door was still closed. He was relieved that he was back, well in time. As he entered, two arms wrapped around him from behind.

"Surprise! I came early, couldn't wait."

"There was a cut jugular..." She placed her index on his lips. "No need to explain, I know what your job is."

"I am hungry."

Digpal brought out a bottle of red wine, hidden in a closet and poured in two glasses.

After the first one, he asked, "More? I will take another one."

"Enough for me, you go ahead."

"Prawns are deliciously cooked, you are a true Goan."

She was looking stunningly charming, in a red top and short blue skirt exposing her shapely legs.

They kept on talking till midnight. They were a small, happy family. Her parents ran a small eatery on Baga beach in Goa. She was in school when her Father was diagnosed with liver cancer, they lost him within a year. Her mother continued running the eatery until her schooling and nursing training was completed. Then her mother closed down the eatery and they shifted to Bombay, from where they came to Rajkot, for a peaceful life. She met Winston in Bombay, where they got engaged and subsequently got married. Only a day after their wedding, Winston left for Abu Dhabi.

He didn't have anything to tell about his family. Only stories of the orphanage, the struggle for food and superiority amongst other children, the two sets of clothes to wear, which they had to wash on alternate days, the medical hostel days, his crush for Ankita and his aloofness amongst hundreds of students, his Vidurpur days and so on. He deliberately omitted mentions of Kalpana and Shabnum. They were tired of sitting on chairs and shifted to bed. They kept sleeping until late in the morning, Jose was not bothered as it was her weekly day off and Digpal had no surgery on that day. Digpal brewed some strong coffee for both of them, while handing her the mug, he had a wide grin on his face.

"What's so funny?" She asked.

"Well… nothing, we are in a strange profession, difficult to separate personal life from professional, or maybe it's my aberration."

"I don't get the riddle."

"Last night a case flashed in my memory," he hesitated for a while, then continued, "he was a newly-wed young man, came to Jiviben past midnight, the resident informed me that he had retention of urine and he could not figure out why."

"Then?"

"I found his penis was grossly swollen and bent sideways from the middle at an awkward angle."

"Strange, isn't it?"

"Yes it is! It was his first night with his teenage wife who was scared to the hilt. He tried to force things, and the poor fellow landed up in hospital with a fractured penis."

"I have never heard of something like this!" then added naughtily, "But you don't have to worry pally. Then what did you do?"

"Just opened, repaired the corpus cavernosa, inserted a cath as splintage and put him on estrogens to keep him cool."

Both of them laughed for a while, then becoming serious, Jose asked, "Isn't it time we consider getting married, Dr Joseph?"

"You are married, Mrs Fernandis."

"Then what are you doing with me in bed? Anyways, Winston is not coming back, since last four years I haven't seen his face; solid ground to file a divorce."

"Give me some time to think, Jose."

She got out of bed, changed and left without saying bye. He felt blank, like a moron. Throughout the next day in his consulting room, they did not talk except for official work. She looked sullen and never smiled. At closing hours, Digpal cleared his throat and said, "Jose, lately I have been imagining my life with you, hope I will prove to be a good husband." As for Jose, it did not sink in for a while, then she began smiling ear to ear, hugged him and gave a peck on his cheek. Digpal was happy that ultimately something positive is happening in his love life.

# HEARTBREAK AGAIN

Following few days passed in a jiffy. His apartment on Kalawad road was ready to be occupied, he put some ready-made furniture in it and shifted there without much fanfare. Joseline helped him set things there. She stopped visiting his house for the time being, saying it will increase the charm and longing for their wedding. She informed him that she already sent a legal notice to her husband and the lawyer is hopeful that it will be sanctioned without much delay.

That fateful evening, he was not feeling like cooking for himself so he ordered food from outside. It was almost 9 PM, he decided to have his dinner when the doorbell rang. As soon as he opened the door, she hugged him tight. She was sobbing, her face buried in his chest. He led her to a chair, brought a glass of water for her and waited for her to calm down. Her beautiful pink cheeks had lines of tears on them. There was a hematoma below her left eye, and her long thick lock of hair was a mess. Kalpana was devastated and spoke between sobs.

"I have decided to leave him. He looks handsome and cultured but is a monster. He suffers from an inferiority complex, a very large ego and is suspicious by nature. It is impossible to live with him. Lately, he found out about our relationship through his sources from Vidurpur, since then he has become very abusive and violent."

Digpal sat near her and kept his hand on her hand reassuringly, though he himself was at a loss to understand the situation.

"My biggest mistake was rejecting you, out of fear and senseless traditions. Now I want to correct that mistake. Let's begin life again, together." Saying that she held both his hands.

Digpal didn't know how to react and what to say.

"You still love me, don't you Digpal?"

"I loved you with all my might, Kalpana, and still have feelings for you, but..."

"But what Digpal? You are making me nervous."

"But now I am committed to someone else." He said as if pleading guilty of his crime. There was silence in the room. Kalpana was stunned; Digpal was bewildered.

Kalpana let go of his hands, stood up and without speaking a word walked out of the room and from Digpal's life for the second time, leaving him sulking in his dining chair, the food kept lying there untouched.

The next few days were dull on the professional front as well. Most of the surgeries were routine, with hardly any challenging one. With addition of more and more super-specialists, his range of surgeries was shrinking, as was happening to most of the general surgeons of those times. The fresh breed of surgeons were comfortable with the super specialities, as they were not trained for performing the full spectrum of surgery. Problem of adjustment was with middle age group surgeons, specially the ones of the likes of Digpal, who were competent and excellent in their work. He noticed that a general surgeon had a more holistic approach towards a patient's problem.

Joseline too seemed to be preoccupied and absent minded, unlike her usual self. The legal proceedings of divorce did not turn out to be as easy as was anticipated. Winston was not agreeing for mutual settlement and the one sided divorce process was lengthy. She avoided her relationship with Digpal out in the open, as it would weaken her case and she might have to let go of alimony, which she did not want.

Overall the mood was a bit gloomy for both of them. The shadows of the event of Kalpana coming to his place, further deepened the gloom. Or maybe he was feeling a presentiment of some mishap!

One of the mornings in OT, Digpal and Jainil were opening an abdomen for cholecystectomy through a small subcostal incision; he used to call it mini-chole. He used some small width modified Dever's retractors, manufactured by Varghese, the Thane based instrument manufacturer, with a fibre optic light at the tip of blade. On opening the peritoneum, a mass formed of omentum, transverse colon and jejunum, was seen on the under-surface of the liver, where the gallbladder should have been.

"We will have to extend the incision, bad adhesions. Even the liver is looking cirrhotic."

Liver was nodular and hard to feel. He slowly dissected free the adhesions, and suddenly a gush of pus filled the operative field. After sucking and cleaning, a bunch of stones, size ranging from 3 mm to 10 mm, were seen lying in the false cavity formed by the adherent viscera. The inferior wall of gallbladder had completely necrosed.

"Adhesions have saved her life." The surgeon commented.

They removed calculi and the remaining part of GB, resulting in oozing from the rigid gallbladder bed. However compression with coagulant soaked mop, cauterisation and intravenous injections of vitamin K and coagulants, solved the problem. He asked Jainil to close, and as was about to turn away from the table, a shortish, very fair young man entered the OT.

"I am Naresh Virani, newly appointed visiting surgeon, may I come in?" He asked in a very sweet voice.

"You sure can."

"What's being cut?" Again in the same sweet manner.

"Cholecystectomy." Jainil responded.

"Who does open chole, nowadays?" Naresh remarked, with a short laugh.

Digpal left for his office. Though he did not like the comment and the sarcasm behind the artificial manners, he was in no mood to counter. In his office he found Jose, once again, in her bubbly mood, looking very pleased with herself. At the first opportunity, Digpal asked, "You are looking very happy today, it seems your divorce has been sanctioned."

Joseline's smile vanished, she spoke hesitantly, "Dr Joseph, you know it's not easy to change things as per our will. Winston is coming this Friday. Both of us are flying to Abudhabi on Monday. Mother will be staying with her brother at Panjim for the time being, then he will take her too, after making necessary arrangements. I am sorry doctor, I know you will understand."

She couldn't meet his burning eyes, and meekly slipped out of his room. Digpal was angry, depressed and irritable, all at the same time. Wondering how to readjust to life now and at the same time Naresh Virani entered.

"Sorry, couldn't talk much in OT. I am a Laparoscopic surgeon. You can take my help for lap surgery, don't hesitate."

Already in a foul mood, Digpal retorted, "Wish you luck, Dr Virani. I will not need your help, but anytime you make a mess during lap surgery, I won't mind chipping in. I feel laparoscopy surgery is becoming popular because of clumsy open surgeons and is market driven." He knew he had made a new enemy on board.

On the weekend he called up Ballu, asked him if he was free for dinner at Diu, he had some important matters to discuss. Ballu, as usual without giving a second thought, agreed immediately. He was badly in need of a shoulder to cry on, a friend to confide in, who better than a selfless friend with a big stomach to keep secrets in.

It was a warm evening, with a breeze from the Arabian Sea. The open air restaurant was right near the beach, had a well stocked bar, and the chef was good at preparing seafood. The owner was Ballu's old buddy and they used to get special treatment. Both were quiet, Ballu waited patiently for Digpal to speak. After two large, the latter uttered, "Nice breeze."

"You haven't come here to comment on the breeze." Ballu taunted.

"I have a midas touch Ballu. Whichever girl I touch, gets settled in life... without me." He blurted out a hollow laugh. Slowly he opened up and narrated the events of the recent past, his relationship with Joseline and commitment to marry her, the dramatic entry of Kalpana leaving her abusive husband, his refusal and then Jose ditching him. Ballu listened to him without interrupting, with an occasional 'hoon' and 'oh'.

"What should I do now? My emotional life is in complete mess; it is affecting my professional life and relations with my colleagues."

"*Bewakoof* (you fool), call Kalpana just now! Beg, cry, apologize, do whatever and bring her back into your life; she is your true love."

Digpal, agitated, tried reaching for his next peg of rum, when Ballu held his hand firmly, "Call her now." Her phone was switched off. He then called up the HR manager and asked him to contact Dr K. S. Rathore, as he needed her help in a case with gynae co-pathology. "Dr Digpal, she left the job 10 days ago, and she has left India too, shifted to the US, but no idea about the city or state. We don't have her contact number as well."

He thanked Vineet, hung up the phone, then facing Ballu, asked in a choking voice, "What now?" Such an emotional response was unusual for his kind of upbringing, but the combined effect of turn of events, presence of a true friend and the high blood levels of alcohol seemed to be the reason. "Get drunk, forget them and get good sleep. From tomorrow, do your work, your surgery which you love more than anything else." How right he was, Digpal wondered!

# GUILTY OR NOT GUILTY?

On the work front, although his spectrum of work was shrinking, still there were patients who preferred him as their tried and tested surgeon. They felt safe in his hands. He was getting good work and money too. He had paid back his loan money for the car and comfortably paid back monthly instalments for his home mortgage.

To stay updated he used to attend state and national conferences, sponsored by the hospital. Pharma and gadget companies sometimes offered him overseas luxury trips and lucrative schemes which he would bluntly turn down. He would rudely refuse requests of false medical certificates or special treatment to important persons of society. His attitude got him the label of an uncooperative and whimsical consultant. Some of his old poor patients from Vidurpur still came for his opinion. Some of the children, with his post hypospadias repair fistula would come for repair.

As he had promised them free surgery, he would request the management to waive off their hospital bills. What he did not notice was that his minimal investigation policy, prescriptions of fewer drugs, and number of free cases was brooding resentment against him in the management. He had good relations with colleagues, but most of them were married, and he felt awkward visiting them socially. A lifestyle which he could never have imagined of, added some kilos on him, mainly in the middle. The gain in weight concealed his rickety rosary on his chest and marginally improved his complexion.

Most of the cases were elective surgeries. The rich would come for their minor surgical problems, ingrowing toe nails, lipomas, sebaceous cysts, corns and so on, generally making a lot of fuss about their problem and asking repetitive questions. He would occasionally lose his cool and even refused to operate upon such over demanding patients. These were the people who labelled him rude and complained to the management. With the number of Onco surgeons increasing, even benign lumps in breasts disappeared from general surgeons' operative lists! But patients belonging to the middle class, still came to him.

There used to be monthly review meetings with the management. For initial few years, Digpal was given gentle warnings for his ways, but as the time went by, management began disliking him for his non commercial attitude, however they still wanted to retain him, for his sincerity and regularity.

Every now and then, there were patients or their relatives, who demanded laparoscopic surgery; some of them even thought it was a method where 'laser' is used, and nothing is being cut! He was tired of explaining that appendectomy is a 15 to 20 minute surgery which can be done through a small crease incision, which will be subsequently invisible. Almost the same was the case with groin hernia, where he preferred a transverse crease incision, and the complication rate was near 0, which could not be said about laparoscopy. The likes of Naresh started telling openly that since he doesn't know laparoscopy, he is giving such excuses. Those were early days for laparoscopy in India and surgeons were still in the developing phase of expertise.

Dr Dhiraj Rathi was a new entrant in the anaesthesia department; who came from Rajasthan, was competent and friendly. Dhiraj was unmarried and clever, with good business sense. He advised Digpal, to go for laparoscopy training, as it's the future of surgery.

"You will be thrown out of the profession, if you don't join the bandwagon," he opined.

Digpal was convinced, and decided to go for lap training in a Mumbai hospital, at the earliest opportunity. Radhabai was an unusual patient for Golden hospital. She came with her husband Shyamji. She was wearing a cheap synthetic saree, her blouse seemed to be hanging on her shoulders. She was hardly 36 kg, grossly underweight for a tall lady. Her husband was shorter than her, looked poor but healthy. On first look Radhabai seemed to be suffering from tuberculosis or malignancy. She complained of severe pain in lower abdomen, Dysuria, fever off and on with chills for two years. They had three children, and had shifted from Rajasthan a few months ago to a small village near Rajkot, where Shyamji was running a small grocery store.

She became pregnant 3 years back in spite of copper T, placed four months prior to that. Medical termination was done in a district hospital in Rajasthan, but the Gynecologist couldn't find the contraceptive device and in search of that she did her laparotomy, but failed to find Copper T.

Digpal admitted her, and the reports surprised both, him and Jainil. Her urine report showed plenty of RBCs and pus cells, as expected and the plain X-ray showed a bladder calculus the size of a tennis ball was staring at them. An abscess with adhesions on the fundus of uterus, was reported in USG. Jainil was excited, "We must post her in tomorrow's list, it will turn out to be interesting! but where is the copper T?" Digpal responded only with a smile.

Next morning they opened her through a Pfenenstiel incision, opened the urinary bladder extraperitoneally, and removed the calculus, placed a cath and closed the bladder meticulously.

"Let's knock out the uterus now." Saying that Digpal opened the peritoneum, and as was expected, there were adhesions on the top of uterine fundus. As soon as he dissected away the adherent omentum and gut, pus gushed out of the cavity. They did her hysterectomy and washed the pelvic cavity.

"Will you ask Priti, as we have to write her name in the operative team."

"Sure will." Digpal knew Priti and Jainil were more than just friends!

"But where is the T?" Jainil was still curious.

"Let's close her up, first."

After the surgery was over, Digpal asked him, "Keep the stone on a hard surface, and break it with the orthopaedic hammer."

Jainil complied, and everyone including Dhiraj, and the nurses clapped- the intact copper T had jumped out of the broken stone!

"Now review the X-Ray, a faint T shaped shadow is visible in the opacity of calculus. I had noticed it the very first day, but did not want to kill the surprise.The abscess is the result of excavation by our gynec friend to dig out the lost treasure."

Radhabai recovered quicker than he expected. His next worry was, 'will they be able to pay the hospital bill?' Here, Dhiraj allayed his anxiety.

"They can afford it Sir, they only look that poor. It's their lifestyle." He proved to be absolutely right. Shyamji, not only paid the bill happily, but tipped the lower staff and thanked the surgical team profusely. When Radhabai came back for follow up after a fortnight, she had already gained 5 kg, and was all smiles. The couple stood with folded hands, and placed a box on the surgeon's table.

"What is this?"

"Laddoos for your kids, doctor *saab*."

"But I don't have kids."

"Oh! some problem?" Radhabai sympathised.

"Yes, I am not married," said Digpal with a straight face.

"Can't believe! you don't look Gujarati. Are you Marwadi? We can find a girl for you if we know your caste." 'How quickly we become personal', Digpal wondered. He ignored her question.

"You are okay now. Continue the same medicine and come

back after three months for urine culture and sensitivity."

He searched for the laparoscopy training schedule, found one 10 days basic diploma course in a reputed Mumbai hospital. Dhiraj said, it's a good course with renowned faculty. He applied for study leave. The management not only sanctioned his leave but offered to sponsor the course fee too. He applied for the training program and got registered. He planned to leave next Sunday, to join the course from Monday morning.

Saturday evening his doorbell rang. That Saturday evening, he did not go to Diu, instead, decided to pack for his trip and was reading 'In Spite of Gods', and found it an interesting insight into the way the country thinks and works, through the eyes of a foreigner. It took him some time to recognise Father Samuel. His beard had turned completely gray, he had lost his thick mane, only a few sparse strands of hair were left there. He looked weak and in spite of losing a few kilos, was still overweight. Both of them had moist eyes. Digpal touched Father's feet, who in turn hugged him, kissed his head and mumbled "God bless you, my son."

He arranged for his rest in the guest room, prepared a quick dinner then sat with him to talk. Father narrated his medical history and purpose of his visit. He had been suffering from a large groin hernia, which was operated for the first time, eleven years back. It recurred within 6 months, then was operated at a mission hospital in Madhya Pradesh, but has recurred again and is very painful now. He had multiple comorbidities– diabetes, hypertension, coronary artery disease and asthmatic bronchitis.

"God had been very kind to me to give me so many problems, lest I forget him," smiled the Father, "but he has created you also, to solve my problem."

Then Father Samuel updated him, regarding the mission and the orphanage. Thakur Digpal Singh Chouhan is no more.

"He remembered you when he breathed his last, probably wanted to tell you something, but God beckoned him very quickly.

Rest in peace, good man." Father made a cross. It was a personal loss for Digpal. The zamindar was so supportive throughout his studies, and kept a tab on his progress.

"Syed Ahmed Ali, the accountant, has become very old and weak, and now his son Iftekhar is looking after his work. The two nuns, sister Mary and Sophia shifted to Kerala, and Dr Banerjee still visits the orphanage to render his free services. He often remembers you and mentions you to the children to motivate them to study hard." Digpal cancelled his laparoscopy training, and requested the organisers to give him another slot of training. They agreed to the request without much fuss.

Next day Digpal took Father Samuel with him for hospitalisation. Got his complete medical check-up done, controlled his diabetes with insulin and consulted Dhiraj to discuss the anaesthesia for him. Dhiraj opined that he is not very fit for full fledged anesthesia, he will inject him with a local block which will be much safer. As was planned, Dhiraj injected a local nerve block, and intravenous buprenorphine, an analgesic, many times more potent than morphine. Digpal sutured an oversized polypropylene mesh as inlay graft, after doing his orchidectomy. Surgery and postoperative recovery was uneventful.

On the fourth postoperative day, Father packed his luggage and was ready to go back to Indore. Digpal wanted him to stay for a few more days. "You are not fit to travel Father, stay for some more days." He requested.

"Thank you very much, but nothing will happen to me. You are a godsend blessing to humanity my son, continue the good work, amen." Father Samuel boarded the train, leaving him sad and alone, again.

Coming back from the railway station, he took a longer route, via the outer ring road, as he was not in a hurry to go back to his empty apartment. On the way, he noticed a newly built Gurudwara near the highway; stopped there, covered his head with a kesri *'patka'*, gifted by Ballu, and sat to listen to the soothing *'gurbani'* which he did not understand, but felt much better. He was coming out, when a Sardarji offered him *langar* before leaving.He happily complied, as he always relished the community meal of Gurudwara.

After a month, once again, he registered for the laparoscopy training program and booked a room in a nearby hotel. All other trainees were much younger than him, in the small batch of six surgeons. Almost all of them were from Gujarat and Maharashtra. Every morning from 8 AM to 2 or 3 PM, there used to be live demonstrations of surgeries. The afternoon session was for theory lectures and evening 5 PM onwards used to be self training on dummies and simulators. Time was unlimited for the last session.

During the live demo, the trainees were allowed to hold the camera during surgery, by rotation. The faculty were amongst the best in the profession. Digpal was not very comfortable while assisting. His hand would often waver from the operative field while holding the camera and at the same time looking towards the monitor. The operating surgeon used to lose patience with him on occasions.

During the evening 'hands on' training sessions on dummies, he proved to be the slowest learner of all. By the time he came back to his room, he often felt depressed. He remembered one extraperitoneal hernia repair demonstration by an eminent faculty from another metro city, very clearly. The patient was an eighty years old gentleman with unilateral Inguinal hernia. As the faculty was giving a preoperative briefing to the trainees; Digpal asked, "Why can't we just do an open hernioplasty on him? It's a half hour no risk job, can be done under local anaesthesia, and time of hospitalisation is no constraint at this age."

Everybody looked towards him with disdain. The wise faculty gave him a, 'from where have they brought this fool,' look; but outwardly let out a smile and said, "Then how will you learn, doctor?" Everybody had a good laugh, at his expense.

The eminent faculty made a tiny hole between umbilicus and pubic symphysis, introduced an instrument to make space then some air and then a mounted Ballun in that space. The lower abdomen started swelling, and within minutes the swelling began to spread on the abdomen, then on the chest and neck. The old man started becoming breathless. "Tracheostomy, quick." The faculty shouted, losing his cool. The local surgeon did a quick tracheostomy, started oxygen. The patient's SPO2 improved and dyspnea reduced.

"We will have to abandon TEP today, shift the patient to ICU." The faculty instructed. Digpal wondered, what did anybody gain? Learned a possible complication? Rest of the surgeries went very well. Since it was a basic course, only appendix, gallbladder and hernia surgeries were demonstrated. By the culmination of training, he made up his mind to begin doing some simple lap surgeries.

On the final day of training before the farewell dinner, actual videos of blunders and complications were screened to caution the trainees, and they were really scary. One of the recordings showed a surgeon dissecting the cystic duct of GB, continued to dissect, cut and clamped the common bile duct, right up to the duodenum! Nobody knew if the patient survived or not. Another one showed the right hepatic artery being clipped and divided, mistaken for a cystic artery. Slipping of clip or ligature from appendicular stump and cystic artery were other mishaps noticed. Thermal injuries resulting in delayed perforations of the gut were also of occasional occurrence, depending on the learning stage of the surgeon. After the dinner, all the trainees exchanged phone numbers and addresses. He particularly liked a young surgeon Piyush Patel from Vapi, a private practitioner from Nasik, Mustak Ahmed and Satish Grover from Medical college Vadodara.

"You were right about that day, about the old man's hernia." Ahmed commented.

"Yes, even today majority of surgeons all over the world say for hernia surgery, open method is better." Grover opined.

"And it was live demonstrated that day," Piyush Patel laughed.

After coming back to Rajkot, for many days, he could not muster the courage to do lap surgery independently. One fine day, he decided to remove an appendix by laparoscopy. He requested Naresh to stand by, which he agreed gleefully. Digpal took over one and a half hours to remove a simple and straightforward appendix!

"Doesn't matter, you will gradually learn. The problem is you started quite late." Naresh commented, concealing his smile. Digpal was depressed and demoralised, he wanted to kick himself. Naresh narrated the story of his surgery with some exaggeration, to every possible person known to him!

Digpal did not have to wait very long to pay back. Naresh called him to take a look at a patient he had operated two days back laparoscopically, for bilateral Inguinal hernia. "He is not looking good, can't figure out what happened." Naresh said in a worried tone. Patient was a 50 year old male without any comorbidity. He had marked tachycardia, tachypnoea, high fever and a distended abdomen.

"Open him up ASAP Naresh. He has peritonitis, probably a colonic perforation. His only chance of survival is the earliest possible surgery."

"You will have to operate, Dr Digpal, I will assist." Naresh sounded nervous. The patient was from a rich class admitted in a luxury class room. They did a laparotomy the same day. As was expected, there was a rent in the colon due to cautery burn; the peritoneum was filled with fecal smelling pus. Digpal did his sigmoid colostomy, and washed the abdominal cavity repeatedly.

"Will have to remove the mesh too, it will be a nidus of infection."

"Whatever you deem correct," Naresh said meekly.

When they came out of the operation theatre, a group of

worried and angry relatives and friends were waiting anxiously. Digpal and Jainil left Naresh to deal with them.

"We don't have to worry, he is good at it. Quite a soothsayer, more of a salesman than a surgeon." The senior man whispered.

That day's consultations had a pleasant surprise waiting for him. A couple in their thirties was waiting for him, with a good looking girl about 10 years old, dressed in a pink frock and matching ribbons in her hair. When he called them in, the couple looked familiar to him, but he could not place them. They came and touched his feet. He looked curiously towards them, when the husband indicated towards the girl, and said, "She is Digansha, the one with a big pot on her head." Now he could recognize them, 'so she is the one who had a huge meningo-encephalocele.'

"Oh! That's great! I'm so happy to see her grow up so nicely. How's she doing in her studies?" Cerebral development could be a concern in such children.

"She is brilliant, doctor. Once she started understanding things, we told her about you and the surgery, and why her name is Digansha." Said the mother, her eyes moist. Digansha turned out to be a chirpy and naughty child, who demanded chocolates from Digpal, and he in turn was so happy that he sent an attendant to bring a big box of chocolates for her and asked her to come again, to meet him. Fortunately there was no sign of hydrocephalus as well. 'This is the biggest incentive of this profession. No amount of money can buy this joy', he thought.

Mr. Kishanji Nagar was an eminent person of Saurashtra region. A learned professor in the University who later became the Dean and subsequently Vice Chancellor of the University and was leading a retired life for the last ten years. He was widely adored and respected for his knowledge and integrity. His son became a builder and amassed huge amounts of money, but could not get the kind of respect his Father commanded, for obvious reasons.

Kishanji Nagar was admitted under the care of the physician

for deep jaundice, which turned out to be obstructive in nature. On further investigations, the cause was found to be carcinoma of the head of pancreas. Mr Nagar was 82, diabetic, hypertensive and had a history of hemiparesis in the past. He was on pacemaker for cardiac arrhythmia. Since the malignancy had invaded the surrounding tissues, and looking into so many associated medical conditions, any major surgery was out of question; but all the same his obstructive jaundice required some palliative procedure. An expert endoscopist of Mumbai was consulted who suggested bile duct stenting. As per his terms, he flew from Mumbai by a chartered plane with his assistant and equipment, performed stenting within half an hour, stayed for another hour to watch on the patient and flew back, in the same plane, his fees greater than a month's earnings of a consultant like Digpal. 'Efficient and professional' he thought.

Digpal was also involved in the day to day care of Mr. Nagar, along with the physician and a cardiologist. Mr Nagar's bilirubin started reducing but the pain did not. He complained of severe upper abdominal pain, which burrowed backward and severe back pain too, which did not respond to usual analgesics. He was put on tramadol and then pentazocine, but the effect lasted for a very short time.

Digpal would often sit with the wise man and try to absorb some of his philosophy of life. The professor once said, "Young man, remember when you retire, you will have a lot of spare time to look back on your life. You will be really happy, if there is no burden on your conscience, that you have not cheated anyone for money, power or success. Not success, but the means and fairness of your journey matters. At the end of the day, you will be at peace with yourself and will happily proceed to the journey to the next world."

'Did his son ever bother to listen to him?' Digpal wondered.

One day, he was sitting with Kishanji, holding his hand, as he was in agony in spite of heavy analgesia. The senior man asked him to bring his ear near him, and whispered, "I have lived enough and am satisfied with my life, I am under tremendous agony. What you people are doing is only prolonging my agony, and process of death, not life. I hope you understand, being a sensitive human being. Please help me with a smooth passage from this world."

Mr. Nagar's wish took some time to sink in. He was taken aback by the request. "I can't do this Sir, I am here to save lives." Saying that he quickly walked out of his room, to hide his moist eyes.

As the days went by, Kishanji Nagar's agony kept increasing. He was put on a heavy dose of narcotic analgesic, which were effective only for a few hours. Everytime Digpal visited the old man, he would beg with the same request of euthanesia. Digpal too wished the old man's suffering would end as early as possible. He was not going to improve or go home, that was for sure.

One morning, Raghavji Nagar was waiting for him outside his office. He requested to see him in his office in privacy. "My Father is suffering a lot, doctor. There hardly seems a chance of his improvement. We all know the outcome, tell me what can be done?" Raghavji said, as they settled in the chairs in Digpal's office.

"We are trying our best but he is deteriorating and as you mentioned, there is no hope of improvement."

"Doctor, I know you are a conscientious surgeon and a very sensitive human being, that's why I have come to you with this request." Raghavji hesitated for a moment then added, "You can facilitate his journey to heaven, painlessly. It will end his suffering."

Digpal did not expect this, he had guessed Raghavji must be unhappy that we are not doing enough for his Father, and he would seek another opinion or shift him to a bigger centre.

"Well... I can't do this Mr Nagar; this is unethical and illegal. I am sorry," he stood up, "anything else I can do for you?"

Raghavji stood up, "Think doctor, think from a humanitarian point of view."

To someone else, he would have offered a big bundle of money, but the shrewd businessman he was, he had done his homework well. He knew offering money to this man would be counterproductive. He left the room and left Digpal thinking.

That evening, there was the usual monthly review meeting of the chairman with all the departmental heads. After initial formalities, the chairman faced Digpal and spoke in a far from polite tone, "Dr Digpal, I want to remind you once again that we are running a profit making health business here and not a charitable hospital. Your monthly reports are becoming progressively dismal. Your number of special investigations are very low, you are prescribing low price drugs, your number of general ward and free patients are very high. The hospital sponsored your laparoscopy training and you have hardly done any lap surgery since you returned from training. Will you explain?"

"Mr Chairman, I don't consider my profession a business; moreover I don't believe in burdening my patients with unnecessary investigations and expensive medicines and tonics. As for laparoscopy, I believe a big number of surgeries which are expected to be done by lap, can be done safely and with better outcome by open method. Only a few surgeries are better done laparoscopically. I learnt that at my age if I try my hand at lap, I will not only spoil my track record but the hospital's reputation will also be at stake." Digpal was cool, "Moreover the patient will have to pay more financially and by more complications. About the poor patients, I feel, we can not shy away from our social responsibility."

"In that case, I may have to ask you to resign, unless you want to be sacked unceremoniously." Pramod Soni was at his worst temper.

"That you cannot do, as we have signed a bilateral contract for ten years, which is binding on both of us." Digpal got up, turned and left the room, without bothering to listen to Soni's response.

On his way back home, he seriously considered leaving this hospital, and he was sure they would happily relieve him. But what was occupying his thoughts were Mr. Nagar's request, which did not allow him to sleep.

He was lying in the bed with shoes on, the feet jutting out of the bed. Well after midnight, he splashed his face with cold water and like a zombie, picked up a ten ml and a five ml syringe from his drawer, thrust them in his coat pocket and walked to the hospital. It was 2 AM, everything was quiet. The guard was asleep, he entered from the rear of the hospital through the janitor's exit. He reached the casualty operation theatre, the casualty doctor was sleeping in his duty room and a nurse in the pantry. From the anesthesia tray, he filled 10 ml of diazepam and in 5 ml syringe, he filled succinylcholine, sneaked out and reached the third floor VIP ICU, where the sole patient was Mr Kishanji Nagar. A middle aged nurse was snoring softly with her head resting on the table. In the ICU, the lights were kept very dim and monitors were switched to silent mode, as Kishanji did not like the beeps of monitors. A drip was going slowly through a cvp catheter.

Digpal was perspiring profusely in the air conditioned room. He did not even look towards the face of Mr. Nagar. He first brought out the 10 ml syringe filled with diazepam. His normally very steady hands were shaking uncontrollably. He pricked the latex of the drip set with the needle of a syringe and the entire room and lobby flooded with bright lights and cacophony!

"Catch him." Were the first sharp and loud words he heard.

Ramilaben Naik, the middle aged nurse barged in, switched on the monitor and shouted, "He has killed Keshav *kaka*. It's a straight line on the monitor." The action and dialogue sounded pre-rehearsed.

The security guard pulled his hand and the casualty medical officer and resident on duty were there immediately. Pramod Soni and Naresh Virani miraculously appeared on the scene within minutes. Soni called someone on the phone and in a matter of ten minutes A.C.P. Surendra Sinh Rathod arrived with a sub inspector and two constables, followed by a howling Raghavji nagar.

"Arrest him." Ordered Mr Rathod.

For a few seconds Digpal was dumbstruck with the sudden onslaught. Trying to gain his composure, he stammered, "I did not inject anything." But beyond that, he had no defense.

Raghavji Nagar, dramatically caught him by collar and shouted, "You were supposed to save my Father, instead you killed him! You villian."

Digpal was surprised, "Raghavji, you only requested me to..." Raghavji started crying and howling even louder; Digpal's voice was lost in the din. He quietly surrendered, and was taken to the local police station. The sub inspector completed the paperwork and threw him in the lock-up room of the police station. After some time ACP Rathod entered the lock-up room alone and closed the door behind him.

"I didn't kill him Mr Rathod, he was already dead, which I did not notice at that time." Digpal said.

Rathod slapped his face hard, "I know that you bloody orphan. My wife left me because of you, now pay for it for the rest of your life."

Next day Ballu came rushing from Vidurpur, "I am sure you did not do this. I will hire a good lawyer, you will be out on bail within 2 days."

"I did not, but I attempted." Digpal confessed.

His bail plea was rejected, every evidence was against him. The court held that if he will be released on bail, he can temper with the evidence and influence the witnesses.

Digpal was shifted to Rajkot jail from the lock-up as an undertrial accused. He was kept with ten prisoners in a room meant for six. Sleeping on the floor, common dirty toilet, unhygienic food and abusive co prisoners would have not bothered him much, as it was not very different from the conditions in the orphanage, but the preceding seven years of good life had changed his habits. 'How quickly we get addicted to luxuries.' He wondered.

Sitting in a corner, he smiled to himself sarcastically and spoke to himself, "You can't change your fate, you are a worm and will remain a worm of filth, you are destined to live a dog's life." His thoughts were interrupted by a slap of a heavy hand on his shoulder, "So, you are the doctor who killed his own patient. what a shame!" A burly, bearded, heavy set dark man, about four inches taller than him stood towering in front of him, flanked by four inmates. One of them ordered, "Stand up chu***, nobody sits in front of *bhai.*"

He stood up quietly in front of Jaleel Khan, a dreaded bootlegger from Porbandar. He had murdered a policeman during a raid on his den and was serving for life in the jail. Even from the prison, he was supplying alcohol to inmates and the jail staff. He had tremendous clout in the jail and called the shots there.

Gradually many of the inmates began to come to Digpal for medical advice. As they knew him more, they would come to him for all sorts of problems.

Harish came to meet him in the prison and assured him that he had connections and he would get bail for him from the high court. His bail plea was rejected by the High court as well.

After a few days, some relatives of Jaleel khan came to meet khan in the jail visitor's room. Jaleel Khan came straight from the visitors room to see Digpal.

"You are a very good surgeon, I came to know?" He asked in

a mild tone.

"Well," is all he could say, but was surprised by the changed behaviour of Khan.

"You saved the life of my nephew's daughter." Digpal did not understand the reference.

"Rafiq the prawn merchant from Veraval is my nephew."

"Oh! you mean Rumi? Yes, she is a very sweet child, and was very critical when brought to the hospital." Digpal now remembered the infant with intussusception and gangrene.

After that day, his status in the jail changed completely. Jaleel Khan even arranged a mobile for him. "Now you can talk to your family."

"I have no family, Khan, only some friends and countless patients."

He called up Ballu who assured him that he, Harish, Dhirubhai, Ramjibhai's sons and many of his well wishers are trying their best through their channels to help him get justice.

One early morning, there was a loud cry from one of the bathrooms. Some of the inmates searched for the source. In most of the bathrooms the latches were broken, so bringing out the sufferer was not a problem. Two of the inmates brought out a very thin man from one of the bathrooms. He was known as '*Tidda*' (a grasshopper), nobody knew his real name. Tidda was holding his right forearm with his left hand and was shouting in pain. He described that he slipped on the wet floor and while falling down, to prevent the fall he outstretched his right hand and all the body weight was borne by the hand. Digpal examined his wrist; and found he had a typical dinner fork deformity of Colles fracture of the forearm bones. The team of inmates took him to the small dispensary attached to the prison. It was very early in the morning and the medical officer and compounder were not expected until 10 AM.

Digpal searched for plaster bandages and gamjee pads, asked one of the prisoners to bring half a bucket of water, instructed a hefty person to hold the upper arm of Tidda near his elbow, and another one to hold his thumb in one hand and fingers in another hand. He asked the latter to give a strong pull, and he himself pressed the fracture site which reduced with a click. Tidda took a sudden gasp and blurted out the choicest of cuss words for all three, who in turn had a hearty laugh. Digpal applied gamjee pad and wet plaster bandages in the flexion position of the wrist and held it until it was set.

By the time the Medical officer came, the plaster had completely dried. The doctor got an X-Ray of the wrist done and found the reduction in perfect position. The MO was all praise for Digpal, and the two exchanged their introductions. Sorav Sahu belonged to Odisha, and was on deputation from CRPF. While the doctor was preparing the medical report, Digpal discovered that Tidda's real name was Manoj Verma.

"I would have referred him to an Ortho surgeon, but you did an excellent job." The MO said.

"It was a simple job." Digpal said, humbly.

After that day, the doctor got special permission from the Jailor for Digpal to help him in his work. He would sit on a wooden stool near the MBBS doctor, who was much junior to him, and helped him diagnose and plan the treatment of prisoners.

Digpal had been in jail almost a year and half now. His friends and well wishers would come to meet him off and on. Some brought homemade food for him, many of them were his patients. Their love and affection was a huge consolation for him, and made him feel that his selfless work has not gone in vain. During that period only, Ballu came to see him. He was in quite an upbeat mood. He informed him that with the help of Ramjibhai's younger son Yogendra, they found a very dynamic high court advocate, who is not only a lawyer, but in criminal cases conducts his independent investigation to find the truth, and fights cases based on those facts and evidence. His success rate is above 90%. The lawyer has a team, which includes a hacker as well, who can retrieve information from CCTVs and computers. He further informed Digpal that the lawyer will come to see him, to listen to his version. Due to repeated failures in the court, Digpal was not as hopeful as Ballu was.

After a week, the lawyer Navroz Soonawala came to see him. Navroz turned out to be a young amicable person who keenly listened to Digpal's version of the incident, and the background of the mishap, and left with reassurances before the meeting time was up.

One day a guard came looking for Digpal; there was a phone call for him. Mukesh was on the other end of the line from Surat. After inquiring about his well being, Mukesh said that a case of 'high fistula in ano' has come up, and if he does a conventional fistulectomy both the sphincters will be cut and the patient could become incontinent. What should he do?

"Stain the fistula with methylene blue and core out the fistula, like a tube completely, up to the rectal mucosa. Do not leave any doubtful tissue or stained part, and most important are the post op dressings, which the surgeon must do himself. Amongst common reasons of recurrence is residual tract and careless dressings."

"Your time is over, hang up." The prison guard warned.

Digpal and Mukesh had to bid good bye, Mukesh too was relieved, otherwise he might have had to listen to a lecture on Fistula in ano.

Navroz took his computer wizard to Rajkot and asked for the CCTV footage. In the footage, the evidence against Digpal was played again and again by Navroz, and when they zoomed on the monitor, they noticed that when Digpal entered the ICU, there was a straight line on the monitor instead of normal ECG activity of a live heart. Navroz jumped with excitement.

"This means Mr. Nagar was already dead when my client entered the room and tried to inject the sedative!"

Then they went to the hospital and demanded the night's CCTV footage before Digpal entered the hospital. They studied the footage and found that half an hour's footage had been erased, before Digpal even entered the premises.

"Can we retrieve that part?" Navroz asked his expert. "Yes I can."

On retrieving, what they saw was hugely surprising! The exterior camera showed that Pramod Soni and Raghavji left in a car, just before Digpal's entry, and a police jeep could be seen on the road outside the campus. Since it was not within the reach of the camera, it could not be seen clearly. In the indoor camera and ICU's CCTV it was clearly seen that the middle aged nurse, who was pretending to sleep, came in the ICU 15 minutes before Digpal entered, injected something in the IV line, and the SPO2 started falling from 95% to 60, 40, 10 and then 0, and the cardiac activity stopped. She stood there for a while, looking toward the monitor, then went back to her desk, rested her arms and head on the table and pretended to be sleeping.

The court, as usual took its own sweet time, and after six months Digpal was acquitted of murder charges. The judgement read, "The defence has provided convincing evidence that Dr J. S. Digpal did not commit the crime of murder of Mr. Kishanji Nagar, but he went to the ICU with the intention of mercy killing of his patient. This is a shameful and deplorable act by a doctor, who is supposed to save lives. The court orders Digpal Singh to two years of simple imprisonment. As he has already served two years of imprisonment, he should be set free."

The court further ordered to file a case against the nurse. Later on it was found out that she was paid a hefty sum by Raghavji Nagar and assured by Pramod Soni and ACP Rathod, that no harm will be done to her. Since so many big people were involved in the case, and nobody was interested in punishing the guilty, the case was hush hushed and buried in files.

# PART TWO

When Digpal was to be released from the prison, a small crowd of inmates, Jaleel Khan, Tidda nee Manoj Verma and dozens of others with MO Dr Sahu and his compounder gave him a tearful farewell. Reaching the gates, Digpal smiled and said, "Now please do not say, *'awjo'* (Gujarati for 'come again')." Everybody laughed with moist eyes and wished their hero happy days in the future.

In the prison office, the jailer shook his hand and gave him his belongings and dress to change. In order to be released, someone has to take the custody and responsibility of the person. While signing in the register, he noticed that as expected, it was signed by Balwinder Singh. Adv. Navroz was sitting in one of the chairs to complete legal formalities. Digpal had a vague idea about the hefty fees of high court lawyers.

"*Vakeel sahab*, I am extremely thankful for everything you have done for me, I will pay your fee as soon as I get my bank cheque book and other documents, please bear with me till then." Digpal requested.

Before Navroz could answer- "It's already paid, doctor, you don't have to worry about money." Yogendra Ramji entered the room and holding Digpal's hand said, "Welcome back to freedom."

"Thanks Yogendra, I will pay you back."

"You have already paid it many times, doctor, by saving our Father's life."

Digpal was overwhelmed by the answer. He knew he had saved many lives by his surgical expertise, but wondered how many felt gratitude like this?

As he stepped out of the jail premises, he heard the familiar booming voice of Ballu in a semi-singing mode, "Welcome back dear pally!" And engulfed his thin frame in a bear hug. Digpal had become thinner and darker, his hair was cut short and a beard had grown making his face even darker. His cheeks had withdrawn, turning his dimples into creases. Gradually from the sides appeared Dr Harish, Dr Dhiraj, Radhabai, Dhirubhai, Rafiq with his wife holding the hand of a five years old very cute girl and many others who looked familiar but he could not recollect their names. There was a round of hugs and handshakes, Digpal's eyes were full of tears which he did not try to conceal.

"She must be Rumi." He asked the little girl's Father.

"Yes! And she knows who you are." Rumi left her mother's finger and came to Digpal and held his hand. Digpal was crying profusely. 'How wrong I was about people not having gratitude towards doctors'! He thought.

Harish was sporting a diamond studded gold spectacle, "You seem to be doing really well, Harish."

Harish smiled and forced a stack of a thousand rupees bills in his hand, "Keep this for time being, if you need more, don't hesitate."

Digpal, putting the bills back in Harish's pocket said, "Thanks buddy, I will definitely ask for help when needed. Just now I can manage with my savings. Now you better go back to Bhuj, your practice must be suffering."

Harish, a very sentimental man, hugged him and left with moist eyes. Others too offered him every kind of help, but he declined to take any. Gradually all of them left except Ballu, who told him to come with him to Vidurpur, as he had brought Digpal's car.

"I will go to my apartment dear, you have already done a lot for me."

"Which apartment? It was confiscated by the bank when they

stopped receiving instalments, moreover, they considered that you will be in prison for a long time, so they auctioned it already."

Digpal noticed that he had become numb to bad news. The information by Ballu would have disturbed a normal person, but the events of the recent past and then the imprisonment had further hardened him.

"That's okay, I will stay in one of your motel rooms and pay the rent. I need all the available newspapers in Vidurpur. I need a job."

"That should not be a problem." Ballu, knowing his friend, did not contradict.

Ballu's dhaba was on a highway and there used to be travellers stopping there overnight. He had constructed four rooms with basic facilities on the second floor. The first floor was his residence and the ground floor was the *Dhaba* (a highway eatery).

"Rooms are very ordinary, will it be ok for you?"

Digpal laughed and indicated towards the jail, "See where I am coming from!"

Both of them hopped in Digpal's car, they had a lot to talk about. Digpal had stories of Jail and Ballu had stories and gossip of the town.

From the very next morning, Digpal vehemently started searching for a job. He did not have to wait too long, he found one within a week. There were vacancies of teaching positions in a private Medical College located in the tribal belt of south Gujarat. The name of the village, Pipalkheda, did not inspire much. It was part of Narmada district of Gujarat, bordering a similar tribal belt of Maharashtra and Madhya Pradesh. But the name of the college was pretty impressive, the 'Jagat Narayan Patel Institute of Medical Education and Research' in short JIPMER. Digpal smiled, so he will be going to Pondicherry! There were walk-in interviews between 9 AM and 5 PM.

Ballu gave him an emotional farewell, both of them finished a bottle of Old Monk; then in a slurred speech said, "Go away *bhaaji* (elder brother), go away. This land is not for you. South Gujarat is a very good part of Gujarat, people are *bindaas* and broad minded, wish you best of luck." And Digpal was like, "I cannot forget you, there will be no Ballu there..." They were sitting on a carpet on the floor, drinking and eating from a low table. Gradually their speech became more and more slurred and they rolled on the floor, right there!

# TEACHER DE NOVO

With his modest luggage and certificates, Digpal reached Bharuch by an overnight train. From Bharuch he boarded a bus for Rajpipla. He inquired about Pipalkheda at the bus stand and he was told that only 2 buses go to Pipalkheda everyday. The first bus had left about an hour ago and the other bus would leave in the evening. A decent looking man advised him to go by a *chhakda* (a modified three wheeler) to Pipalkheda, which he could get from outside the bus stand. Digpal located a '*chhakda*' outside the bus stand, but it already looked loaded with fifteen passengers though it is supposed to seat eight! The driver asked him to hop in, another five to six passengers will be accommodated in it, he informed. When the *chhakda* began its noisy journey, about twenty odd passengers were stacked together merrily to be dropped at different destinations on the way. On the way, a talkative teacher from Pipalkheda passed on some valuable information, that nobody knows Medical college or 'JIPMER', he has to get down at Shriram hospital, attached to the college, which is a good 2 kms away from the village and is situated on the state highway. It was only 30 kms from Rajpipla but took three hours to reach the destination.

The campus was huge, with an imposing, new medical college building alongside an old Hospital building. On the left side at the edge of campus was a small hillock, on which a beautiful temple with its flag could be seen. In the medical college, hardly any activity was seen, but patients and staff could be seen moving in and out of the hospital building. Life seemed to move in slow motion, staff did not seem to be very particular about the uniform, and an ambulance and a few vehicles were parked haphazardly on the large empty ground in front of the hospital.

As instructed in the ad, he reached an office where the board outside read 'Dr H. H. MAHANT, Dean.' On a stool near the door was sitting a yawning peon, whom he asked if he could go inside to see the Dean. He directed his head towards the door and said, "*andar jata raho* (go inside)."

Inside the office, the Dean was discussing some administrative matter with a chubby man with bags below his eyes. 'He either has renal problem or is an alcoholic', Digpal thought. He introduced himself and the purpose of his visit. The Dean asked him to take a chair and introduced the chubby man with baggy eyes as Dr P. P. Prasad, Medical Superintendent of the hospital, who had a distinct Bihari. The Dean went through his documents-

"You have an excellent academic record and almost 20 years of work experience, but it can not be counted toward a teaching post. You can be appointed as Assistant Professor and if you wish to stay in the campus, you can be given additional charge of a full time surgeon, for which you will get additional salary." Digpal readily agreed.

He was allotted a 1 bedroom house on campus. On the backside of the building were some 22 houses arranged around an oval shaped garden with a lawn in the middle. 2 of them were 3-bed rooms, 5 of them 2 bedrooms and 15 were 1 bedroom houses; all on the ground floor only, as space seemed to be no constraint. There was no pollution, no noise except the chirping of birds and hourly sound of a gong and an occasional sound of temple bell, which was very pleasant to the ear. He fell in love with the place instantly.

First day in the college and hospital was introductions and understanding the working pattern. HOD of surgery was Prof R. P. Mishra, who would come once a week from Vadodara for signing papers and administrative formalities. There were almost a dozen faculty in the Department of Surgery on record, but none stayed locally. Most of them would come on the day of inspection by the Medical Council. Same was the story of almost all the departments. Gradually the facts about the workings of newly mushroomed private medical colleges dawned on him. A skeleton staff would come everyday and were paid regular salary, all others who showed at the time of inspections were given different 'packages', depending on the 'supply and demand' principle of the market. There were agencies too, which would supply teachers to such colleges, on demand. There were some teachers who commuted from nearby cities like Ankleshwar, Bharuch, Vadodara and Surat. They would come once, twice or thrice a week, depending upon their negotiated conditions.

The doctors who were available during all the working days of a week were one Physician, one Paediatrician, an Anaesthetist, a gynec. and now himself as full time surgeon. Additionally a teacher each for Anatomy, Physiology and Biochemistry came regularly to teach first year students. Strangely, the HOD of O&G lived on the campus only. He had retired from a reputed medical college of Mumbai and preferred the peaceful life of Pipalkheda. Every department had a resident, not necessarily an MBBS.

Since the college was new, there was only one first year batch, he did not have to do teaching duties and his work was only clinical. As he settled in the simple non-air conditioned consulting room, a tall, fair young man with well oiled jet black hair entered the room with a broad smile;

"Good Morning Sir, I am Amit Jadhav, your resident." He pulled a chair and sat opposite him. Amit was a local lad, son of a teacher and farmer, working in Shriram hospital since its inception six years ago. He knew everyone and everything inside out, and loaded him with so much information by lunchtime that Digpal began to feel as if he had been working there for years.

The patients were in stark contrast from those of Golden hospital and so were the facilities. Majority of patients were tribals, poor, uneducated, ignorant, made no fuss and were faithful. They had an unusually high pain threshold and the effect of simple analgesics or antibiotics was excellent. They were least concerned about the method of surgery or the kind of anesthesia to be adopted. Size of incision, scope, laser, infrared or cryo did not matter to them- all they wanted was to be cured of their problem. They preferred to stay in the hospital till their wound healed and sutures were removed as it was not easy for them to go back and forth from the village to the hospital. For Digpal, who had never been very comfortable with the fussy, rich and suspicious patients of Golden hospital, this was a pleasant change.

Everything was straightforward there as only simple and cheap drugs and suture material was available there; most of the patients were not able to afford costly drugs and suture and the surgeon had to compromise in the quality of surgery.

He got a glimpse of the kind of people in hardly two days. In the evening, a young tribal man was brought into the casualty. Amit called him up to take a look. The dark, short young man was lying quietly on the examination table, without any signs of pain or agony on his face. When asked about the problem, he just lifted up his loincloth. His scrotum was soiled, raggedly torn and both his testes were hanging naked outside the scrotum.

"How did this happen?" Amit asked.

"My bullock tore with his horn." Answered the young man coolly.

"Then what did you do?"

"I killed the bullock." Digpal was taken aback.

"Why did you do that? He was just an animal! How many bullocks do you have?"

"Only one, the one I killed."

"I will repair your wound, and you will be alright, but your bull won't come back." Digpal was a bit irritated.

"Leave it Sir, these people are like this only, they live only in the moment." Jadhav whispered in the surgeon's ear.

Under local anesthesia, Digpal cleaned the wound, washed the testes with dilute povidone iodine and trimmed the ragged margins of the torn scrotum. Then Amit asked, "Will it be possible to house the testes back in the rags?"

"Yup, easily. Scrotal skin has a lot of margin for stretching and expansion due to rugosity and laxity. Actually you can house four in that." Digpal added in jest.

As he finished his comment, he heard a hearty feminine laughter. Digpal raised his head looking for the source. A lady in a doctor's apron, a bit taller than the average Indian female, responded to his look, "Dr Diksha Deshmukh, I am here to poison your patients."

"Digpal Singh, surgeon and assistant professor, joined recently."

"Welcome to the jungle, hope you survive a fortnight. I am injecting him with pentazocine to relieve pain."

Once the repair was done, all three of them removed their caps and masks. Digpal noticed she was in her mid-thirties, wheatish, ordinary looking but charming, with black brown hair cut at the level of her shoulders and looked generally happy. She was wearing a top and jeans, unusual in those surroundings. Digpal wondered if she was married. As if reading his thoughts, Amit informed him when they were alone, "She doesn't live on the campus, commutes from a nearby Industrial area. Her husband is in a Managerial post in a factory and has a teenage son. She is here because of her husband. As such they belong to Pune. She is a very competent Anaesthetist and very sincere too."

Madhya Pradesh and Maharashtra borders were not very far from there, and that too was the tribal belt. Patients from these states also used to come to Shriram for treatment, generally in an advanced state of disease.

One day, a short, dark, thin tribesman from bordering Madhya Pradesh, came with pain in his right buttock radiating to the back of his thigh, for a long time. Generally, it was not easy to get an accurate history of symptoms; even the age of the patient was difficult to ascertain correctly. He could be anywhere between 20 to 35 years of age. Digpal examined his gluteal region, and a faded scar of about one inch could be seen on the buttock. He did not remember if he had sustained any injury. Digpal requested an X-Ray, and to everybody's surprise, a very clear opacity of an arrowhead could be seen in the gluteal region.

The next morning, Digpal opened up his gluteal region under spinal anaesthesia and found the arrowhead stuck obliquely in the gluteus maximus muscle, brushing the sciatic nerve near its emergence from the sciatic foramen. The arrowhead was removed neatly and the muscle repaired. The arrowhead was surprisingly very clean, sharp and devoid of any rust or wear. As he held it up in a big Kocher's forceps, "What a shot!" Was the surprising comment of Diksha.

In Golden hospital, he would have been forced to refer the case to orthopaedic surgery, Digpal mused. They had injected him with tetanus toxoid, preoperatively.

"Arrange for 5000 units of Tetanus immunoglobulins for him, Amit." Looking at Amit's curious face, he said. "These dormant foreign bodies can harbour Tetanus spores for decades, and they may get activated when disturbed."

"Let's go to the canteen for some snacks and tea, I am hungry. Ma'am, mind having a cup of tea with us?" Digpal offered Diksha.

"I can have tea, as many times as offered," was her response.

"Same pinch." And they all laughed. Digpal noticed she would laugh at the slightest pretext, and heartily.

The 3 of them, Digpal, Diksha and Amit developed an immediate camaraderie and would often sit together in canteen or OPD to chit chat and exchange views. The poor tribals did not go to the private or trust hospitals of bigger cities, for want of conveyance and funds. Moreover, they did not feel very comfortable in urban areas. Even in this hospital, they reported when the stench of gangrenous limb became intolerable for everybody, or the liver abscess became so big that hardly any healthy liver remained after drainage. Gastric perforations were common, probably because of cheap illicit alcoholic brew. Late appendicular or enteric perforations were also not uncommon. Sickle cell anaemia and malnutrition were also common. Diabetes and hypertension were rare, it seems these are the gifts of modern life to humanity. Whenever diabetics were detected, the majority were pancreatic diabetics. He observed one more strange trend. Except Wednesdays, the hospital charged very nominal fees for treating the patient. On Wednesdays, it was completely free. More than half of the work of the week would come on that single day. Even emergencies like peritonitis and obstructions would wait for six to seven days, to reach the hospital on Wednesday. The usual teaching in Medical colleges is that such cases must be operated within 24 to 48 hours, otherwise the mortality is very high. But the people there defied all logic and scientific knowledge! They had tremendous resilience and pain tolerance. A 6 or 7 days old perforation or obstruction, in severe septicaemia would come untreated, but even after such delayed surgery, the majority survived. The only difference was that lengthy surgeries were done at the surgeon's own pace in modern centres, where speed did not matter. Here Diksha coaxed him to be quick and wind up as early as possible. The condition of patients and the anaesthesia facilities were not conducive to a relaxed pace of surgery.

Since there were no super-specialists in the hospital, not even visiting ones, the variety of surgery in the General surgery department reminded him of the initial years of Jiviben hospital of Vidurpur. The kind of surgeries he had been missing in Golden hospital were again in his fold.

Many of the tribals had converted to Christianity in that area because of active missionaries in the interior. Lucy was a 5 year old daughter of such converted tribal parents. Lucy was anaemic, emaciated, underweight, irritable and hardly looked a day older than 3 years. Her mother gave a history of chronic constipation since birth, for which she would take her to a local practitioner, who would hand her some or other laxative. Since she was home delivered by a *'Dai'*, no qualified doctor had ever examined the baby properly. Her perineum was always soiled with liquid stools, was the mother's observation. Digpal examined her abdomen, which was studded with lumps of different sizes and consistency; some pitted on pressing with finger. He cleaned her perineum and found that the anus was absent and liquid fecal matter was coming out of the vaginal opening. He decided to examine her under general anaesthesia. He observed that she had an imperforate anus, with a very small, almost a fistulous opening in the vagina, through which only liquid stools and gas could come out.

The 'lumps' were faecoliths collected since her birth, for five years! What an extreme case of ignorance, negligence and medical inadequacy. The state was also at fault, they were not providing basic minimum medical care to its citizens. This was not a solitary case, he came across many cases of suffering due to the shortfall of proper medical infrastructure in the rural and mofussil areas of the country. Most of the facilities and qualified doctors were concentrated in urban areas.

Digpal planned a sigmoid colostomy as the first stage and to remove faecoliths from the colon. It turned out to be much tougher than his expectations. He had done a loop colostomy to remove fecoliths from both the ends, but it was impossible to remove them with the finger. Then he used cystolithotomy forceps to remove the lumps of feces, some of them calcified. almost more than an hour passed, and since Lucy had developed a megacolon as well, the liths continued to come in large numbers. Diksha warned him to stop, as the child was weak and frail. Experience had taught Digpal that never contradict or force your Anaesthetist to stay safe. She suggested that he could continue after a few days. Lucy was hospitalised for 20 days and they did five sessions of fecolith extraction. With supportive treatment and improved diet, she started gaining weight. Her mother was taking good care of Lucy's colostomy.

Lucy's parents brought her for a follow up every month, and generally the child was happy to meet him and addressed him as 'Uncle'. Her irritability had gone and she became active and cheerful. Digpal had operated upon many anorectal anomalies, but none reporting so late, at age 5.

After 6 months, he did her definitive surgery and subsequently closed her colostomy.

Work was good, he was satisfied on the professional front, but his work as a teacher was still naught, as there was only a first year batch in the college. Only time he felt like a teacher was when some group of students would sing a 'Good Morning Sir' in unison while passing by in the corridor.

During breaks or free time Digpal, Diksha and Amit would go to the canteen for tea and snacks. Of late Prof Shinde had also joined them. Dr Shinde, after retiring from Govt. medical college of Mumbai, joined different private colleges, before landing in Pipalkheda. He said he had multiple medical problems, and he wanted a place where he did not have to do any clinical work, was peaceful and non polluted. He did not want to stress himself at all. He lived on campus, and did not use any vehicle.

The hospital had employed a young, full time obstetrician and gynec, Sangita Panchal, who commuted from a nearby town where she lived with her parents. She generally did obstetrics and minor procedures and no major surgeries.

The group would discuss different topics every time. Once they began discussion on the reservation policy of the government in medical colleges. Diksha and Amit vehemently opposed the reservation policy. They said it must be strictly on merit basis, by making non meritorious doctors the society is risking the lives of its citizens.

"You all are from the privileged class, it's easy for you to score good marks. Have you ever seen the pathetic conditions, poverty and filth we live in? Can we compete with you people? Where is the sense of equality with us in everyday life? All of you want us to remain in the same shit we have been living in for centuries." Dr Shinde's voice became bitter while talking. Facing Digpal he added, "You must also be from the same privileged class Dr Singh."

Before Digpal could think of an answer Amit said, "The living conditions of SC/ST should be improved instead of giving them reservations."

"Admissions by capitation fee is also a kind of reservation for undeserving candidates of rich class." Digpal commented. The discussion continued for some more time without reaching any consensus, like in the rest of the country.

Once Dr Shinde told Digpal, "You know, even today when there is a crime in the village, the police raid our 'basti', beat up people, rape women, round up youngsters and throw them in lockup, beat them up and then release them next day." The latter only listened, stunned, but later on weighing the things, he was not much convinced by Dr Shinde's version. It may be a rare occurrence or exaggeration.

A few months later, when the canteen was closed down during vacations, Amit had gone to his village for a short visit, Digpal offered Diksha, "I make very good tea and omelet, we can go to my apartment for that."

"I can come to have tea, but not an omelet, I am vegetarian."

While preparing tea, both of them talked about the working conditions of 'Shriram' and the kind of cases they had encountered before they came here. Gradually they switched to personal matters. She talked about her family, that her husband is a highly qualified chemical engineer on a big post in a chemical factory. They have been married for eighteen years and are parents to a 13 year old son and an eight year old daughter. She sounded worried about her son. He was quite a handful and not interested in studies. Digpal placed the tea mugs on the small table, pulled a plastic chair across from her and sat, listening keenly.

"I think he smokes and may be into drugs as well."

"I don't have much idea about parenting, but teenagers can behave like this, and generally it is a passing phase." While speaking Digpal placed his hand on hers reassuringly.

"Thanks pal, but he gives me a lot of anxiety." Said Diskha pulling her hand away.

Though he had placed his hand unintentionally, he muttered a lame 'sorry' and noted that he should not do this in the future. After that incident, the two of them were never alone in his apartment.

Once the canteen reopened, all four of them started meeting again to talk on different topics. Sometimes only Digpal and Diksha would go to the canteen, their friendship becoming more and more informal, and started discussing personal lives. Digpal, still unmarried, asked her opinion regarding a medico or non medico spouse. She thought for a while then said, "I am happy in my family life, but sometimes I feel it's not very easy to communicate with your non-doctor husband. Certain compulsions of our profession are unique, moreover sometimes you want to discuss some medical problem, which is not possible. Though he is very understanding, sometimes he looks suspicious when I mention my male colleagues, or maybe it's just my imagination."

"That's right, though I don't have any first hand experience, but I would like to go home and discuss cases with my wife, or ask her opinion."

"I have observed that generally male doctors are absolutely comfortable with their homemaker wives, the doctor husband gets all the attention and respect of his spouse."

"Are you sure? Aren't the wives bored to hilt, when hubbies are too busy with their work?" Digpal argued.

"Married life, for that matter life itself does not have a 'one size fits all' formula." She concluded, to close the discussion.

Then Digpal started opening up about his upbringing, life in an orphanage and affair with Kalpana and the short stint with Joseline; and how Kalpana could not muster courage to ask her parents, and so on. She was listening to him very keenly, at one point she remarked offhandedly, "If I were her, I would have run away with you." Her comment surprised him.

While walking back to the hospital, they noticed the gynec resident rushing towards them, "Sir, can you come urgently to see a newborn baby? She looks abnormal, her viscera is outside."

"You too, have a look." Digpal told Diksha, "She may require anaesthesia."

# EXOMPHALOS MAJOR

They rushed to the labor room where the new born baby was in a tray, wrapped in a sterile hospital towel. A big part of the anterior abdominal wall was missing, and the intestines and some part of the liver was also exposed. The exposed part of viscera was enveloped in transparent film with the peritoneum and the cord hanging from the lower part of the film.

"This is an exomphalos major, will need an early surgery, can not keep the viscera and peritoneum exposed for long." Digpal addressed Diksha, "Will it be possible to anaesthetise her?"

"Why not? Babies are stronger than they appear."

Digpal covered the exomphalos with saline soaked pads.

"Okay then, we will close this tomorrow morning."

After that moment he kept on planning the surgery. During his Paediatric surgery residency days, a primary closure with release incisions used to be done. Success rate of that surgery was very poor, most of the neonates used to die either due to respiratory distress or shock of surgery. Digpal could hardly sleep, but ultimately reached a foolproof solution. 'Why can't I use the tensionless closure principle of hernioplasty'? He thought.

The next day, he dissected the skin away from the fascia of abdominal wall, all around the rim of defect, then on both the sides, sutured two strips of polypropylene mesh enough to cover the defect with the same suture material. He then sutured the two strips together, without tension.

"Sir, how will this help?" Amit asked.

"Now I will keep tightening the two strips by trimming them bit by bit, and suturing them again every alternate day, until the abdominal wall can be closed without any tension, and without mesh. I have no Idea, how long it will take."

"Where have you learned this technique? I have never seen this anywhere, in Pune or Mumbai." Diksha asked curiously.

"Nowhere, I have neither seen, heard or read this technique. I thought of it last night. this must work, I am confident."

As per his plan, he kept on trimming and tightening the mesh. This did not require any anesthesia. Within 5 weeks, the two opposing margins were near each other, and were ready to be closed. The final closure required anaesthesia.

Diksha, after closing, said, "You are superb Digpal. Are you going to give this technique your name and prepare a case report?"

"Was not possible without your help, and no, I am not going to give it my name or prepare a paper.I do not know if someone somewhere else has used this method; moreover I can only work and that's it. You may call it my weak point."

Diksha could not understand what was wrong with this man.

Meanwhile, his car was dispatched by Ballu through a driver. The person who drove his car from Vidurpur to Pipalkheda refused to accept any remuneration, as he turned out to be the Father of one of his paediatric patients, operated by him at Vidurpur.

Dr Shinde generally did not leave hospital campus, Amit too stayed in campus only, but accompanied him occasionally for trips to nearby towns, Ankleshwar or Bharuch.

His circle of friends began to expand slowly, as a young Physician (internal medicine), Arif, joined the hospital. During spare time, they would play volleyball on campus along with the hospital staff.

Arif turned out to be good company in discovering new

places to eat, especially non-vegetarian ones. His smoking habit irritated him, and they generally had few exchanges of words in that connection.

One afternoon, when Arif and Digpal were coming back from one of the outings, they noticed some policemen trying to control an angry crowd. Almost a dozen muscular men in religious robes were sitting on the floor, in a row, with backs resting against the wall. They had received varied injuries on their faces and other parts of their bodies. 2 of them seemed to be badly injured and were lying on the stretchers. Digpal asked one of the police officers, "Why are these disciples battered like this?" Before the officer could respond, a local, small-time leader jumped in, "They are not disciples, but they are goons of Haridas *Baba*.They deserve this battering, don't treat them doctor."

Digpal did not respond, and proceeded to examine the men in robes.

Most of them had Hematomas of different sizes and shapes, a few black eyes and some lacerated wounds but no grievous hurt. Even the two apparently 'serious' cases were blunt trauma only, without any sign of internal injuries. They were tough muscular guys, most of them from Uttar Pradesh and Bihar, seemed to be professional henchmen of the *Baba*. "Are they okay, doctor?" The police officer asked.

"Yes officer, nothing much it seems, they are pretty used to thrashing."

Police arrested them and took them in their jeeps, after they received primary treatment.

The story behind this episode turned out to be interesting. The owner of the medical college was a local politician named Jayantibhai Jagatnarayan Patel, popularly called Jayanti Jagat or JJ; who had been elected as a member of legislative assembly as well since the last ten years. He was quite popular for his helpful nature and running the free Shriram hospital, amongst the villagers of the area. However, running a medical college was an expensive proposition, and his funds dried up. He took a heavy loan from Hariram *Baba*. The grapevine was, the *Baba* used to fleece money from his disciples and ran a lucrative black money lending business. When JJ could not pay the interest or return the money within the stipulated time, *Baba* sent his goons to arm twist JJ. The latter was alerted by his informers about the impending danger, and he sent word to villagers all around to come in large numbers to counter the attack. It was said that more than 5000 villagers responded to their leader's call, and the outcome was there to be seen!

The loan was never paid back to the *Baba*, and he had to let go of it. After a few years, the *Baba* was arrested on sexual molestation charges of one of his female disciples.

Diksha and Digpal became friendlier as the time went by. Even when others were not there, the two of them would go to the canteen, and sit and talk during their free time. None of the two bothered about the murmurs and oblique smiles of staff members and students.

During one of the slack days, while he was sitting alone in his office, in came Savita Kapadia, an employee in the administrative office. He had noticed Savita a few times, she was good looking, had a full body, big eyes and the most remarkable feature were her full, well curved lips. Once, while she passed by, Arif had remarked, "What a sexy dame, Pal Sir."

Savita had vague complaints like headache, insomnia and pain in the abdomen of indeterminate duration. Digpal jotted down the complaints and said, "I will call the nurse and examine you."

"Why call the nurse? You can examine me, I have full faith in you."

Digpal ignored her request and called a nurse to remain present, while he examined her. As was expected, there was no positive finding. He prescribed her some placebo and advised her to come after a week.

The very next day, during the post-lunch break, there was a knock on his door. Digpal generally despised interruption in his siesta, unless it is an emergency; moreover since the last few days he felt a loss of appetite, weakness and malaise. Groggy and irritated, he opened the door and in came Savita. She quickly closed the door behind her, held his hands, turned her face up towards him and whispered, "Doctor, don't you think I am beautiful?"

"No doubt you are beautiful, Savita, but please leave me alone. You should not have come to my home like this. You better leave." Saying this, he proceeded to open the door. She did not move, "What do you see in Diksha? Why is she always sticking around you? What's wrong with me?"

"Dr Diksha is a friend, and I don't owe you any explanation. You better leave now." He was angry now.

She left, thumping her foot, leaving behind a worried Digpal. He stood in front of the mirror and told himself, "I am no macho or handsome man. Why is she after an ordinary looking dark man," and suddenly he was alarmed, "with yellow eyes!"

# THE WORLD IS YELLOW

He changed and headed straight to the laboratory and gave his blood sample for liver function tests. After an hour the lab technician brought the reports to his office. Arif had already come to his office knowing about his ill health. Arif was alarmed to see his reports-

"Your bilirubin is way too high, and LFTs are also deranged. We must get your USG and Australia antigen done." Then added, "We had been roaming together all the time, and I never noticed the ictrus! Shame on me."

In 2 more days he turned from yellow to orange with complete loss of appetite and aversion to food. He felt perpetually nauseated. His ultrasound did not show any obstructive pathology but his hepatitis B antigen turned out to be positive. In retrospect he concluded, it might be because of accidentally pricking his finger with a suture needle during a surgery, about two months back. That time he did not take it seriously, only changed his gloves and rejected the needle. After a month, that patient had come back with jaundice. He was hospitalised, a glucose drip with vitamins accompanied by bedrest.

His only job was to lie in bed and think. He tried to focus only on the positives of his past. He did not want to remember his Golden hospital days. His most pleasant memories were of Jiviben hospital, when he had little money but a lot of happiness. The camaraderie with colleagues, lots of surgical work, pristine beaches of Diu, the lively dinners and drinks with friends, most of the time with Harish or Ballu. The beautiful and serene temple of Somnath on the seafront, the place always filled him with peace. But the history of Somnath filled him with anger and disgust. Anger for the invaders who repeatedly looted and vandalised it and more so for the local rulers and common men, who could not save it from a handful of foreign attackers. Though, he thought, after centuries, it is wrong to be judgemental.

The ever-recurring memories of Kalpana and the beautiful moments with her again came back, while he had all the time to mull over.

Digpal requested Arif to give in writing about his ill health to Dean Mahant and Medical Superintendent P. P. Prasad. As it was not certain, when he will be antigen negative, the management decided to appoint a locum surgeon in the department. On the very first day of joining, he visited Digpal.

"How are you doing, doctor?"A very fair, a bit short, plump young man was standing near Digpal's bed, "I am Sanjay Vyas, pass out from Jamghodiya, newly appointed surgeon." Vyas extended his soft plump hand towards him. Digpal shook his hand weekly. "Better sanitise your hand now, I am B-hepatitis positive, though not known to spread by skin contact, but still." He could muster a faint smile.

"Don't worry, and don't worry about the surgical work as well. The patients won't miss you."

Digpal noticed an air of overconfidence and a tinge of ego in him. 'This is dangerous', he thought. Moreover, he knew Jamghodiya was a private medical college with high capitation fees. Many undeserving candidates with rich and doctor parents got admitted there by the power of money. He was not very sure of the standard of such institutes. Sanjay Vyas left after discussing the working module of Shriram hospital with Digpal.

In the evening, Diksha visited him with her husband Ojus. He was a tall hefty man, with specks of gray in his thick lock of hair. Digpal found him amicable and well mannered. "She speaks very highly of your diagnostic skills and surgical expertise; It's a pleasure meeting you, wish you an early recovery." He could not see any shade of envy in his voice. They had brought some homemade snacks for him, which he happily accepted.

During his three week hospitalisation, Amit and Diksha visited him every day during lunch hours, and brought extra food to share with him. He would eagerly wait for the lunch hour.

In the late evening Savita visited him with her husband, who was a diminutive, thin and pale looking man, almost three inches shorter then Savita.

She introduced him as Jayantibhai, who uttered a faint *'Namaste'* and sat quietly, without speaking a word, during the visit. Savita was chattering non-stop about all kinds of hospital news, gossip and rumours.

"I will attend to you during nights, as you are alone and on IV fluids." Savita offered.

"I am ok, used to staying alone, thanks."

"But you are sick and will require assistance, what say Jayanti?"

Her husband shook his head in affirmation.

After that, she sat every night in his room, for three consecutive nights. On the fourth evening he requested her, "I am off IV fluids now and feeling better; please don't come now, and thanks a lot for your concern."

"I am waiting for you to become fit, want to find out why she hovers around you, must be something." She winked, "I am feeding you *kesar* milk every day, not for nothing."

Later on Amit informed that she had been married to Jayantibhai for name sake as a cover for relations between JJ and her. Jayanti has a menial job, and the couple lives in an apartment on campus. She did not even change her surname after marriage. "I am not interested in her or her story." Digpal told Amit.

Diksha came to know about Savita's night duties and taunted, "You need a lot of nursing care in the night, it seems!" He just smiled in response. 'Envy is an integral part of the female psyche;

even though I am just a friend, she doesn't like the proximity of another female to me!'

In a week he was feeling better but very weak, his appetite was still poor and he was passing dark yellow urine. Arif got his LFTs repeated and looked worried.

"Your Bilirubin is rising, it's 24 mgms. I am putting you on oral steroids, is it ok with you?"

"You are the quack, Arif, do whatever you think is right."

Methylprednisolone was started in high doses, and within a few days his LFTs began to improve, his appetite started improving to an extent that he felt perpetually hungry and could think of nothing but food! He requested Amit to bring him some cookies and salty biscuits that he munched on intermittently for the whole day. He started feeling better within a week, when one morning his phone rang,

"Can you come to OT for a while? I know you are not well but it's necessary." The OT nurse was on line.

Sanjay was standing in his operating gear, with a nurse assisting him. He had opened the scrotum of a young man, who looked around twenty to him.

"Sir, this fellow seemed to have a TV hydrocele, but on exploration, there is no fluid, only a very enlarged testis. What should I do now?" Sanjay sounded subdued, his air of overconfidence missing.

"This is a testicular tumor, should be a Teratoma, at his age." The senior man opined.

"Now what?" Sanjay asked.

"Extend the incision up to inguinal region, don't fiddle with the testis, or you may spread the malignancy. Try to trace the chord as high as you can, even beyond the internal ring. Now apply a vascular clamp on the chord." Sanjay followed the instructions. "Now with a knife, give a deep incision on the testis, almost through and through."

"Did you hear the gritty sound and feel of the knife?" Digpal was excited.

"It is a Teratoma for sure. Normal testicular tissue is soft and pouts out on incising the tunic, this is cutting like a raw pear. Go ahead with high Orchidectomy. Next time, elicit fluctuation and translucency tests in all scrotal swellings." He started feeling as if his legs would give way "May I leave? I am feeling weak."

"Thanks Sir." Sanjay said meekly. "Should I write your name on the papers?"

"Don't, I am not a moron to miss a tumour for hydrocele." Digpal retorted.

"You never make any mistakes?" Sanjay was offended, insulted in the presence of nurses and Anaesthetist.

"All surgeons make mistakes and errors of judgement. Some are less skilled than others which is understandable, but this is not an error, this is a blunder. I am sure you did not even touch the patient." Retorted Digpal in a cool voice.

"I am not a second proff student, Sir." Sanjay was sarcastic.

"Then keep repeating such blunders." He slowly walked back to his room, angry and sad at the same time. He was tired and slept till evening. When he got up, Diksha was sitting on a chair, reading a book. Noticing he got up, she ordered tea and snacks from the canteen.

"I am hungry." Digpal said, "I am perpetually hungry since Arif has started steroids."

"Yes, and it is beginning to show, your cheeks are rounding off." She smiled and fetched a pack of cookies from his side cupboard. He started devouring the cookies.

"It was pretty unpleasant this morning in the OT," she said.

"Yes, there was no need for me to be so rude, after all he is a young surgeon."

"But he too should have behaved like a junior; he had called you for help and you came in spite of your ill health." Diksha tried to console him, "I have noticed he is overconfident and sometimes arrogant too. He tries to do surgeries which he might have never done before, takes hours to reach the lower third of ureter or a high retrocolic appendix. An Anaesthetist's nightmare!"

There was a knock at the door and in came Sanjay Vyas, "How are you doing?" He asked sweetly.

"Not bad."

Nobody spoke for a while, there was an awkward silence.

"I am sorry for my behaviour, we must respect our seniors. How often our teachers used to reprimand us in Medical college for minor mistakes, and during residency, the senior resident would insult us in the wards so very frequently. I have come to apologise."

"That's ok Sanjay, I too was harsh, maybe due to my ill health;" Digpal pointed towards the small table, "help yourself with cookies and tea." All three were relieved and started talking about their teachers and their whims and wits.

After they left, Amit came with home cooked food, which they shared and meanwhile he updated Digpal about the new happenings and rumours. Come night and in came Savita with a thermos full of *kesar* milk.

"I am ok now, and already gulping down lots of calories, you needn't bring this milk." He tried to avoid her.

"I can't wait to see you fighting fit, and you know why."

"Hepatitis B can be transmitted by contact, it may take months to become negative."

"Will keep track of your reports." She told naughtily.

He breathed a sigh of relief once she left.

In another week, he shifted back to his apartment. Arif began to taper his steroids, though he still felt hungry all the time. He took a shower and stood in front of a full size mirror, where a fat stranger was staring into his eyes. He had put on lipids at all the wrong places, his face looked round and fair, a small paunch and two buffalo humps were decorating his middle!

His Australia antigen was negative after three months and he gleefully joined work again. Arif would visit him regularly to monitor his progress. When his report turned negative he came to congratulate Digpal. "By the grace of Allah you have recovered quickly and completely."

"I thought it was my immune system and your treatment that made it possible."

"You don't believe in God?" Arif was surprised.

"I don't know about his or her existence, consider me ignorant."

"You are saying this because you don't know about the real God, the one and only Allah."

"I know none of the gods, faceless or the idols, and I am not interested in finding out. I believe in my work and humanity, empathy and integrity. I have seen many hardcore religious persons who are corrupt and dishonest."

"If you have no faith, how do you get peace of mind? Where do you find solace and support when you face problems and failures?" Arif asked.

"I am at peace, and even if I am not, I don't mind being restless, worried or sad. It is part of human nature and life. I don't seek support from some imaginary power." Digpal responded.

"You are hopeless."

"Why not have a cup of hot ginger tea to cool down?" Digpal proceeded to brew tea on his coil heater.

First day of return was only outdoor patients, then the three of them, Digpal, Sanjay and Amit went for rounds in the wards. Sanjay seemed to have done a good number of surgeries, but none very major. When they stood near the bed of a young patient, Sanjay told proudly, "This is the lap appendectomy I did yesterday, will discharge him today."

"Well done Sanjay." Digpal said.

"He took two hours to remove this normal appendix." Whispered the accompanying nurse in his ear. After the rounds, Sanjay asked, "May I stay here for a few more days and work with you, till the end of this month?"

"Sure you can, I will be delighted." He said.

They worked together for a month, and Sanjay became his fan forever. When the younger surgeon was to leave, Digpal arranged a small party in the canteen. Dr Shinde, Diksha, Arif, Amit and Sangita were present. After the formalities and exchange of pleasantries, Sangita informed that she had resigned and was getting married very soon. Everyone wished her a happy married life.

When they were about to disperse, Digpal asked Dr Shinde, "You admit women with advanced gynae problems for teaching and examination purposes, what do you do to them, once your purpose is served?"

"We send them back." Dr Shinde said.

"Why should they not be cured of their conditions before sending them back, don't you think, it's inhuman and selfish?" Digpal was bitter.

"Frankly dear, you know my medical conditions, I can not stand the stress of surgery anymore. As for Sangita, she has limited competence. She was doing obstetrics and very limited surgeries, other visiting faculties are only for namesake. What can we do?" Shinde tried to defend himself.

"I am a local, and I have to listen to all the criticism of the hospital." Amit intervened.

"Do you mind if I operate on them? Please do not send them home just like that." Digpal requested.

"Do you know what kind of cases they are? Large fibroids, procedentias and bad prolapses. Even malignancies, with very bad general health, almost all are anaemic.

I have no objection if you operate, enjoy!" He gave out a hollow laugh.

"Thanks a ton Dr Shinde! Diksha here is great at knocking them down and bringing them back. Is it ok with you Diksha?" Digpal was happy as a child, who got a new toy!

She just nodded her head in affirmation.

"I will monitor their cardiorespiratory condition." Arif offered.

"Great! it's done then. We start working on it from tomorrow." Digpal was upbeat. But happiest was Amit. He was the local lad, people knew him and he was concerned for them.

"I will be missing all the fun." Sanjay remarked.

# GYNAE SURGERIES

Next morning, when Digpal, Amit, Diksha and Arif reached the gynae ward, the scenario was quite depressing. The women there were anaemic, underweight and looked as if they had lost all hope of cure. In all there were 8 women requiring surgery. They decided to operate one each in their operative days, in addition to their general surgery cases.

Dr Shinde who was already there, took them to a bed where a 50 years, lean and thin, dark lady was lying, with one eye lost probably because of infection or injury, a small opaque nodule was there instead. Dr Shinde indicated towards her, "She is comparatively fit. She has a 6 x 6 inches posterior fibroid, which bleeds off and on. She has been here for the last 15 days, you can begin with her."

Under spinal anesthesia, when Digpal picked up a scalpel to incise, he heard murmurs near the door, and in came a bunch of about 20 students, led by Prof Shinde. Digpal gave him a curious look. Prof Shinde spoke with a wide grin, "As I told you, I am Gavaskar, was a great player in the past but now I am a commentator. Go ahead with your surgery."

Digpal became self-conscious for a second, then overcame it and began the surgery with his usual flare. True to his word, Prof Shinde began with his commentary for the benefit of students.

"He is making a transverse crease incision on lower abdomen, this is called a pfannenstiel incision, pronounced fenensteel but begins with a 'p' which you will have to mug up. He is coagulating bleeders, the white layer is rectus sheath and laterally transversus and oblique muscles of abdomen. He has retracted the recti laterally, the glistening white membrane is peritoneum..." He went on and on with every minor detail, until the whole uterus with the fibroid, its adnexa and cervix was removed.

'He really is an excellent teacher', Digpal thought.

After the peritoneum was closed, he began to suture the sheath, when Shinde asked, "Why are you closing with interrupted sutures, and not continuous ones?"

"Wherever strength is required I prefer interrupted sutures, more reliable and less ischaemia of edges, material does not matter much."

After the surgery was over, the Professor commented, "You did a neat and swift job, didn't look like you are not a gynec."

"He always does." Diksha said.

"You seem to be his big fan." Shinde smiled obliquely.

"He deserves that." Diksha quipped.

Digpal had already slipped out to the side room to write post-op orders and operative notes. He asked Prof Shinde, "Should I write your name in the papers as the main operating surgeon?"

"It hardly matters, this is the last village of the universe, nobody is going to bother you with legal tangles." The Professor assured.

Every operation day, he would operate on a gynaec case, four uterine fibroids of various sizes, three uterine prolapses and a large ovarian cyst. The history of the last one was a comedy of ignorance. She and others thought she was full term pregnant and the baby was not coming out. The old and wise women of the village tried various methods from massages and application of different types of concoctions on the abdomen. Then she was taken to a semi-educated medical practitioner who injected her with different drugs to induce labor. When everything failed, she was brought to Shriram Hospital, where she was diagnosed as having a huge ovarian cyst. Technically ovarian cyst was one of the simplest surgeries with a literally 'huge' outcome.

One of the challenging cases was a huge fibroid, stuck in the pelvis and refused to come out of it. The middle aged lady was bleeding per vaginum leading to severe anaemia. Anesthesia too was challenging in that case but Diksha managed her well under Epidural block. Digpal divided all the muscles on the way transversely for better exposure. He did not hurry to reach the uterine vessels, but systematically divided the branches, which had fanned on the sides of Uterus. Gradually the uterus was free and the whole fibroid with the uterus could be pulled out of the pelvis with a sucking sound, resulting in an easy approach to the uterines.

Prof Shinde was always there, sometimes standing on a short table to peep inside the abdominal cavity.

Uterine prolapses with varying degree of perineal injuries with urinary difficulties were other unfortunate cases. All of them were completely preventable with good obstetric care.

During one of the breaks, the small group of Digpal, Prof Shinde, Amit and Arif were discussing the pathetic condition of obstetric care in the rural areas of our country. Shinde said, "It is because the majority of gynecs prefer bigger cities, for better life and more money. Especially a married lady Gynecologist can not decide the place of her work on her own."

"Even a lady Anaesthetist can not decide the place of her practice, she has to hang on to her husband." Diksha commented.

"Unless both partners are like-minded doctors, and don't mind living in a rural area or a small town." Amit said.

"What I have observed is, most of the specialists choose a branch or sub-branch, in which chances of earning big bucks are maximum, like assisted reproduction, radiology, cosmetic dermatology, and the upcoming joint replacement surgeries and cardiac bypass surgeries. Qualified general practitioner is becoming a rarity. The most important doctor for the common man is the GP." Digpal was bitter, "Capitation fee is highest in branches where there is more money, nobody bothers about the aptitude of candidates and need of the society."

"Yes, MBBS family physicians are fast becoming an endangered species," Amit said, "people in general are at the mercy of backdoor allopaths, degree holders of other pathies, practising modern medicine. Even a large number of unqualified quacks are practising in slums of cities and villages."

"Doctors too have the right to a good life, they too have a family, their children too have to go to good schools. You are talking about impractical idealism." Arif countered.

"Then, what are you doing here, in this godforsaken place?" Diksha asked.

"Most of us are here for a short time. Like Sangita left, you are here only as long as your husband is here. Everybody is temporary here. I will also move to a city, get married and settle in private practice." Arif retorted.

"All except me," Digpal said

"Me too, it's my home." Amit concluded, "Let's celebrate service to the poor and needy, with samosas and tea." This turned the topic into a lighthearted conversation.

Life was busier, with the addition of teaching to his duties of surgical work and voluntarily accepted gynec surgery. Not that he was complaining, on the contrary, it reduced his loneliness.

Amongst gynaec surgeries, apart from ovarian cysts, he found uterine prolapse surgery easy, except that, he had to be careful while dissecting the urinary bladder from the anterior vaginal wall. As time went by, he ventured into non-prolapse vaginal Hysterectomies too, for that he repeatedly studied the operative videos on his video player. He was particularly impressed by the 'hydro dissection technique' of a North Gujarat-based Gynecologist; injecting large amounts of isotonic saline around the cervix, which made dissection easy and bloodless.

Whenever the resident of obstetrics asked him to do a caesarian, he would happily comply. He loved the outcome of the procedure- a new life and a safe mother.

Life was good. He had a place to live, enough money for his survival, good food, friends, a lot of work, students who liked and respected him and a peaceful quiet place. But still, there was a big void in his life. He felt very lonely during the night. He longed for a female partner by his side, someone with whom he could share his most intimate secrets, fears, griefs and joy.

But, time does not stop, and one morning, he noticed the first strands of silver on his side whiskers.

# SERPENS MORDEAT

At times, he felt that his life was a game of snakes and ladders. Whenever life was good and hunky dory, something would pull him back.

Digpal had completed four years at Pipalkheda. Many things had changed. He was Associate Professor now, Diksha had left as her husband joined a job at Pune, Arif had started his private practice in Bharuch, got married and was doing well. Prof Shinde had receded in his shell. A new anaesthesia diploma holder from Surendranagar joined after Diksha left, and Digpal found him quite average incompetence. The posts of Gynaecologist and Physician were still vacant.

There were reasons for these changes. The reputation of 'JIPMER' of Pipalkheda was going downhill, the Medical Council had found many deficiencies in the institute and there was a strong rumour that the college would be derecognised. As there were no new student admissions, the funds were drying up. The staff had not received any salary for three months. Staff members who went to the owner to request money would have a small amount doled out to them. Students were going into depression, they had lost hopes of appearing in examinations and in turn, had stopped studying.

The evening tea gatherings, the discussions, jokes and laughter had become a thing of the past. Amit has been married for the last 6 years and now fathered a baby girl. He used to remain busy with the newborn and would leave the hospital early, sometimes even absent from duty at the slightest pretext. The flow of patients had reduced, as the hospital had stopped the 'free treatment day' and hiked the charges, though they were still a fraction of private hospital charges.

Digpal was even more lonely now. During his melancholy he would often rewind his good times of past; the informal friends of Jiviben, Harish, Dinkar, Ravindran, the omnipresent Sarang and mood elevator, ever reliable Ballu. The rosy days with Kalpana, her touch, the Mumbai trip and the painful separation. The intoxicating dinners at the pristine beaches of Diu, that was an ointment for all traumas. The romantic nights with Joseline and her sudden exit from his life. The unforgettable night when Kalpana left her husband to be with him forever; how unfortunate one can get, he wondered!

But unfortunately, he was, he sarcastically smiled to himself; otherwise, who would leave their newborn son on the steps of a church on a rainy night, or have to go to jail on false allegations and live with criminals? To console himself, he would say to himself, "I am very lucky, in spite of all the odds, I became a master of surgery which gave me the power to heal and make a difference in the lives of thousands of sick and suffering." He sometimes would get up, past midnight, and open his 'Love and Baily's short practice of surgery', he relished it more than any novel.

Remembering his friends, he replayed the conversation with Diksha, when she told, "I would have said 'yes' and run away with you"; and he was so very pleased to hear that! He had asked, "Why would you have said 'yes' to someone whose background, religion, caste and family is a mystery? Venture to share your life with an underdog brought up in an orphanage?" And her answer, not only quietened her frustration but watered down his quest to find his family and roots. She said, "Because your identity is you, yourself. A good, honest, truthful and empathetic human being, without caste and religious biases. Your religion is surgery, and you excel in that, you don't depend on any lineage for your introduction. Kalpana should have come with you, for what you are."

Reminiscing the conversation, he felt peace and solace, but was still lonely. He had never felt so lonely in the orphanage or even in the prison!

Prof Mishra, HOD of surgery summoned him in the office. As he entered his office, the Professor told him to close the door behind him and take a seat.

"Do you know this college is derecognised and you may not get paid anymore as JJ is in financial crisis?"

"Yes Sir, I have some inkling."

"The Government of Gujarat is partnering with private players to open 6 Medical colleges in the state. You better try for a job in one of them. I would advise, don't try for colleges near Ahmedabad or Baroda, there will be a lot of competition with locals who have connections. Better to opt for a smaller place where not many are willing to join." Advised the senior man.

"Thanks a lot for your valuable advice, Sir."

Prof Mishra was a talkative man, enjoyed talking of rumors and grapevine. He described the owner, JJ's war of words with the MCI strongman; the latter asked for a hefty bribe for arranging recognition for the college, and in turn, JJ gave him his piece of mind with the choicest of cuss words in Gujarati. This derecognition was said to be the result of that conversation. "Your experience certificate may not be valid for the next appointment." The professor warned.

Digpal participated in the conversation by nodding his head and an occasional "Yes Sir."

"I am going on a long leave to my home at Vadodara, Dean Mahant may also not be available after some days; You can collect your certificates from Prasad."

Digpal took leave from his senior, to plan for his next course of action.

OPD was routine. Hydrocoeles, goiters, peptic ulcers, liver abscesses, Buerger's disease and so on. A girl of about 10 years came to his OPD with her parents. She looked apparently healthy, went near enough so she could touch him, wearing a big grin. He then looked towards the parents and said excitedly, "Is she Lucy? really?"

"Yes uncle, I am Lucy." The girl said before her mother could respond.

"How is she doing?"

"She is doing very well, doctor; except, for a few weeks, she has to take laxatives to pass stools."

Digpal examined her, the abdominal scars were sound without any herniation and found that her anal opening had stenosed slightly. He explained to the parents that her anus has narrowed slightly and he would make it bigger. He gently dilated the anal openining with lubricated dilator and advised them to increase fibre intake in her meals. He was more than happy with the results; these are 'small dividends of a surgeon's life' he thought.

From his last four years experience of working in the tribal belt; he had observed certain differences in the disease pattern from urban areas. The incidence of anorectal problems, constipation, malignancies of rectum and colon, Gallbladder diseases, appendicitis was much less in the tribal belt, as modern fast food was unknown there. Carcinoma of breast too was rare, but if at all it occurred, they would report when the growth has either fungated or spread everywhere. GI cancers generally would land up with acute obstruction. However, incidence of gastric ulcers with perforations, liver diseases were common due to rampant consumption of hooch, 'tadi' and 'mahuva' alcoholic brews. Congenital anomalies were also common because of poor or complete lack of antenatal care. There were upsides too, they never demanded prenatal sex determination or female feticide, as gender discrimination and the superstition of compulsory last rites by the son, and the continuation of paternal lineage by the son, was non existent. The anxiety of marrying their daughters and arranging for dowry was also the prerogative of so-called 'high caste' and 'civilised' society of this country. Moreover, couples rarely came to consult for infertility.

In spite of the uncertainties, he wanted to continue working there, at least for a few more months for various reasons. His paediatric patients with congenital anomalies, where staged procedures are done, would be left in doldrums with incomplete surgical procedures. He did not want to leave them like this. The students were in the final year of their curriculum, they would be shifted to another college for their final examinations and their syllabus was yet to be completed. The teachers of the recipient college may not be interested in them, or they may become subjects of the fellow students' butt of jokes as they were students of a derecognised rural college.

After mulling over the situation, he decided to call the students for his proposal. Barring a few, most of the students were sincere and were keen to learn. Once the majority was there in the classroom, he expressed his plan,

"As you must be knowing that this college is on the verge of closing down and you may be shifted to colleges in Surat or Baroda. I wish you fare at par, or even better than the students of recipient institutes. We have yet to complete our syllabus of surgery; I have no idea about other subjects. I can survive here, without a salary, not more than two more months. If you all agree, we can have double and prolonged sessions of learning, seven days a week. Not only should you have clear concepts of the subject, but you should be able to express what you know, on paper and by speech; and for that we will have weekly assessment tests. You will have to write answers and also must be able to stand here and be able to speak in front of the whole class. I want your whole hearted cooperation." Saying this he waited for their response. There were murmurs in the room, then their representative Jay Parmar stood up, "Sir, we are ready, but we have a request, you will have to accept a token amount of 'guru dakshina' from us." Then Abhilash, the batch topper too, got up and said, "Yes Sir, please." And with him all the students stood up and repeated in chorus.

"I am overwhelmed with your request; my guru dakshina will be the feedback from the recipient colleges, about your excellent performance." His eyes were moist.

The next couple of months were gruelling, for him and the students. He had to finish off with all the staged surgeries of congenital anomalies and complete the corrective procedures of complications and had to conduct prolonged teaching sessions. He would conduct weekly tests and coax them to speak freely in front of an audience. He used to correct not only their subject but their diction and language as well.

His farewell from Pipalkheda was simple but emotional. PP Prasad, Prof Shinde, Amit and a few of other colleagues were present. There were no big lectures, only some hugs and handshakes by colleagues and 'feet touching' by students. Menu was very basic, as hardly anyone had extra money to spend.

He had already applied for teaching jobs in new semi government colleges and opted for remote places. He got an appointment as Associate Professor at a place, near the southern tip of Gujarat; a coastal town, called Tithalsar. During the interview, he was informed that he was appointed only because no one else was available for that college. The interviewer did not conceal that he was not fully eligible as he was coming from a de-recognized college of a god forsaken place. He did not mind the comment and accepted the appointment.

A day before he had to pack his luggage and leave for Tithalsar; there was a knock at his door at around 11 PM. Wondering who could be there at this hour, he opened the door and a shadow covered in black shawl pushed him aside and barged in.

"This is the sixth time I have tried to meet you in privacy, but did not get the opportunity. I have no seventh time, like the spider. I have come to bid a farewell." Savita said, removing the shawl. This time he did not tell her to leave, but closed the door; as he too was longing for a feminine company.

Before going back, she offered, "I can recommend JJ to pay you your pending salary, before you leave."

"And, if he asks, why are you favouring me, how will you explain?"

"That's my headache, I know how to get things done."

"Thanks and no, thanks; I don't need favours." Digpal replied.

She picked her shawl, covered herself completely and headed towards the door,

stopped and asked, "Was Diksha better than me…?"

"Now you are talking bullshit, she was only a friend." He answered angrily.

She laughed, opened the door and slipped in the dark.

# INITIUM NOVUM

In 2003, India was well into the 21 century. Electronic gadgets, colour televisions, computers and mobile (cell) phones were becoming commonplace. Because of the efforts and policies of previous finance ministers, results were showing. The infectious effect of high salaries in the IT industry could be seen in other sectors as well. A new upper middle class was emerging in the country.

He was surprised by the salary offered by the 'Morarji Desai Medical college' of Tithalsar town. It was almost four times that of Pipalkheda. The college was named after India's past PM, Shri Morarjibhai Desai who hailed from a nearby village of Tithalsar.

With his modest belongings when he reached Tithalsar; he noticed it was a serene, quiet town with lots of greenery and water bodies, some of them formed by the hightide of the Arabian sea. The national highway joining Delhi and Mumbai passed by it and had a railway station of the same route. South-East from it was an Industrial town, 30 kms away and southwards along the coast was the union territory of Daman.

He met the Dean of the college to submit his joining report. The Dean turned out to be an amicable and helpful person. He informed that for time being the college is running in a makeshift building, meant for nursing college; and the hospital is running in the old Government civil hospital building. The college, hospital and residential buildings were under construction, and Digpal was supposed to find his own accommodation. "Till you find your own living space, you can stay in the government circuit house," Dean said.

To reach the HOD of surgery, he had to wade through the melee of patients with their relatives, hospital staff running with gurneys and wheelchairs carrying patients of varying seriousness, nurses in their uniforms, and doctors with or without their white coats and stethoscopes. He could make out the surgeons, as they were not carrying their stethoscopes and were in informal dress. The corridor was as crowded as Surat or Patna railway station. 'This is the place, he will love to work'. Digpal thought.

The HOD, Professor Dayaram Parikh, turned out to be a soft spoken idealistic Khadi cled Gandhian, who welcomed him in the department, and explained to him the working pattern of the department. There were four units in the department; unit 1 was headed by the HOD, unit 2 by an associate professor Dr Rasiklal Patel, unit 3 would be looked after by Dr Digpal and since there was one associate less, unit 4 too was also supervised by the HOD. Each unit had a unit head, 2 assistant professors, 2 senior residents, 2 junior residents, as it was only the first year of the college and no fresh graduates were available.

The ground realities were interesting. The 2 assistant professors, Pritesh Patel and Yogesh Tandel, both local boys, turned out to be enthusiastic young men, who knew their job well and were hard working. He could not see any SRs and JRs! He was informed that SRs are local Private practitioners, who would come only on operation days, that too to hone their laparoscopy skills, on the poor patients of civil hospital. Their posting was only to fulfil the mandatory MCI requirement; similarly the JRs were also very irregular; they were fresh graduates preparing for PG entrance examination and were disinterested in their work. In the OPD he was assigned a separate office but he joined his 2 juniors in the work, as there was a long serpentine queue of patients.

In the surgery OPD, just beyond the entrance; behind a small table cluttered with investigation forms, patients' case papers and a stethoscope, sat a young junior resident (JR), who would write a short history of the patients and send them to Assistant Professors. A little distance behind the JR sat the 2 assistant professors, Pritesh Patel and Yogesh Tandel, sat side by side behind two tables joined together. Both of them had an iron stool beside them, for the patient to sit. Along the wall were placed two examination tables in a row to maintain the patient's privacy, hung a green curtain which had become dirty by repeated handling.

Another reason he sat with the 2 young men was, he wanted to learn the working pattern of the hospital. As for the academic part, there were no students for the surgeons to teach, as it was only the first year of the college. After one year the students would start coming to them for clinical teaching.

The treatment in the hospital was completely free of charge, even the meals were provided free to the patients, as it was a Government run hospital. Majority of the patients were from low socio economic strata and served a fairly large area. Since the town was on the railway main line, a big number of patients used to pour in from the neighbouring Maharashtra state and they sung praise for the kind of treatment and facilities provided by the Gujarat government and the then chief minister of the state.

While in OPD, he noticed a thin dark boy of about two years, holding the finger of his mother accompanied by her husband. They looked like manual labourers. They stood near Tandel who asked about the presenting complaints; in response, the mother removed the child's half pants and pointed towards his groin. "Oh, its undescended testis," mumbled Tandel, then spoke aloud "you will have to take the child to Surat Civil hospital; we don't do this here."

"Why do you want to refer him?" Digpal intervened.

"He has left sided undescended testis with hernia; we don't operate this here."

"Admit him and get routine investigations done; and post him on the next operation day." Tandel followed his advice.

When the family was sent to wards, Digpal said, "Now onwards do not refer any paediatric case; for that matter no case should be referred without my consent. They are poor people, they somehow reach this hospital from their village. Going beyond is not easy for them; we should try to solve their problem here only, as far as possible."

Tandel was pleased at the prospect of learning from this modest looking man.

The operation theatres were old like the building, but they were equipped with central oxygen, suction and modern integrated anesthesia workstations. General surgery OT was meant for one operation table, but to meet the workload, two tables were accommodated in the room. Two teams of Surgeons with nurses, OT boys and Anaesthetists, made it pretty crowded and a bit noisy; unlike the imagination of a layman who form its mental picture by movies and TV serials.

A good looking short lady, apparently in her forties, was fiddling with the buttons of the anaesthesia machine. "Dr Asmi Jain, HOD anesthesia and Ma'am, this is Dr Digpal, our new unit head." Pritesh introduced them. After exchanging formalities, Digpal asked, "I will be doing his orchiopexy with herniotomy, what will you be giving her?"

"Caudal epidural." She informed.

"Fine with me."

By the time Digpal reached the table, scrubbed and gowned; the child was already anaesthetised and the nurse was painting the operative site with antiseptic.

"I will need a number fifteen blade and bipolar cautery."

Tandel stood right behind him on a short stool and spoke in his ear,

"Will you explain the steps of surgery Sir? Actually, the college from where I did my PG, is a big one in the capital city and we had no exposure to different sub-specialities. We had separate departments of Paediatric, Onco, Uro and so on; but here we have to do all kinds of cases."

"Don't worry, will narrate during surgery; I am fortunate to be from the pre-subspeciality era." Digpal smiled behind the mask.

Special paediatric instruments were not available in the OT, only a few mosquito arteries and two Adson's forceps with bad tips were kept on an instrument trolley with an adult set of instruments.

"I prefer a transverse crease incision, commencing from just above the pubic tubercle." While speaking, he incised and cauterized the small bleeders, incised the fascia and picked up a soft whitish tissue in his forceps, "Undescended testis is associated with an inguinal hernia, unless the organ is very high up in the abdomen." He picked up the sac and cautiously incised it between two forceps, "The small testis is hiding inside the sac." He picked up the small organ with a bit separated epididymis and curled up cord, "Now comes the tricky part; the wall of sac is blended with the cord and needs to be separated to get some length; for that we can inject normal saline just behind sac wall to separate the two."

"Do we have any lap cases today?" A bald head with a few strands of hair on it, jutted inside the OT through partially opened flaps of door.

"Ya, there are 3." Tandel answered, in his high pitched thin voice, "Me and Pritesh will do one each; you can remove the appendix." The bald head disappeared.

"He is Dr Vinayak, senior resident in our unit, a busy private practitioner; comes here to practice lap surgery on our poor patients." Tandel did not like him, it seemed.

"Seems, we won't get lunch till 4." Asmi mumbled. Though there were ten Anaesthetist in the department; she had to stay to supervise, especially the lap cases.

"The cord should not be under tension, or the testis will atrophy; the testicular artery is already very thin and delicate;

now we will keep the testis in subdartos pouch and..."

"Nobody is listening; Tandel Sir has left for his lap chole." the nurse interrupted.

After closing; he looked towards the head end, "Thanks Dr Asmi for the excellent anaesthesia."

"Thanks to you Dr Digpal; frankly, I got the opportunity to inject a caudal epidural, after fifteen years; after my residency days."

On another table, Pritesh Patel was slowly dissecting the calot's triangle to skeletonise the cystic duct and artery. Looking toward the monitor Digpal commented, "You are dissecting beautifully, and the magnified organs look lovely."

"Yes, they do." Pritesh said, and continued slowly.

'How difficult it is for the older generation, to dissect, while looking towards the monitor, we were taught to keep your eyes towards our hands and operative field'. Digpal thought.

"Unfortunately, I don't have the patience like you," he commented.

Next case in the list was an obese middle aged woman, having a large post hysterectomy incisional hernia. Digpal was to operate upon her.

"I will assist you, in the hernia; will finish this off in another twenty minutes. I have heard, you are good at hernias." Pritesh said.

"Fine with me, it will take that much time to commence."

Ragini Desai, Assistant Professor was the Anaesthetist for the obese hernia case. She induced and then connected her to the ventilator after adjusting respiratory rate, volume and amount of volatile drugs. How difficult it might be for Diksha, working in the meagre facilities of Pipalkheda, Digpal wondered.

The patient had a huge belly, which looked bigger due to the hernia. Some part of hernia had been reduced inside by the relaxant administered by the Anaesthetist. It was a lower abdominal hernia, following hysterectomy, done five years back, through a vertical incision.

"Expect lot of adhesions." Digpal commented. By the time he scrubbed, Patel too was ready to assist.

With a clean sweep of the knife, he gave an elliptical incision around the thinned out skin; "These vertical incisions are notorious and ugly."

"Gradually everything will be done by laparoscopy." Pritesh said.

"Maybe, as long as patient doesn't suffer surgeon's long learning curve and ego, of not converting to open, even if things go out of hand." Digpal responded.

"Maybe." Patel knew the senior man's bias against Lap surgery; so did not take the discussion further.

It took them more than two hours to clear the adhesions; then closed the peritoneum and Digpal began to make space between hernial ring and peritoneum.

"This dissection can be avoided by onlay graft." Patel said.

"As far as feasible, I would prefer inlay graft only; it gives mechanical advantage and chances of recurrence are very very less."

He passed four number 1 polypropylene sutures, one each in four directions, to tuck the mesh below the heria ring, then with one zero polypropylene sutured the edge all around; placed two thin, perforated suction drains above the mesh; "Will you close Pritesh?"

"Sure Sir."

Digpal went to the surgeon's room and asked the wardboy to

bring a cup of tea for him; he had started feeling at home in the new set-up.

All in all, there were ten cases for surgery that day; Yogesh Tandel did the second lap chole, and lap appendectomy was done by Vinayak who removed a near normal looking appendix in two hours. 'What's wrong in removing the appendix, with a two inch low crease incision in fifteen minutes! The incision is almost invisible and results are excellent.' Digpal thought, but did not say anything, lest he would be labelled retrograde.

Gradually Digpal made new friends and acquaintances; had a very good rapport with his colleagues in his unit, and even other units. He never hesitated to help juniors from other units too, whenever they needed help. He learnt a few things about his dipartment, like Prof Dayaram was a good surgeon but seldom got time for surgery, because of administrative burden; Dr Rasiklal, the other associate and unit head was least interested in surgery and rarely scrubbed for surgery, he had some chronic ailments and aptitude problems not properly understood.

During an impromptu meeting in the hospital canteen, Digpal proposed that they should have monthly dinner meetings, where they could discuss clinical cases and interesting surgeries in an informal atmosphere.

"But where? Seems, you already have something in mind." Paresh Makvan, a very senior surgeon, who still was assistant surgeon, as he joined teaching quite late; asked curiously. He had heard that Makwan only ran unit two, as Rasiklal was disinterested to lead.

"Can we go to Daman, on every last Saturday evening, for the academic feast?" Digpal asked and almost everyone jumped to the idea; as Daman was a union territory and booze and non-vegetarian food was available aplenty there. They decided to ask the HOD too to join.

"He may not like the idea; he is a staunch Gandhian, teatotaller and vegetarian." Tandel opined.

"Still we should ask." Digpal said.

Thinking, there would be a lot of academic discussion, the professor agreed. Rasiklal Patel declined to come, as per Makwan who was part of his unit. "He does not come to any parties or meetings, and has some reasons of his own."

The first meeting was quite disciplined, many of them narrated interesting cases. As the dinner was to begin, Tandel asked Prof Parikh if they could have a drink, and he said, "Go ahead, I will have a soft drink." Everybody else gleefully ordered his choice of hard drink and bitings. Daman had a good choice of seafood for bitings. After the second round of drinks, the surgeons became louder and more boastful, but still everything was within decent limits. After finishing his helping of vegetarian food, the professor suddenly remembered some important commitment and excused himself from the meeting.

After the Professor left, the conversation became louder, more boastful, dotted with the choicest of Hindi and Gujarati cuss words. Someone started singing and then there was no stopping series of Bollywood songs. One practitioner asked,

"Dr Digpal, you are so senior, might have done lot many surgeries, you didn't narrate any."

"Mine was not a very illustrious career, nothing much to tell." Digpal said with a smile.

The group dispersed past midnight; the meeting was a big success; majority appreciated Digpal's idea.

With the help of an OT nurse, he could get a small single bedroom house near the hospital. The owner had gone abroad and wanted to rent it out to some good person. The house had a fully furnished small sitting room, a kitchen and a small bedroom;and was situated in a middle class locality.

Across the narrow street, in front of his house lived one Ramakant Mistry with his wife Madhuri, a teenage daughter and his old Father. He found them helping and affectionate; often was invited for tea and snacks, whenever time permitted.

Once Ramakant's old Father called him and said, "Doctor, I had a burn on my leg about three years back; Madhuri is dressing it regularly but it is refusing to heal; can you do something about it?"

Digpal had a look and felt, it was a Curling's ulcer.

"Can you come to the hospital tomorrow? Let's see what can be done."

Next day, he removed a small piece of tissue from the edge of the ulcer for histopath, and sent it to the lab.

Seven days passed after that but there was no sign of histopath report, coming from the laboratory. He decided to go himself and find out where it was stuck. Since it was an old building, there were haphazard extensions. Lab too was in such an extension, near the hospital canteen. As he entered the lab and asked about the report, the clerk cum technician indicated towards the next door, "Ask madam."

As he entered the room marked 'Histopathology' on a small plate above the door, he could see a lady bent on a microscope, her open lock of black hair cut upto D-12 level were covering her face because of her posture. Through the hair her long fair neck and profile of fair complexioned cheek was visible. Without looking up from the microscope, she asked, "Yes?"

"Ma'am, I..."

"Wait a minute." She interrupted him, without lifting her head. He was becoming impatient like a typical surgeon; when she straightened her head and turned 180 degrees on her swivel chair to face him. Oh! She was so beautiful; Digpal dumbstruck for a few seconds. She had a question in her eyes; 'they are so expressive' he thought.

"I am Dr Digpal, associate in surgery, came in connection of HP report of one Ganpat Mistry; it's more than 7 days."

"Kamna Mehta, Assistant Professor. I am sorry for the delay; I was on leave so all the HP work is pending; why don't you have a seat?" She indicated towards a revolving steel stool. Suddenly, he was in no hurry to leave. When she smiled, he noticed a row of even white teeth behind her shapely lips; there was a shallow dimple in the middle of chin; and as she had stopped looking through the scope, she wore thin rimmed glasses on her sharp nose making her beautiful eyes look even more attractive. There was no bindi or vermilion and was not wearing a mangalsutra, he quickly noticed.

"I think, I had a look into the slide you are talking about," she searched in the paper, she was scribbling, "Yes, Ganpatbhai has a squamous cell carcinoma of skin, well differentiated and slow growing."

"Yup, I suspected Curling's ulcer." Digpal commented.

With her facial features, complexion and accent of language, she must be from North India, he guessed. 'Will find more, if I get the opportunity,' he thought.

"I have been here for three months, came to the lab for the first time; it's beautiful."

"What is beautiful about it?" She gave out a small laugh. He wanted to say 'you', "Well... because it is near the canteen; can we have a cup of coffee?" He offered.

"Thanks, some other time; I have a lot of pending work; will send the printed report to your department."

'You are going too fast', he warned himself. He reluctantly left the lab to join his juniors in OPD.

After finishing their work, when they were having having their cup of tea; Digpal brought her name in the conversation,

"Ganpat Mistry has SCC, had been to the path lab and talked to Ms Mehta."

"Isn't she beautiful?" Smiled Yogesh "She is a divorcee, comes from Mumbai and joined about a year back."

"Oh!" Digpal was curious but did not show that. Was he happy to know, she was a divorcee!

In the next list, he did a wide excision of Ganpatrao's SCC and put a skin graft on the raw area, fixing it with a quick dissolving fine suture material.

"You did not keep the graft in normal saline?" Tandel asked.

"I don't. I think, if we let the natural body fluids remain on the inside of the graft, it will take up much better." Digpal opined.

Next case was a big prostate, more than 150 gms, as per sonologist's assessment. The visiting urosurgeon did not turn up that day, as he was busy in his private hospital; moreover, he would have not risked removing a big prostatic adenoma with the old resectoscope which kept on going out of order repeatedly.

"Let's refer this case to Surat medical college." Pritesh said.

"Why should we?" Digpal intervened "We can do a Freyer's, here only."

Pritesh being senior most Assistant Professor, due for associateship in an year, did not like his opinion being turned down. Tandel volunteered to assist and confessed that they were not exposed to this surgery.

"Good; this way you can get the feel of the gland, hands on." Digpal said.

He explained every step of the conventional Prostatectomy to his junior; explaining every step in detail and letting him get the feel of the tissues. After a big adenoma, the size of a shade smaller than a tennis ball was removed; Vinayak entered in, peeped in the operative field and asked, "What's being cut?"

"Freyer's prostatectomy." Tandel answered.

"Primitive." Vinayak said and winked towards the anesthetist; noody responded.

Tandel whispered inside his mask, "*Saala chu\*\*ya.*"

They had a long list of cases; Tandel quickly connected foley's with continuous irrigation and left to scrub for the next case. Digpal too began to scrub for penoscrotal junction hypospadias.

Whenever he got an opportunity, he would slip out to the pathology department and Kamna too seemed to be waiting for him. Generally they would go to the canteen to have tea together; and with every meeting they began to know more and more about each other.

"If you don't mind asking me, what went wrong about your relations with Mr Mehta? You may not answer my question, if you don't want to." Once he asked.

She gave out a short laugh, "He is not Mr Mehta, he is Mr Bhatia, a chartered accountant in Mumbai. We met in Delhi, when I was studying in Lady Harding Medical College and he was doing his CA in the same area; we used to commute by the same Metro every day; became friends and one day he proposed. He was well behaved, tall, fair, handsome and with a bright future; moreover we are also Punjabi Mehtas; so there was no reason to refuse, I readily agreed." Kamna continued, "After marriage we shifted to Mumbai, where, after some experience with a renowned CA, he started his own firm and was doing very well. I also got a job as a pathologist in HN hospital, and was getting good experience there. We were married for 6 years, then…" She kept quiet and Digpal also did not poke any further. After a while they resumed conversation on more general topics.

# POENA SINE CULPA

That Saturday was emergency duty for unit 3. As per protocol, SR is first on call, AP second on call and associate was seldom required to come; but SRs rarely attended any emergency, so AP used to be first on call and associate was called for bad cases or medical students and staff members.

One AM, his phone rang; Hamid Shaikh, a new AP, was on duty; he sounded worried, "Sir, there is a bad head injury, accompanied by a rowdy group; can you come?"

"In ten minutes." He responded.

In the casualty, Hamid had already started a 10% Dextrose drip, a shot of antibiotic and steroid each. Two staff members were trying to control the delirious patient. He was around 35 years, shabbily dressed, sporting a short beard, was semi conscious and restless, pupils were equal and constricted, chest was clear, abdomen had some free fluid, a hard liver with sharp edge and was smelling of cheap country liquor. There was a small lacerated wound on the parietal region with a big haematoma.

"Can we get an emergency head scan?" Digpal asked.

"I have already inquired; our machine is out of order; we have to send the patient to a private centre; and they will charge."

"I will talk to the relatives," the senior man said.

It was a group of about ten persons of almost the same age as the patient; all of them drunk; they were talking and abusing loudly.

"Babubhai's condition is not good; we can assess properly, only after the effect of alcohol wears off; he needs an emergency head scan for which he is to be sent to a private centre and they will charge for it." Digpal tried to explain the situation.

There was some discussion amongst them, then one of them said, "We are just acquaintances, he is from Bihar and lives alone here; we can't afford a scan, you treat him as you can."

He told Hamid, "Watch him closely for fresh signs; he may require tracheostomy; can bleed, as he has cirrhosis also."

Next day, his agitation had gone but his coma deepened, pupils dilated and stopped reacting; respiration was irregular. Hamid had already done tracheostomy and the nurse was suctioning it, at regular intervals. By afternoon, he was put on a ventilator. At around 11 PM, Dr Dayaram called up,

"There seems to be some problem with your patient with a head injury in the ICU; better attend him immediately."

"Yes Sir." He responded, and jumped out of bed.

Outside the ICU, a small mob of 25 to 30 men had assembled and were talking loudly in an agitated manner. In the ICU, the duty doctor was writing notes on the case sheets.

"He expired half an hour back; since it is a medico legal case, we have to get his post mortem; but the mob outside is not ready to listen and is in a violent mood." The duty doctor sounded worried and scared. There was one guard outside, two nurses and a wardboy.

"I will talk to them." Digpal went outside and called, "2 of you, please come here"

About ten people came towards him.

"Babubhai had a bad head injury and was critical; we tried our best but could not save him; as it's a police case, we have to request a post mortem, and for..."

Before he could complete his sentence, one of them shouted,

"He is the one, they killed our brother and now want to

mutilate his body." And something hit his head; another stone was hurled which hit the window pane, shattering the glass. The guard, duty doctor and nurses closed the ICU door behind him and hid inside the doctors' duty room. His face was wet with blood gushing from forehead wound; as he pressed his hand on it to stop bleeding, someone kicked in his abdomen. He fell down and some more goons joined the party of kicking and abusing him. Before he lost consciousness, he could hear the police siren.

He woke up in the surgical ICU, his wound on forehead sutured and dressed, a drip was running through an angiocath introduced in his forearm vein and he could hear the beep of a monitor connected to him. For a few minutes, the faces around him were blurred, then slowly he could make out the calm face of Dr Dayaram, tense and fidgety Hamid Shaikh, Yogesh tandel without his naughty smile and worried face of Kamna . He turned his head upwards where Asmi Jain was standing on head end with laryngoscope blade jutting out of her apron pocket. Noticing him regain consciousness everybody smiled.

"You had a concussion; chest is clear and there are swellings on your flanks; will get a portable USG and lab workup to rule out internal injury; but don't worry, you will be fine." The HOD spoke in his usual calm manner and left the SICU. Digpal uttered a weak 'thank you' while the former was leaving.

"See, the beautiful pathology department is here to investigate." Tandel whispered in his ear and winked.

"Shut up, " he spoke in a weak voice, then turning towards Asmi he asked, "How come you are here at this time? No case in OT today?"

"The whole staff is on flash strike; this kind of behaviour can not be tolerated." Asmi spoke with a tinge of anger.

A nurse came to his bed followed by a wardboy who was holding a bottle and a urine pot. "Doctor you have to give urine for checking." She spoke in a heavy south Indian accent, "All of you leave him alone." She encircled the bed with a mobile screen.

After an hour Kamna was back with his reports.

"Reports are okay except for plenty of RBCs in urine." She said waving the report.

"The buggers generously kicked my flanks," he gave out a short laugh, "but luckily my spleen didn't give way, thanks to the bony cage." Looking towards her worried face he added, "Why looking so tense, me not gonna die so soon; most of the renal injuries heal by conservative treatment; there is not much bleeding, my hemoglobin not falling."

She sat on a metal stool near his bed, softly holding his hand between the palms of her hands. The beeping sound of the monitor suddenly became more frequent, "My pulse starts racing by your touch, here is the evidence." He smiled. Continuing holding his hand, she spoke seriously, "In this short period you have become very important to me; have started liking you; I must accept, I used to wait eagerly for your visits to the lab and our tea meetings."

"See, how dark my hand looks in your hands; think again! Maybe when you listen about my past and background, your thoughts may change."

"That's not very important to me." She replied.

"Still." He said.

Their conversation was interrupted by rolling in of a portable USG machine on a trolley pushed by a Radiology technician followed by a plump young man, who smilingly addressed Kamna with a 'Hi Dr Mehta'.

"Hello Dr Sheth." Kamna responded "Dr Mukund Sheth, AP radiology and Mukund, hope you know your patient."

"Yes; the famous surgeon Dr Digpal." Mukund said, applying jelly to the probe.

"And, when did I become famous?" Digpal asked, "Since

being thrashed?"

"Don't say that; you are the talk of the hospital, for your knowledge, surgical skill and helping attitude." She spoke with pride in her voice, as if she herself was being praised.

"Liver, spleen and other viscera looking normal." Mukund was giving a running commentary while sliding his probe on his abdomen. "Except a haematoma around the convex surface of your left kidney, but no active bleeder." Digpal and Kamna both thanked him in unison.

As Digpal's vitals were stable, he was shifted to a private room facing the front of the hospital. Advantage of that was, the duo could get some privacy. He slowly and systematically narrated about his early days in orphanage, his medical education by scholarship money and charity by some kind donors; His Vidurpur experience, his failed love affair with Kalpana, about his dear friend Ballu, and death of Sarang.

When he mentioned about his childhood, her eyes were moist; and when he narrated the incident of Kalpana's refusal, her reaction was, "She was an idiot."

She keenly listened about the corporate hospital experience; commitment with Jose; the drama of reappearance of Kalpana; backing out of Jose; the false allegation and jail term. She commented, "You have gone through a lot."

"Life is no bed of roses." He smiled; then continued with his Pipalkheda experience and the friends he made there. Somehow, he avoided mentioning Shabnum and Savita and told himself that they were inconsequential in his life story.

Suddenly he noticed something, "Why are you not going to the lab? Are you on leave?"

"All the doctors are still on indefinite strike, this is the third day; it won't be called off until the authorities take some stern action against the culprits and assure safety of hospital staff." She replied.

"Oh! I thought it's only for a day." He slowly got up and walked up to the window. A small group of young doctors was sitting in front of the main entrance; some of them holding placards. Scattered on the open lawns, in front of the hospital, were patients with their attending relatives and friends in different postures. Most of the patients were either lying down on mats, dirty bed sheets or sitting on bare ground.

"Can you help me go there?" He indicated towards the open ground, in front of the hospital.

"I will have to ask the HOD." She was reluctant.

"Please." He pleaded.

"OK then; but only in a wheelchair." He readily agreed.

She wheeled her to the front entrance where the young doctors had gathered. As the duo reached their, the young doctors stood up, and began to shout slogans,

"We want justice." "Punish the culprits." "Stop violence against doctors."

He stayed with them for some time, thanked them, then asked Kamna, "Can you take me to the open ground?"

Amid the scattered lot, were patients of fractures; one with gangrene of lower limb; some of them orthopneic due to cardiac or respiratory problems; a teenage girl with a big goiter; a middle aged man with distended abdomen and so on.

He came back to his group of colleagues. Sitting on the wheelchair, he addressed them with folded hands- "Dear friends, I greatly appreciate the support and solidarity shown by all of you, as a reaction to this unfortunate incident. I fully endorse that nobody has the right to manhandle the well meaning medical and para medical fraternity; but please, do not punish these suffering people because of some goons..." As he was speaking, policemen on duty, laymen from the attendants and journalists from local TV channels surrounded him and began video recording; at the same time they heard the siren and could see a motorcade coming towards the hospital. From a luxury car alighted the Health minister of state surrounded by bodyguards and bureaucrats. He promised the striking doctors and Digpal, a very stern action against the culprits; also promised them of posting some policemen in the hospital for the security of doctors. There were some heated discussions by the young medicose, but the wily politician convinced them to call off the strike. Everybody knew that many of the promises were false, typical of politicians; 'but this is how the world works', Digpal mused.

# POSITIVUM MUTATIO

Back in the room, when Digpal was alone, he analysed Kamna's reactions to his story. She was the first one, who was not taken aback by knowing that his last name was Joseph, about his bringing up and his anonymous family; his past history of imprisonment and his financial status. And then he was very sure, beyond any doubt in his mind, that she was the one, he wanted to share his life for as long as he would live.

What followed was surprisingly smooth. After a week, when he recovered reasonably; he decided to propose to her. As she came into his room and like every day, began to open the tiffin; he spoke with some effort, "Kamna."

She asked in a most casual way, "Have you thought of some date?"

"What date?" He asked, surprised.

"Date of our wedding, what else?" She smiled. And they both laughed and laughed.He was suddenly very hungry after a long time. She bent and gave a peck on his cheek.Then he noticed that they never went beyond occasionally holding each others' hand; unlike his previous outings! 'Has he grown old', he wondered. He will turn fifty in the coming year.

Though still feeling a bit weak, he was back to work two weeks after the violent episode. He would sit in the surgeons' room in OT premises, instructing his unit to call him only when necessary. One of the cases on that day was of bladder calculi, one of the simplest of surgeries. Hamid being junior most was going to operate upon the middle aged man. The plain X-ray was a bit unusual, 5 calculi of varying size were arranged like beads of a garland, the biggest being the size of a betel nut.

Hamid opened the bladder, held one of the calculus in stone holding forceps, but it refused to come out; he tried another one, same result. Hamid called Pritesh for help, he told he will be scrubbing for a lap chole; Yogesh had gone to ENT OT to attend to some 'on table' emergency there. Hamid sent a nurse to summon Digpal, who came and peeped in the bladder, "Are they in a diverticulum?"

"No, but they seem to be attached to something." Hamid said. Digpal scrubbed and put his finger in the bladder. He felt a string attached to calculi, reaching the inferolateral wall of the bladder. He followed the string, coming out of the bladder and passing through the medial end of the conjoint tendon! He recognised the 'string' as polypropylene suture, divided it outside the bladder and pulled it in and removed it, along with the chain of calculi formed on it.

"Hamid dear, that's why, we should always be sure that the bladder is empty, or drained by an indwelling cath, before hernia repair. See there is a hernia repair scar on that side. The surgeon, unknowingly passed the suture through the bladder while doing a Bassini's repair; and that formed a nidus for formation of calculi; now close everything."

"Thanks Sir, it was interesting." Hamid replied.

It was a long operation list, as usual. Vinayak and one Dr Sunil Dhodiya, both private practitioners, on the post of SRs, who would come to the Govt. hospital to hone their laparoscopy skills, were preparing for a lap appendectomy of a very thin and emaciated young lady. Her abdominal wall was so thin that the light of scope could be seen clearly through it!

"A 2 inch crease incision would be more than enough to knock out her appendix in less than 15 minutes." Looking towards the patient, Digpal commented.

"We want to practice lap appendix, you have any problem?" An irritated Vinayak retorted.

"Go ahead and enjoy." He said and went back to the room; he was still feeling weak.

He went back to the OT after an hour, and the duo were still searching for the appendix. Digpal looked towards the monitor and was suddenly interested in the case.

One of the two caught hold of a chord-like structure and told excitedly, "I have got the appendix." Digpal looked towards the monitor keenly and spoke in a firm voice,

"Stop, and leave that structure; and don't do anything; I am scrubbing." Listening the fag end of Digpal's sentence, the Anaesthetist took an audible sigh of relief, uttering a long "Haash!"

"What you are holding is not the appendix."

"But we had identified the cecum as well." Dhodiya objected.

"That is not cecum, it is dilated hypertrophied ileum, seems to be a case of chronic obstruction at I/C junction; remove the scopes." He could not hide his anger.

Digpal opened her abdomen through a right paramedian incision; did a right hemicolectomy with ileo-transverse anastomosis.

"It's a case of ileocecal tuberculosis giving rise to chronic obstruction; you would have killed her, had you dissected and cut the mesentery." The two surgeons did not utter a word; neither an apology, nor a word of thanks. 'Nobody seems to have inculcated any manners in these arrogant surgeons; and they are brought up in happy families, unlike me!' Digpal wondered.

The last case was a thirty years old man, lean and thin, chronic smoker, having Buerger's disease and dry gangrene of a leg. Digpal, Pritesh, Tandel and Hamid; all four of them stood around the patient, to decide the level of amputation; which was not easy. The limb looked alive upto the middle of leg; but all the major pulsations, except a weak femoral, were absent; even the doppler was not of much help.

"Let's hold the amputation for a few more days; and do a lumbar sympathectomy first." Digpal said.

"Who does Lumbar sympathectomy nowadays for TAO?" Pritesh opined with some sarcasm "Even during our PG, we never saw anybody doing a lumbar sympathectomy."

"You can see now." Digpal smiled "It may not have any effect on the diseased arteries but the healthy collaterals will dilate and help us decide the level of amputation and the stump will heal better; moreover, it will give you a good idea of retroperitoneal dissection and structures."

"I will assist." Tandel said, "Me too." Hamid was enthusiastic, "But explain to us the steps."

Under spinal anesthesia, with the patient placed in lateral position, the surgeon cleanly placed a four inch incision in the flank, cutting the skin and fascia; patient was devoid of any fat; split the oblique muscles in their direction, and asked the two assistants to retract the muscles. "Can you identify the peritoneum and its reflection from the posterior abdominal wall?"

"Clearly," agreed Tandel.

"You don't have to use any instrument to separate the peritoneum from the posterior abdominal wall." Saying that, he quickly used his hands to push the peritoneum forwards, keeping his left hand on the retroperitoneum. Then he told Hamid to gently retract the peritoneum with viscera, anteriorly.

"You can see the psoas muscle running obliquely from the vertebral column; the major vessels, ureter, lower pole of kidney and so on."

"Beautifully seen." Hamid agreed.

"Just medial to the border of psoas and erector spinae, lies the sympathetic chain; we will leave the first lumbar behind and remove the second and third ganglia with the chain between them."

"Why leave first?"

"He won't ejaculate, if you cut that." Digpal replied.

After the closure, Tandel felt the limb with the back of his hand, "It's already warm."

"It may be because of spinal given by Dr Desai; let's check after it wears off." Digpal said.

"Yes; it will take its own time; your surgery was over in thirty minutes." Anaesthetist was impressed.

"Now we can amputate the limb after a few days, giving him a good stump for prosthesis," then addressing the patient he warned, "Hariram, you continue smoking and your other limb will also be gone."

Things were changing, and they were changing for good; both in Digpal's life and college. A new state of art building of the Medical college and hospital was near completion. The new operation theatre complex had a proper surgeon's room, a changing room for every speciality and modern modular OTs. His personal life was also coming on track; work atmosphere was good, colleagues genial and co-operative; and his love life was going great; but looking into his past experiences, in this matter, he was keeping his fingers crossed!

Kamna and Digpal had some discussion regarding the rituals and day of wedding. She wanted the wedding on an auspicious day to be decided by 'Muhurat' and by Hindu rituals. Digpal was skeptical about the rituals and *muhurat*; he said, "I don't believe in these superstitions; however if you insist, I have no problem with the Hindu *vidhi*; but first we can do a legal registered marriage then I will get it approved by any of the gods of your preference. By the way, your first wedding might have been done by proper rituals and on an auspicious day with horoscopes matched, and I need not remind you of the outcome." Listening to this, her expressions turned somber;

"I am sorry Kamna, it was rude of me." He apologised.

"Rude, but right. Okay, I am convinced." Holding his hand she told.

Ultimately they agreed for court marriage on a week day, then *'saptapadi'* in an Hindu temple followed by a reception dinner on Sunday. They decided a date of the coming month; as he was in a hurry to get wed-locked before he turned 50. They decided to take 5 days' leave for the wedding and agreed that they will go to Indore for three days, for their Honeymoon.

The very next day, the Dean called him and instructed him to go to Mumbai, for the purchase of some surgical instruments and select the latest equipment for operation theatres.

Digpal asked Kamna to come along; she hesitated for a while, as she had unpleasant memories of her life in the mega city.

"This time, you are going with a better company; moreover it's a very big city, you may not encounter any of your past relatives; the city doesn't belong to them." With some coaxing, she agreed. Since it was only a day trip, they did not book any hotel.

On the way to Mumbai, his memories of the trip to the city with Kalpana, came back. Vidurpur to Mumbai was a long journey, in a general unreserved compartment, in which they were sitting, sticking together, waves of excitement passing through their bodies with every movement of the train. This time, the journey was only a little over two hours, in an air-conditioned coach, and they were not getting hyper excited but were spontaneously holding each other's hand without trying to find an excuse to do so. Looking outside the window, he reminisced about Kalpana's passionate kiss at her uncle's Andheri residence, bringing a smile on his lips, Kamna noticed that, "Kalpana?" She asked; he did not say anything.

"First love is difficult to forget." She said without any shade of envy.

"Yes, but I don't believe in brooding over missed opportunities, what is bygone is bygone, best is to look forward; and the 'forward' is beautiful and promising." He smiled and squeezed her soft hand.

They got down at the crowded Mumbai central station and suddenly Kamna shrieked, "My purse, my purse." Digpal noticed a short, thin teenager running with her purse; he tried to chase the boy but the latter vanished in the crowd.

"What was in the purse?" Digpal asked.

"My whole month's salary, credit card, identity card and the purse itself was Gucci." Her eyes were moist.

"Let's go to the police post, they generally know these goons; take heart." He tried to console her. It was a long platform and the police post was near the entrance. They proceeded towards the entrance, when he felt a hand on his shoulder.

"Hey *dacter*, how are you?" He jerked and looked towards a smiling, thin, tall figure, in tight jeans on his stick like legs and a duplicate Nike T shirt on his barrel chest. Digpal took a few seconds to recognise him, then shouted with excitement, "Tidda!"

"Thank God you recognized me; but you are looking worried and *bhabhji* is looking very upset?"

Digpal explained the incident.

"Don't worry, your friend knows all the punters of this area." Tidda spoke with an air of overconfidence, "You and *bhabhiji* relax on this bench, and wait for a few minutes; no need to go to the police." He indicated towards an empty bench and vanished in the crowd. Kamna asked curiously, "Who is he, with a funny name, Tidda?"

"Oh!" Digpal hesitated for a while, "My prison friend; actually his name is Manoj Verma."

"I see; are you sure, he will be able to…" And before she could complete her sentence; Tidda reappeared with a bag hanging in his thin hand, "Please check if everything is there, or I give that punter a nice thrashing." A boy with two disposable cups, was following Tidda who said, "Have some coffee, you will feel better." They did not refuse.

"Everything is there; thank you very much," Kamna said in a relieved tone.

Digpal and Tidda chatted for some time; the former asked about other jailmates.

"And how is Jaleel Khan?"

"He is no more; his abdomen became very big and he started vomiting blood," Tidda informed.

"Oh, so sad." 'Must be cirrhosis of the liver', Digpal thought.

After a while they bid good bye to Tidda and proceeded to their destination.

During the trip, they had all the time to discuss their likes and dislikes; and with past experience, Kamna knew small things matter in married life.

Kamna was vegetarian, but did not mind him having non-vegetarian food, "I can even prepare omelets and boil eggs, my Father was non-vegetarian." She said, "I love vegetarian food of North and non-vegetarian food of South India; especially seafood of coastal Maharashtra." Digpal opined, "Our country has a mind boggling variety of cuisine; even I can cook some, moreover I am great at household work."

"Relieved to learn that." She said and both of them laughed.

When she asked if he liked to travel, he said, "As yet I have travelled only to attend conferences, that too in India; never had enough money to go overseas, you might have seen other countries?"

"Many." was her answer. He knew she belonged to an affluent family.

"Which country did you like most?" He asked.

"Switzerland; but our own Himachal and Kashmir are equally beautiful; but the difference is infrastructure and cleanliness."

"Yes, cleanliness is a big issue with us; especially spitting is a disgraceful habit."

During their return journey, only two of them were there in the first class coupe'. They were quiet when Kamna suddenly asked, "Do you like children?"

Digpal smiled, "Very much. I like paediatric surgery because I love children; they are honest patients, they will cry only when hungry or in pain; but the poor things suffer many a times because of the foolishness and misplaced emotional decisions of their..."

"I am asking about, 'our' children; you obsessive surgeon; and not your paediatric patients."

"Oh! sorry; and yes, I would like to have our own, as many as possible; but age is against us."

She did not smile or laugh, "I am sorry pal, I didn't tell you before; I can not bear your children. My subtotal Hysterectomy was done for multiple submucous fibroids with intractable bleeding; I don't possess a uterus now." He listened keenly, "My husband Nitin said I am useless now and asked me to agree for divorce by mutual consent. My in-laws too were of the opinion that if I can not give a successor to the family, what use am I?" Digpal held her hand firmly between both of his hands and kissed it.

"That is not everything, my love; we can adopt a baby or

even 2." He smiled reassuringly "There are a lot of orphans out there, they need parents, a family. Who else knows this better than me?"

She looked relieved, "You really have a golden heart dear."

"And your ovaries are intact," he winked, "so, the hormones are still kicking!" Both of them laughed together.

Back in his small apartment, once again, he stood in front of a full-length mirror, like he did 25 years back, when he fell for Kalpana; switched on all the lights of the room and keenly analyzed himself. Some strands of gray were visible in his jet black mustaches and whiskers and some silver was seen on the frontal part of scalp. "So, you are the would be bridegroom! You look more like a Father of one! Anyway, atlast, congratulations." He pulled his small paunch in and turned to look into his profile, and caressed his 'little lady' birthmark, near the root of his neck, as if talking to his birthmark!

In the common room for teachers; Kaushal Patel (In that part of country, every second person's last name was 'Patel'), Assistant Professor from unit II, proposed, "Since Dr Digpal is getting married a month after, let's organise a pre-wedding surgical meet cum party, this weekend, at Daman; not sure he will be allowed to attend such parties post marital." Everybody laughed, clapped and agreed. Seems, surgeons keep finding excuses to party; a rare idea where everybody agrees unanimously!

"As usual, we can discuss surgical cases, tips from our senior colleagues and I propose, this time we can include some senior practicing surgeons as well." Pritesh suggested; and nobody objected, as the parties used to be contributory.

Prof Dayaram expressed his inability to attend, for other commitments; everybody knew he was not very comfortable in such an atmosphere and vice versa was also true. Rasiklal, another associate, as usual did not turn up; rest of the surgeons, some practitioners cum SRs, and senior private surgeons from

Vapi, were present. The get together started on a sober note; pleasantries were exchanged; introductions completed, simultaneously with the first round of drinks. A very dynamic surgeon, Akhilesh Sharma described his successful laparoscopic surgeries where he could remove malignancies and perform anterior resections of carcinoma rectum; a really commendable job. Everybody appreciated it. A practitioner described his experiences with a recent technique of hemorrhoidectomy; there was some hot discussion regarding the best method, bands, cryo, laser or stapled hemorrhoidectomy? Someone has suggested hemorrhoidal artery ligation, by locating it with doppler. Hamid, sipping his lemon drink, asked Digpal, "What is your opinion?"

"I prefer only those methods, where larger population is benefited with minimal cost and complications; my preference is a neatly done submucos excision of piles." Some agreed, some did not; and the topic was changed.

Once the second round of drinks was over, Tandel stood up,

"Since this meeting is about Digpal Sir's end of freedom and I had been working with him since little over two years, he has given many pearls of wisdom to his juniors. Before we finish our third peg, I think it's time to share some of them with you."

"Shoot." Someone spoke in a slurred voice. Tandel brought out a paper from his pocket and continued in spite of increasing murmurs "Simple skin sutures are better than mattress, if conditions permit; they should be applied loosely, with a very thin gap between the two cut margins; this will give the best scar."

"Place the incision in skin creases, transverse are generally better than vertical or oblique; even for groin hernia or appendix."

"I would prefer lap for these." A practitioner commented.

"You sure, the patient will be benefited?" Digpal asked; the effect of the third peg was becoming evident on him too.

"Yes, why not, I need not enumerate the benefits." The practitioner retorted.

"And how many deaths have you seen by open hernia surgery?" Digpal said, and the surgeon started thinking; "I will tell you." Digpal continued. "I have seen one death and one seriously ill patient, transferred from a private hospital to medical college after lap hernia. His colon was perforated, and we had a tough time saving him. Should I name the surgeon?" The discussion stopped there.

"Friends, friends; let me proceed. Improvise surgery and adjust your speed as per patient's general condition; you want a live patient, not a great surgery." Tandel continued.

"Whatever that means, continue." Another slurred comment.

"Small things matter; surgeries like circumcision should be done with all seriousness, a casually done job can ruin someone's sex life for ever; make a small dorsal slit on prepuce to prevent postop paraphimosis."

"Yeah, one of my patients had that problem." Commented a young surgeon.

"Any stage of appendicitis, patient must be operated upon; conservative treatment is a waste of time."

"You mean, even from a lump?" A curious surgeon asked, "I won't do that."

"Can be done, if your handling is delicate and your tactile sensations well developed." Now Digpal answered instead of Tandel.

"In very old and frail patients of prolapse rectum, it's better to place a folded strip of synthetic mesh around the anal shincters, a bit higher up than a Thiersh's wire."

"Really? Can that be done?"

"Yes; I have seen him do that, gives excellent results,

moreover mesh stimulates lots of fibrosis, which helps." Pritesh confirmed.

"Paediatric patients are not small adults, they are different, don't venture unless trained; while treating think of another 50, 60 or 70 years' good quality life."

"Agreed, I won't touch them, they are very noisy." Speeches were getting slurred.

"Bleeding vessels, which don't have a name, won't kill the patient."

"What is that bullshit?" Another comment.

"If you do an unindicated surgery for that extra buck, it will have more complications than usual."

"Happened to me once." Alcohol works like truth serum sometimes!

"You may forget your theory, but don't abandon common sense."

"If you try to pass the buck, by referring a serious patient to a bigger city; chances are, only a cadaver will reach there. You are a general surgeon, operate right there."

"And get beaten up like our friend here." Indicating towards Digpal, a surgeon told.

"Next..."

"Enough, enough, you are wasting such good whisky by this serious surgical talk, stop it now." Someone started shouting.

"Okay, okay, I will cut it short, to only one more," Tandel agreed, "Laparoscopic surgery in good hands, and done for judi...judishus indications, is boon, otherwise..."

"Leave it, we know, what is his opinion about lap surgery, because he does not know how to do it. Let's have our fourth peg." Sharma's tolerance had reached the edge.

"Leave it Yogesh, will discuss some other time, this particular topic, when everybody is sober and see reason, but I am sure, a day will come when all surgeries will be done by Robots and surgeons will lose human contact completely." Digpal responded.

"Attention everybody." Hamid, who was a teetotaler said, "Kaushal here is a very good singer, he will sing a Kishore Kumar song."

Kaushal began to sing, and many joined, turning a solo to a chorus; someone started reciting ghazal, and others began to use the table as tabla. After the fourth peg some of them began to embrace each other, calling them as brother and *'jaan'*. The party ended on a happy note, forgetting the reason for which they had met in the first place!

Next day was Sunday and surgeons, except teetotalers, who were at the party the previous night, were looking for paracetamol tablets in their side drawers, tobe gulped down with strong coffee. This Sunday was emergency duty of Digpal's unit. He too was splashing his face with cold water in the morning, when his doorbell rang; Akhilesh was on the door.

"Please come in." Digpal invited him in.

"Had an extra peg last night, I am sorry if I gave out some rude remarks. But, do you really think laparoscopy surgery is over hyped?"

"Yes and no; it definitely has given a new life to the dying general surgeon. But don't you think, not only are we overdoing it, but feeding the psyche of society that it is some magic wand, which cures without cutting; and we know that it is not true."

Before their discussion could go any further, his phone rang. Hamid was speaking from the OT, "I am trying to remove a stuck tumbler from the rectum of this psycho for one hour, under heavy sedation. It is refusing to budge; can you come."

"Ten minutes, and call the on duty Anaesthetist." Digpal said, in spite of his throbbing headache.

"He is already here." Digpal excused himself and Akhilesh left, unconvinced.

He was there in less than ten minutes. "Can you administer spinal to him?"Anaesthetist injected spinal lignocaine, sphincter relaxed, but the tumbler was so badly stuck, that it did not move, moreover there was lot of edema at the anal verge and the edge of it was 2 inches above the verge. It was stuck upside down and every instrument to hold it would slip from it.

"Can we get an obstetric vacuum cup from the neighbours?" Digpal asked.

He applied the obstetric cup in the tumbler and started the suction machine; the cup got stuck snugly inside the tumbler, and he steadily began to pull it downwards.

"Mangubhai is a known psychotic patient, taking irregular treatment. Last month, he had come with a wire in the urethra; his wife had already left him." Hamid informed. Meanwhile Digpal had removed the tumbler, there was some bleeding from the anal verge, which was controlled by pressure.

"And her wife's name is Babita." Digpal commented.

"How do you know?" A surprised Hamid asked.

"Read this, '*Mangubhai ane Babita no lagan par saprem bhent*'." (Gifted with love on occasion of the wedding of Mangubhai and Babita.)

# MYSTERIUM RETEGIT

Only a fortnight remained for their wedding when Digpal decided to attend a day-long seminar, jointly organised by the Gynecologists' and Surgeons' association of Surat, and do some shopping for their wedding. He despised driving in the congested city and decided to go there by train. The city turned out to be a shoppers paradise; apparels for both, men and women, diamonds, ornaments and cosmetics were available aplenty. He felt like a pauper in that city. After attending the seminar and finishing off with some shopping, he reached the railway station well before time. He had enough time to mull over the day's happenings and rerun them in his mind.

Two of the lectures interested him in the seminar; 'Dealing with complications during and after gynaec surgeries', and 'Role of general surgeon in gynaec surgeries'. Though, he felt that there was not much of the difference in the two topics; as he remembered, many a frantic calls from the Gynecologists during surgery, for trauma to urinary bladder, large intestine or adhesions of previous caesarean section; even very large fibroids for their proximity to ureters, for internal iliac ligation and so on. It was this kind of mutual help and coexistence which made the profession so unique.

But what made the day so memorable was the speaker. She was from Florida, USA, introduced as Kelly Smith by the anchor and seemed to know her subject very well. Digpal was sitting in the last row, when she stood up and walked to the rostrum to deliver her talk; tall, fair, bespectacled, hair cut short, wore western formal Digpal noticed. Despite the jacket, her beautiful figure could not be missed. As soon as she began to speak, he got up from the last row and could find a seat in the front row. Though the accent was American and voice deeper than it used to be, Digpal could have recognized it, even in the cacophony of the Ganesh visarjan procession! As soon as he got up and sat in the front row, she faltered for a moment, which passed unnoticed, except by Digpal. For some time all he could notice was the movement of her lipstick clad beautiful lips; it was only after she mentioned the general surgeon, he began to register what she was speaking about.

When she concluded her talk; Digpal got up and asked, "What I have experienced and could understand from your talk, that for all gynaec surgeries where you anticipate problem, you must have a general surgeon by your side; more over shouldn't surgeons be given a short course to get acquainted with gynaec surgeries?"

"For the first part, agree fully, and we have a full time surgeon in our hospital, who is handy; for the second part, it's the prerogative of policy makers." They met during lunch hours and on a table for two.

"Pal, you haven't changed much." Kalpana was first to speak "You never were a good-looking bloke, but you have become handsome by age, those greys look sexy on you; but could you recognise me immediately?"

"I would, even if you grow a beard," and they both laughed. "What is this Kelly Smith business?"

"In the US, many Indians have their American nicknames; Kalpana was too tongue-twisting for them, and colleagues used to call me Kelly; and Smith is a stinking rich businessman, thirty years older than me. When her second wife was admitted in the hospital, where I worked as an intern, the oldy fell for me. To make a long story short, he divorced his second wife, married me, purchased a running hospital and I became chief of Gynecology and chairperson of the hospital! Now we live separately and are going to get divorced very soon."

"Oh! What an eventful journey!" A surprised Digpal wondered, 'Is she "my" Kalpana?'

"How's your life with Joseline? Must be having kids by now?" She asked.

"We didn't get married; she went with her husband to Oman."

She smiled; 'was she happy to know about his failed affair?' He thought.

There was an uneasy silence. A young gynaec stopped by and addressed Kalpana,

"Hi ma'am! It was an excellent oration." He began to pull a chair to sit, "I wanted to ask regarding…" Before he could complete his sentence she interrupted, "Thanks, buddy; but will you please excuse us for a while, it's personal."

He left disappointed; Digpal gave out a short laugh, "You Americans are too straightforward." But that fellow's interruption broke the silence between them.

"You intentionally mentioned a 'surgeon by your side,' didn't you? Come to the US to be by my side, both in OT and at home." She offered "leave this messy, filthy country; your talents will never be recognised here." She placed her hand on his hand on the table "I am a citizen now, and soon will be a billionaire, once my divorce proceedings are complete; We will have a good life at last."

Strangely, for the first time, Digpal did not feel the excitement by her touch, nor his heart raced, as it used to happen. He said in a calm voice, "Kalpana, thanks for the offer; first thing I am getting married after a fortnight; Secondly, even if I am not, I will not leave my country for any temptation. I was born here, brought up on charity, and became a doctor on scholarship with the tax money of people of India, in a highly subsidised Government medical college; practically free. I learnt surgery on the ordinary people of this messy, filthy, developing country. I love my country, and will ever be indebted towards her."

"For the first part, I am getting a feeling of 'deja vu'; but I am not the same sentimental fool I was; for the second part, I know your impractical idealism. I just tried; can only bring the horse to water."

They parted, with a goodbye kiss on the cheeks; Digpal was feeling light and relieved.

The AC waiting room on platform number one was half empty, when he had come, now it was fast filling in; only one seat by his side remained vacant, there was still half an hour to go for his train's arrival when an old man entered through the main door. He was hefty, fair, a few inches taller than Digpal and carried a stick, though he was not using it for support. He was pulling a trolley bag with one hand; looked around the waiting room, then walked gracefully and with sure steps, towards the empty seat near Digpal.

"May I?" He asked in a polite voice which reflected authority; it appeared that he was used to giving orders. "Sure." Digpal responded, impressed by his courtesy.

The old man arranged his suitcase by his side and pulled out an English magazine from the side pocket. It was a hot and humid day, the air conditioner was not very effective due to the number of people in the room and frequent opening of the door. Digpal opened the top buttons of his shirt.

The old man got bored of reading after a while, "It is a warm day."

"Yes Sir, it's a coastal city plus very densely populated and highly industrialised." Digpal responded. He too was getting interested in the impressive old man.

"But it's a nice city; people are friendly and helpful; everybody seems to prosper here."

"You were here for some business?" Digpal was curious.

"Me? And business!" The old man let out a loud laugh, "I am a retired army man; a full colonel. My daughter lives here; she is married to a diamond merchant. My son in law dropped me onto the platform, then I let him go. And what do you do here gentleman?"

"I am a sort of doctor, a general surgeon."

"Oh! That is wonderful; I have a liking…" He abruptly stopped in mid sentence. Digpal noticed the colour of the old man's face drain from coppery pink to white.

"Are you okay Sir?" Digpal was alarmed anticipating some medical emergency.

"I am good, don't worry. You have an interesting tattoo there." He asked, indicating towards the peculiar birthmark on Digpal's neck, which laid bare due to his open upper buttons of the shirt.

Digpal touched his birthmark, which looked like the silhouette of a lady sitting on her knees fully folded, with head thrown back and open hair, and said, "It's been there since, as long as I remember, it's not a tattoo, it is a birthmark."

The old man was quiet, as if stunned; he kept on looking towards the face of Digpal, with moist eyes; a tear rolled down one of his eyes. He spoke in a hoarse voice, words coming out with great difficulty, the authority and baritone missing, "You have your mother's complexion and dimples, but the features are unmistakably your Father's… that is me."

It took some time, even for the sharp mind of the surgeon, for the meaning of the Colonel's words, to sink in.

"I am an orphan." Said Digpal emphatically.

"Which orphanage?"

"St. Joseph's church and 'God's own children' orphanage, Indore." Digpal answered dryly.

Another tear rolled down the eyes of the colonel and got stuck in creases of his wrinkled cheeks. He began to speak slowly,

"I had been looking for you for the last 8 years. My wife died of cancer, 8 years back. Our only son died in a motorcycle accident, ten years back. I could not trace your mother and you. The only persons, Father Samuel and Digpal Singh Chauhan, who knew the truth are no more. I am your unfortunate Father, my son." He kept his large palm on Digpal's thin, long hand.

"You threw me, a delicate newborn, on the steps of church, on a rainy night. When the whole country was to celebrate the independence day, a symbol of freedom, you took away my freedom, my right to the love of my parents, security of a home, the name of my family. I lost my love as I didn't belong; did not belong to a family, a clan, a religion. I always tried to draw a picture of my parents, or a sister in my imagination, but could not even imagine any faces." Digpal spoke with a suppressed anger, without raising his voice.

"If you will listen to my story and the circumstances I was in, maybe you will understand. Back in my village, I was married, as soon as I completed my schooling; then I graduated and joined the Indian Army as second Lieutenant. I was a commissioned officer and there was nothing in common between me and my uneducated wife. I was a young officer when I was posted in MHOW, 20 kms from Indore, for combat training. During the training, I was badly injured by an accidental grenade blast, for which I was admitted in Military Hospital; it was there where I met your mother. She was a nurse there; sincere, empathetic, intelligent and attractive. Though dark in complexion, her bearing, big eyes, sharp features and the dimples made her look so beautiful"

The colonel was looking towards infinity, as if visualising her. "I fell in love with her and she too responded. Though she was from Kerala and I from Rajasthan; it did not come in the way of our love. She shared a rental apartment with another Malyali girl and alternated day and night duties with her. When she was alone during the day, I went to her apartment; incidentally she forgot to bolt from inside; I went in and what I saw is permanently imprinted in my memory and." The old man stopped for a while.

"Saw, what?" Now Digpal was curious.

"And your neck." The colonel continued, "She had just taken a bath, was wrapped only in a towel; was sitting on the floor on her fully flexed knee joints, the head was thrown back to dry her long black shining lock of hair which were flowing up to her hips. Probably, that was the day you were conceived." The army-man took a long breath, pulled out a water bottle from his bag, took a sip and continued,

"After that day, we used to meet regularly, whenever she was alone in her apartment. One day she informed me that she is pregnant, and insisted that we should get married as early as possible. I had no other option but to tell her that I was already married since my teens and had a wife and a big joint family, back in my village. She cried and cried, but refused to abort the baby, but I was worried that this could create problems in my life. A powerful local zamindar, Thakur Jaipal Singh Chouhan's son Digpal Singh was my close friend; his Father was a member of the managing committee of 'God's own children' orphanage. I confided in him about my situation, and he promised to help me."

As if tired, the Colonel once again stopped, sipped some more water, and then continued. "Both of us made a plan; we informed your mother that she had a dead baby. With Digpal, I went to the outskirts of Indore on his motorbike; with you wrapped in a white cloth and handed you over to Father Samuel, who knew our secret and promised to look after you. Digpal Chauhan who subsequently inherited his Father's place in the managing committee promised to not only look after you but will see to it that you become a doctor which was your mother's wish during her pregnancy."

"Oh! That's why uncle Chauhan used to help me." Things began to become clearer now for Digpal.

"Yes; Father Samuel and Chauhan saw to it that nobody adopts you. We were in contact until 1970 when I was posted in

Eastern command as a Major and fought the famous Indo-Pak war to liberate Bangladesh. We were not allowed to contact any civilians during the war; you were trying to get into Medicine during that period. Distance is a strange thing; Sunitha, your mother went back to Kerala and never wanted that I should contact her; she did not leave any trail. I had splinter injuries during the war, but soon recovered and was sent to North-East, to counter the terrorism there."

"I am not interested in your story, it doesn't matter now," Digpal said dryly.

"Please, my son; some of the weight from my conscience may reduce if you listen to me. In 1975, I was badly wounded during an ambush by terrorists, in which I lost my limb." The army man lifted the right side of his trouser to show his artificial limb.

"I retired prematurely and shifted back to my village; could see my two little daughters growing up, then fathered a son, who died in a motorbike accident. Digpal, don't be surprised, my friend had told me your name; now you are my only son and successor of the huge family estate."

"I am not interested in your property." Digpal was not impressed.

"We are a highly respected family in that part of the country. You will be the sole heir of the name and property; please son, come with me, or the family name will not continue." The colonel was almost begging.

"You are a selfish man; we all are to some extent, but your actions affected many lives. You manipulated and disowned your love; abandoned your son, who lived an orphan's life without any identity, family name, or tag of a religion." Digpal's anger was mounting.

"My son you belong to..."

Digpal interrupted, raising his voice above the din of the train arriving on the platform, "I don't want to know now; I have my own identity, I am a doctor and a surgeon, and that is enough for me."

He picked up his bag, and walked out of the waiting room to board the train, without looking back.

THE END

# EPILOGUE

Digpal was waiting eagerly for Ananya. She will be coming home to celebrate her 18th birthday, with her Father. He had retired from his teaching job four years back, and made this small village 'Dive agar', situated on the Konkan coast, his home. He had purchased a small house, surrounded by coconut and *supari* (betel nut) trees. He was growing vegetables in the backyard for him and his help's personal use. Ananya's birthday coincided with his and Kamna's wedding anniversary. Kamna slipped into a coma, following metastasis in brain from a missed malignancy in her uterus, which was removed 6 years before their wedding. He did not admit her to ICU; she breathed her last at home peacefully, as he refused to put her on life support, and that was Kamna's wish too. They had adopted Ananya from 'God's own children' orphanage, and St. Joseph Church, Indore; two years after their wedding. She was a very sick, underweight infant; the management agreed to allow them to take her as both of them were doctors. As Kamna and Digpal had decided, he would be breaking the news of her adoption, on her 18th birthday.

# ABOUT THE AUTHOR

Dr Gurmit Singh Dadiala BSc; MBBS; MS (Surgery); FICS.

Despite a brilliant academic career, opted to work in a small town hospital, accompanied by his doctor wife. Later ventured into private practice. At the turn of century, joined a medical college as a teacher of surgery to follow his passion for teaching, which he continued till 2016. Writing Hindi poetry and fiction had been his hobby since his college years. 'Magic of Surgery' is his first novel. He lives in Bardoli, Gujarat with his Gynaecologist wife, Archana and 2 daughters.

You Write. We Publish.

To publish your own book, contact us.
We publish poetry collections,
short story collections, novellas and novels.

contact@thewriteorder.com
Instagram- thewriteorder
www.facebook.com/thewriteorder

www.ingramcontent.com/pod-product-compliance
Lightning Source LLC
LaVergne TN
LVHW010314070526
838199LV00065B/5552